PRAISE FOR *WHAT IT TAKES*
JUDE SIERRA

"[STARRED REVIEW] "Tender and beautifully written… Sierra (Hush) uses rich characterization and lyrical writing to infuse this slow-building romance with depth, humor, and pathos. Readers will savor every dip and peak of Milo and Andrew's relationship as they balance the need for safety with the necessary risk of pursuing happiness."

—*Publishers Weekly*

"FIVE STARS…This story was an emotional rollercoaster. Even the happy moments were laced with fear, sadness and anxiety. But Jude kept me hanging onto every word."

—*Bayou Book Junkie Review Blog*

PRAISE FOR *HUSH*
JUDE SIERRA

"In her debut novel, Sierra explores Cam's emotional confinement and burgeoning self-discovery with poetic delicacy… Sierra skillfully captures the frustration of navigating identity and interpersonal relationships for those to whom it doesn't come easy. The subtle twist of fantasy enhances the narrative while also complicating the notion of consent… a worthy read and a valuable addition to the genre."

—*Library Journal*

"The writing itself is full of flowing words and beautiful prose with precisely chosen phrases. The entire book has a specific cadence and tone that indeed compels you to read on."

—*Joyfully Jay Book Reviews*

Idlewild

idlewild

A NOVEL

JUDE SIERRA

Author of What It Takes

interlude 🧩 **press** • new york

interlude press • new york

For Georgie, who refused to give up on either of these men, or on me.

Author's Note

WHEN MY FATHER WAS SEVENTEEN years old he came to Detroit from Venezuela to attend what was then called the University of Detroit. At the age of twenty-one he met my mother, who was raised in Redford, a suburb of the city. After five weeks of courtship they married and, a few years later, left the United States. My sister and I were raised on the stories they and our grandparents would tell of their lives and times in Detroit. Some were heartbreaking: My father and grandmother's recollections of the 1967 riots, for example, were vivid. Some were not: My grandmother never ran out of funny stories about my grandfather's time as a Detroit police officer and her days as a rebellious teenager growing up in the city.

When I was twelve years old our family moved back to the Metro Detroit area. From the moment we first flew over the city I was fascinated. Every few weeks for years, my sister and I would accompany our father and his uncle to University of Detroit Mercy basketball games. This city wears its history beautifully and heartbreakingly, and I never tired of seeking out tiny details of that history carved into her landscape.

While here I've heard so many horror stories, heard people tell how they would never set foot in the city again, heard the stories the rest of the country relied on to paint a picture of this place. However, there are also countless people here who tell stories of hope and resilience, of a refusal to give up, and of love. Growing up, I've watched the changing face of this city. In this moment, Detroit exists in the center of complex issues; so much of Detroit's story could be told, and I have a deep love for this city which informed my desire to tell a story that takes place here.

At its heart, *Idlewild* is the story of two men falling in love. Set behind them is a city they both believe in and love, though understanding her story very differently. There is no easy way to do justice to this city's history—one whose story goes much deeper than the 1967 riots—or the complexity of issues it now faces. Detroit's recent history runs much deeper than this story could do justice to, although it informs so much of this book. Writing this was a huge labor of love, and in the process of doing so, I read many excellent books about the city. If you are interested in checking any of them out, I've provided a reading list at the end of this book, and on my website, judesierra.com.

Prologue

ON THE RARE NIGHTS ASHER manages to drag himself home from Idlewild, the whirlwind of lights that follows from downtown Detroit to his home in Royal Oak slips by in a blur of exhaustion—which is a shame, because nighttime in the Downtown district, especially in the winter months, is glitteringly beautiful. Starting at Campus Martius Park, whether he's headed northwest up Woodward Avenue toward Midtown or east along Monroe into Greektown, whether he's looking toward the changing lights of the Renaissance Center buildings or the stunning mix of architectural styles along all the corridors, Asher finds Detroit so lovely. That loveliness is proof that he's not alone in his desire to resurrect this city from the ashes of its history.

In the morning, when Asher is sleepy-eyed and resentful, especially on rare sunny days, Downtown isn't the same. It's still lovely to him; it awes him, makes him proud to be a part of what the people of Detroit are building. But the path he's been on has been hard, the last six months especially. He's not sure he can enjoy the things he's always loved.

Most nights Asher stays too late at Idlewild to make the half-hour drive home worthwhile. Instead he sleeps in the third-floor loft apartment above the restaurant. For two years now he's promised himself that he'd attend to the apartment he and John had never managed to fully renovate. It was one of the last plans they'd had and they'd not had time to see it through. Now the prospect is too exhausting. The apartment is functional, if a little threadbare. It has a bed, a closet and a shower and a small fridge, a two-burner stove and a small sink, along with about one foot of counter space. Sleeping where he works isn't ideal, but with the hours he pulls, it's often necessary.

The last year has been awful, it's true. Asher had trusted Kaley to help him manage his restaurant while he drowned in paperwork that kept him off of the floor, separated from his staff. Sequestered, he let too many things to slip past his notice, until suddenly he had to face the harsh reality of a too-often empty restaurant and bills he struggled to pay.

March, when everyone begins to hope for a break in the weather, sneaks in and he doesn't turn the page on his desk calendar until halfway through the month. The worst thing about winter is the way hope begins to bloom, even before the foolish crocuses start to peek from the sodden earth. A beautiful warm day, in the fifties and sun shining, tells you winter almost over.

The way things go though, that usually means another cold spell is coming.

March in Michigan is always a series of hopes and heartbreaks, of wetness and never-ending wind that makes his Internet flicker in and out. For the most part, March is dark, muddy and mostly depressing. Asher doesn't deal with tiny hopes when he can help it; he doesn't mind that he misses the nascent crocuses and sporadic warm spells. This way, he also doesn't mind that he almost never leaves Idlewild. He spends the second half of the month struggling to get a grip on everything that's gone wrong.

For too long he's let himself get buried under mounting paperwork; spent his time on the phone with vendors and locked away from the personal half of his business. Asher makes himself leave the tiny closet that is the back office and get back in the kitchen and on the floor with the servers and bartenders, hoping to reconnect with his staff, with the clientele.

But his presence only drives a wedge between himself and his employees, particularly Kaley, who has gotten used to having the run of the front of house. Asher's interference is resented; his attempts to regain authority backfire. It's awful to realize that none of his employees respect him or the business. None of them understand that this is the *one thing*, the last thing that John touched that Asher has sworn to hold on to. In five years, he's lost every employee who knew John.

Late in April, Asher bangs hard against facts he can no longer just worry about, but rather has to face. He's on the verge of bankruptcy, and Idlewild is slipping from his fingers. On the cusp of spring, when May is knocking on the door, Asher bites the bullet and calls a realtor, arranges to put his condo in Royal Oak up for sale and begins to draft a plan for his Hail Mary to save Idlewild.

Saturday he tidies in the kitchen and, for the first time in a week, goes home. It's midday, sunny and warm. The sky is dotted with bulbous clouds beneath veils of clouds sheered thin by wind.

Traffic is ridiculous. Asher's tired enough that he should be annoyed, but he's never hated driving. Something about the solitude in the car, being able to blast music and enjoy it, helps Asher sink into his head space and really feel present. Images from the past week, conversations with the few guests he met, their faces and smiles—all filter through his brain while he bops his fingers to Macklemore's "Can't Hold Us Down." It's not a song about Detroit, but it seems like it. Something anthem-like about it calls to mind those old Eminem Chrysler commercials.

Home smells stale. Asher puts his overnight bag on the armchair and walks around opening blinds and then windows. Dust dances in the air, and he sneezes three times in succession. For a minute he stands, hands on hips, gazing out his window and down onto Campbell. This place has needed a spring cleaning for good year or so.

The one-bedroom apartment is smaller than the condo he and John shared but was perfect for him, with bright open space and clean lines. Leaving their home had been a huge step, spurred by Asher's realization that he not only had to move on from his partner's death, but that he *wanted* to. It's been five years since John died and almost three years since he moved to this apartment. But that's as far as Asher's managed to move into a new life. If anything, he's regressed.

Showering here is a luxury, with steady warm water and all of his products, his own soft gray towels and, best of all, his bed. It's made neatly, warmed by the sunset light spilling through a west-facing window. Naked, Asher slides in. His dark hair is still wet; he'll wake with his wild curls he can't bring himself to dry. His bed is warm and so soft he can't resist it, and he wonders how he ever managed to convince himself that the loft bed is an acceptable substitute.

Despite the time, he slips into a doze; it's restful but not sleep. For once, he's not worried. Something positive is starting. It's a slippery goal and an incredible risk, but he's determined to catch hold, to make this work and somehow, down the road, find the momentum to finally, *finally*, have a life.

Chapter One

DAYS OF CONTEMPLATION AND GUILT bookended Asher's decision to fire his entire staff, to bet everything on a fresh start. Idlewild is closed for a month, long enough to meet, interview, hire and train a new staff, but not so long that Idlewild will no longer be relevant in the Downtown scene. Asher has a short list of candidates and a lot of thinking to do. He's not interested in just good employees: What he really wants is magic. These people are puzzle pieces, and Asher needs to figure out if he can put them together to not just save Idlewild, but make it thrive.

Monday, Asher wakes himself with coffee, which he then takes into the shower and manages to drink, letting the hot water loosen tight muscles. He forgoes shaving. His usual button-down shirt and slacks—his work uniform, casual but professional—are too formal. His jeans have holes worn into them, and the shirt he throws on is old. It's deep green and comfortable as hell, having been washed countless times. Other than to scrub his hands through his curly brown hair, he doesn't check his appearance in the mirror.

Joy, his first applicant, knocks on the back door at eight on the nose. Mentally, Asher gives her one point.

"Hi." She stands straight and shakes his hand. "I'm Joy Chambers."

"Asher Schenck," he says. He leads her in, takes her past the closed office door and the kitchen, onto the floor. He pulls out a chair at a table where his paperwork is spread out. "Do you want some coffee?"

"Oh, no thanks," Joy says. "I had one. Two and I devolve into a shaky mess."

Asher laughs. She's pretty: her cheeks are freckle-dusted, her eyes are light brown and her dyed-blonde hair is pulled into a high, neat ponytail.

"Here's my resume," she says and slides it across the table. He scans it. Experience as a waitress and bartender, references from her last job. Pretty generic. But Asher's been burnt before. Food service culture isn't a mystery to him; most of his previous staff had experience—as well as a desire to party and a tendency to complain about anything and everything associated with the bar, which they were dragging into ruin.

"Why do you want to work here?"

Joy cocks her head and gives him a frank look to return the one he levels at her. "I need work. I've worked Downtown as well as on the West Side. I prefer it here. This place has character. I'm a people person, and if I had to choose, I'd rather bartend here because it's got a vibe. I get to meet more people. I enjoy having regulars."

Asher makes quick notes on the back of her resume as the interview unfolds. He feels pretty good about her answers and he can't really ask her if she's the kind of worker who will sneak shots and alienate customers she doesn't think will tip well—at least not yet. "Okay. I've got several interviews coming up. I'm planning on calling people back for seconds in a few days. Does that work for you?"

"Does that mean you're going to call me back?"

"I think so."

"Awesome."

His gut tells him she's a good candidate. His brain tells him his gut has proven its lack of worth in the past. By the end of the day, Asher has a headache. It's not that he doesn't enjoy talking to people—he'd hardly have opened a restaurant if he didn't. But spending a day analyzing responses, motivations, potential, all while worrying about the future of his business, is exhausting.

He has two more interviews today. He has time to make a quick meal in the quiet of a kitchen that's not filled with the frenetic energy of a dinner rush. The kitchens are dark and the high ceilings amplify even the smallest noises. The air is charged with silence; the hiss of vegetables sizzling in a pan is intrusive. Asher finishes cooking with no desire to linger in what could soon be the shell of a dream, a wish, the site of so much heartbreak.

He's barely finished eating his stir-fry when he hears a knock at the door. He's not expecting any deliveries, so it must be his next interview—twenty minutes early.

"Hi!" A young man stands on the stoop with a wide but nervous smile on his face.

"Tyler?" Asher asks.

Tyler holds out his hand and nods. "The one and only."

Asher chuckles and ushers him in. "You're early."

"I know, I'm sorry. I get antsy when there's a chance I might be late, which means I'm always early."

"There could be worse character traits," Asher says.

Tardiness was a chronic problem with his previous staff. He shows Tyler to the front-of-house table where he's been working. Despite his professed nerves, there's nothing nervous about Tyler's body language. He scans the room and smiles at Asher. He's brought a reusable bottle of water, which he drinks from before making a tiny exclamation and removing his resume from his bag. One corner is bent, but despite this, Asher can tell at a glance that this young man has had training; it's professionally laid out and fuller than most of the resumes he's seen.

"Pre-med at Wayne State?" he asks. "And you just graduated. Congratulations."

Tyler bites his lip. He's young and has charming good looks: rich brown skin and full lips, shocking green eyes. It's those eyes—bright and curious—that most convey his youth. His hair is a bit longer than

Asher might call close-cropped: tight curls a brown so deep they are nearly black. His cheekbones are something to write home about, sharp and striking.

"Yes."

"On your way to med school?" Asher prompts.

Tyler shrugs. "No. I don't know. Maybe."

Asher resists the urge to press for more. Tyler's reticence doesn't seem secretive; this is perhaps a sore topic.

Asher reads the rest of the resume. "So, no experience in food service at all?"

"No, but everyone has to start somewhere." Tyler's smile is equal parts coy and sunny.

"But why here?" Asher gestures at the resume. Tyler has experience working, yes, but nothing close to food service.

Tyler runs his fingers over the deliberately distressed wood of the two-top table.

"I've been here before."

"Oh?" Asher swallows.

"Can I be honest?"

"Please," Asher says.

Tyler stands and pushes his chair in. He walks around the room, trailing fingers over the backs of chairs and then along the bar. He doesn't ask permission before he steps behind it. He doesn't do much—he's not really doing anything—but every movement is contained energy, and his eyes captivate when he turns their force on Asher. His magnetism could be dangerous to anyone who draws that focus. But Asher can see how it could be a fantastic asset to the restaurant as well.

"Well," Tyler starts. Asher tilts his head. "It was kind of a hot mess." The words sting. They're true, but the honesty, the ballsy honesty, makes Asher smile.

"It totally was," he says, then laughs.

"My friend Joy told me it was closed for a few weeks. I'm not sure what exactly that means for you, but I was hoping it meant something new."

"It does."

"I appreciate challenges," Tyler says. He takes a breath and squares his shoulders. "I'm a hard worker. I like people, and they like me."

"It's a lot harder than people think it is," Asher tells him. "Working at a restaurant I mean."

"Oh, it'll take more than that to scare me away. I can do hard."

There's a long pause; he can see that Tyler is repressing the urge to giggle, and Asher has to hide a smile. "Not, um. Oh god… you know what I mean," Tyler says.

"I like you, kid. I have a good feeling about you. I'm not making any decisions now, but I'm fairly confident I'll be calling you for another interview. It'll be more specific."

"Yay!" Tyler bounces on his toes and lights the room with his smile.

Chapter Two

I THINK IT WENT WELL—

Tyler curses when the bus hits a pothole and he accidentally sends the text. He's typing out the rest, swaying with the lumbering progress of the bus when Malik texts back.

In class. Tell me at home.

Tyler sighs. The sky is darkening with clouds. It's late enough that there's not much he can do but go home and wait for Malik, because he wants to share his good news with someone other than Joy. Though everyone seems understanding about his decision to put school on hold, he imagines them hovering on the periphery of his imagination, hoping for a miracle that will fix it all. Becoming a waiter at a ragged Downtown restaurant will not make the top-fifty list of things they are hoping to hear from him, much less the top-two.

Joy told him about this opportunity, knowing he needs not only the money, but also something new. Other than Joy, no one else would understand why he might be excited. Malik's lukewarm response is par for the course in their circle of friends. Detroit is so much more than the Downtown renaissance so often billed as its only saving grace—in many circles of people who've lived in and worked hard for Detroit all along, that's problematic. But Tyler has to admit, he loves its countenance; loves the busy spill of Greektown Friday nights; loves the Woodward storefronts covered in Christmas lights; loves the idea of couples ice skating in January, horse drawn carriages and a brand of romance that's foreign to his life. He never learned how to ice skate, but it would be the most romantic date. It's not his life, and it's not his world, but it glitters with temptation.

He exits the bus at West Grand Boulevard and walks to their apartment. The elevator smells like takeout, and he's already dreading the mess. He left a pointed note for Malik and Brandon on top of a stack of dirty dishes. He can predict the note was ignored and tossed.

He's not wrong.

He deposits his coat in the small hall closet, then wanders into the kitchen, angles a glass around the dishes, fills it and retreats to their bedroom. Malik's left the bed unmade again, and for some reason shoes litter the floor. Tyler shoves them back into their closet and makes the bed, then flops onto it. There's no TV, so he pulls his laptop onto his chest. Sequestering himself in his room is the only way he can guarantee he won't cave and do the dishes. To be honest, Malik and Brandon are probably waiting him out; eventually he always caves.

Malik gets in late; he smells of aftershave and cigarettes and his lips are cold when he kisses Tyler hello. He leaves his coat on the floor and toes off his shoes. Malik's body, thick and heavy, rests on his. He kisses Tyler again, next to his lips and then under his ear. He doesn't say anything; he's speaking with his body. He often does. Tyler can never tell what exactly he's saying or what language he needs to use in return, but the last thing he wants to do right now, with Malik's attention and affection directed at him, is to shut him down. He'll tell Malik about the job later.

* * *

GROWING UP IN EAST DETROIT taught Tyler many things: about the man he wanted to make himself and the man he could so easily become. He learned very early that he didn't fit in—not into his family, not with peers at school. There was always something, a shimmering thread of *himness*, that Tyler knew made him different. The day of his graduation from East Detroit High, Tyler knew he was on the cusp of new beginnings.

"Tyler, baby." His mother pulled him in for another hug and he had to grab the mortarboard of his graduation cap, lest she knock it off. He'd worked hard to get it settled at the right angle to make his cheekbones look fierce.

"Mama," he said, extricating himself with care.

"Oh, don't you go Mama-ing me." She swatted his arm playfully. "I get to be as proud of my baby as I wanna be. High school graduate." She looked at him fondly again and then pulled him down to kiss between his eyes. He wasn't a particularly tall man, but she was definitely short. "*My* high school graduate."

Tyler fidgeted; all of her attention, sweet and direct and soft, made him uncomfortable. Francine Heyward usually preferred to show love in word and actions.

"Soon enough you'll have two more," he said, nodding toward his sisters Gayle and Hope, who were picking their way across the soft lawn to them. It had rained hard the night before. Now they had beautiful early June weather, and the sun was a bright ball in the sky. All three women wore their best dresses and wide smiles. He and Hope shared their father's green eyes, and while Gayle had beautiful dark eyes, Tyler and she were noticeably lighter skinned than their mother or Hope. It was strange that Tyler thought his sisters so beautiful, but those markers passed from his father often burdened him. They didn't need anything from Ross Heyward and hadn't for years.

He accepted more hugs from his sisters when they caught up, and as they waited and chatted, he received a few handshakes and congratulations from his classmates, the ones who never minded him too much. Tyler's mother had always said he had some kind of magic that drew people to him, that made it impossible not to like him. Tyler thought she didn't understand how hard he worked to do that. But she meant well, and when he came out to her she had supported him without hesitation.

Now, though college was on the horizon, a whole new chapter of his life was dawning. It would bring exhaustion of a different kind, but would be worth it, because Tyler Heyward had *plans*.

He was breaking the cycle of barely scraping by day to day, of never getting ahead, of feeling caught in a system that seemed impossible to get out of, and he was becoming a doctor.

Tyler had never told his mama or sisters about his plans. Speaking of a dream always seemed like breaking the veil surrounding it. It was an intimate hope, something close and precarious. Like many things, Tyler concealed it deep inside.

They ate dinner at home. His sister Hope made his favorite foods, green beans with slivered almonds and rosemary chicken. They spent that evening around the small table in the kitchen. Gayle kept them all in stitches with stories about Tyler as a little kid. She was younger than him by ten months. Sometimes those months were nothing, almost as if she was his twin. This was hard for Hope, who was four years younger. But other times those months weighed on him, and he felt years older.

He'd been the first of them to go to work despite their mother's insistence that they could all get by without it. He and his mother had fought about it, but as sweet as Tyler was, he was also stubborn and determined. He'd only been eleven when his good-for-nothing excuse for a father had left, but he'd promised himself he'd work his hardest to be the man of the house and care for his family the way his father never had. And he'd do it in an honest way and make his mother proud.

The night of his graduation, warmed by the happiness of his family, Tyler gave himself permission to be proud of his own hard work and his achievements. He slipped more comfortably into himself and let go of his personas. Rarely was his family all together, not pulled apart by their various jobs. Tonight was a set-aside night. It wasn't goodbye—Tyler wasn't leaving to school for a few months and even then he wasn't going far—though it seemed like one.

After the kitchen was cleaned and Hope had gone up to bed, he felt his way onto the back porch, where Gayle was sneaking a cigarette. One dog barked in the distance, then several more. Tyler lowered himself carefully next to her; she offered the cigarette, and he shook his head. He leaned against the railing of the porch steps. They needed to be painted, one of many small things their house could use that they never find the time, energy or money for. Maybe he'd make a summer project of it.

"Whatcha thinking about?" Gayle tapped his toes with hers.

"Nothing," he replied. Were he to try a home repair in front of his sisters, they'd laugh themselves silly. He'd had a few mishaps in the past and earned himself a reputation he played up whenever they needed cheering; he snuck in repairs when they weren't around. Tyler was capable of a lot more than his family, or most people who knew him, thought. People took him at face value. He had soft features and a lithe, thin body that should have been a dancer's, delicate hands and unusual eyes. It was easier to let them think what they would than to always fight it.

At home he was lighthearted and silly and lovable. He didn't demand attention. With his friends at Affirmations, the LGBT community center, he was femme and funny, the laugh of the party and everyone's pet. At school he was quiet: the achiever; tones spoken a little lower, clothes a little baggier and the line of his shoulders held differently.

Tyler was gifted. And it wasn't just his intelligence, or his unusual prettiness or his sweet nature. Tyler was an actor at almost every moment, a patchwork of personas, a chameleon and a bone-deep people-pleaser.

* * *

"Aren't you going to ask?" Tyler says.

Morning is creeping through their window. Malik groans and rolls away and under the covers.

"It's not even eight," he complains.

"It's ten, you bum."

Tyler steals the covers back, then tucks himself against Malik, who radiates delicious heat. Malik's breathing evens out. Tyler lets himself sigh. Malik won't hear it. Malik hates Tyler being passive-aggressive. However, Tyler doesn't think expressing annoyance is passive-aggressive. He closes his eyes and tries to will himself back to sleep. It doesn't work. He rolls out of bed as quietly as he can. Brandon's in the shower, so he plants himself on the couch and grabs the remote. He assiduously ignores the kitchen. Eventually Malik gets up, dressed only in boxers and an undershirt. He stumbles into the kitchen, then comes out to flop onto the couch with a thump. He hands Tyler a banana. It's sweet that he knows Tyler's hungry, but also infuriating because it's an acknowledgment of what he's not doing. Namely, keeping anything clean.

"All right, all right, tell me all about it," Malik says.

"It was great. I think. He seemed to like me. Considering I don't know shit about restaurants, I'm shocked. He said he'd call about second interviews today?"

"That's a lot of effort to hire some waiters," Malik says.

"Well, that place has been closed for a month now, so I think it's a re-start thing. You remember when we went there?"

"I wasn't there, Tyler," Malik points out. It's easy, as if the reminder that they'd been broken up, which Tyler had deliberately forgotten, isn't a big deal. Maybe it's not to him.

"Okay, well, whatever. A bunch of us went. It was jacked up," Tyler refrains from pointing out that he'd told Malik this when he applied for the job.

"So what, you're gonna go bust your ass for a bunch of white kids at a place that sucks anyway?"

"...alik, come on," Tyler says. He tries not to let hurt feelings bleed into his words, but he does not succeed.

"Sorry, baby," Malik pulls him closer and kisses him, right next to his eyebrow.

"I just, I need the money," Tyler says. "None of this was the plan. I'd rather do this somewhere I'm interested in than somewhere soul-sucking."

"I know," Malik says, tugging. "Come on, you'll figure this out." Tyler sets his head on Malik's shoulder and tries to believe himself.

* * *

IDLEWILD WILL BE THE FIRST job lead Tyler's had since graduating that might pan out. He worries that he might have to take a second job, but he trusts Joy when she said this will be worth it. He's a month behind on rent and lucky that Malik and Brandon are willing to cover him. Everyone's resources are limited though, and owing sits wrong.

He worries over his appearance for far longer than seems warranted and changes his clothes four times before Brandon and Malik take a house vote to stop him.

"Good luck, I guess," Brandon says around a mouthful of cereal.

As Tyler puts on his unlaced blue high-tops, Malik smacks Tyler's ass, then gives him a quick kiss.

The bus makes good time, and Tyler's early again. He goes for a walk, peeking into storefront windows and looking at the buildings. He did the River Days thing out of curiosity and came for Motor City Pride last year, but he's never spent much time Downtown. It's crisp and modern, with nods to old architecture and the city he hears it was. It's nothing like his neighborhood, much less like where Malik grew up.

Tyler walks down Woodward toward Hart Plaza until the Spirit of Detroit statue sits before him. At over twenty feet tall, Tyler has to step back to take it in. In the Spirit's hands are balanced the light of God and family, representative of a world beyond his fingertips. The Spirit sits cross legged, looking down on the symbol of the family unit, while he holds a sphere aloft in the other; both a shiny bright bronze that contrasts with the elegant blue-gray patina of the statue's finish. A verse from the II Corinthians is engraved on the wall behind it. "Now the Lord is that spirit and where the spirit of the lord is, there is liberty." Tyler reads the words over and over for a long time, mulling over the irony of those words behind such an iconic landmark of this city.

When he turns back toward Idlewild, he feels that otherness stifling him, covering him in the whooshing air of cars passing and the smell of city. Here, for the money, he'll be performance art; he'll be the embodiment of whatever will be most desirable for Asher, for Idlewild's patrons.

Today when Asher greets him, he seems more present. Tyler knew this place was in dire straits, but if he needed confirmation, the harried expression on Asher's face when they first met was it.

Although his clothes hint that he's tried to put himself together, his hair is a mess. It's longish, with a hint of curls and is the kind of tousled only some men can pull off. Though deep brown, Tyler can see some gray at the temples. Asher has dark eyes and sports the shadow of a beard. Despite the pallor of his skin that indicates he hasn't gotten sun in a long time and his slightly sloppy appearance, Tyler can't help but notice how handsome he is. He's taller than Tyler by a few inches— most men are. He has no idea how old Asher is—it would hardly be polite to ask—but he thinks maybe in his thirties. That's hardly old, but it's older than he; that's never been an attraction. But, it's working right now. Tyler swallows and smiles.

"So," Asher starts. He sits at the same table. It's just as covered in paperwork. "What are your thoughts about working here?"

"Are…" Tyler eyes him. "Are you hiring me?"

"I am strongly considering it." Asher doesn't smile but his eyes are friendly.

"It would be great to work here," Tyler says. "Really. This building has a vibe."

"A good one?"

"Oh, I don't know. Something here feels right." He wonders if he's making a fool of himself. Tyler sometimes can sense the energy of a person or place. It's nothing he seeks—but some people and places he's encountered just feel *right*.

Empty, Idlewild brims with potential. It's a building with great bones, long but narrow, with high groin-vaulted ceilings and a bar that curves down the length of the front-of-house floor. Cream-colored wainscoting lines the bottom of the walls—he sees it running up the stairs to the second floor—and the walls are a rich deep red that's brightened and warmed by an eclectic assortment of antique lighting fixtures. Wide wooden steps with carved spindles lead to the second floor seating area. The dark wood and walls are offset by light through the large glass window.

"Well, I hope so." Asher looks around, then shrugs. "Or that I can make something of it."

"Just you?" Tyler asks. "That sounds exhausting."

Asher tilts his head with a tiny smile quirking his lips.

"Well, if you wanna take a chance on me, which I recommend, I want to help you with that." Tyler smiles as warmly as he can and is gratified when Asher's eyes catch his. They share a second of eye contact that leaves Tyler short of breath. He looks away quickly.

Chapter Three

Monday is hiring day. It goes faster than Asher thought it might, with almost everyone he called accepting the job, and all but Claudia sounding excited. Claudia was his first choice for bartender, and he saw a lot of potential in her. He isn't going to read much into one phone call. The last thing Asher needs is to work himself into a panicked state while shaping a new staff. Asher's never been given to panic attacks; John used to tell him that the more anxious Asher was, the less likable he became. But back then he had John, who excelled at kissing him out of his funks.

Asher no longer misses those moments with pain, rather with fondness and a wish for the future. He's not sure that he'll ever find love again, but that doesn't mean he doesn't want to.

Asher splits Tuesday and Wednesday into basic front- and back-of-house orientation as well as cleaning. Tuesday, his new cooks, Santos and George, get the abbreviated Idlewild tour; they won't be spending time in the front-of-house with the servers. Instead Asher shows them the front kitchen with the cooking lines and prep coolers. The back kitchen has a wide steel prep table and metal storage shelves for assorted pans, containers and dishes. The walk-in fridge and freezer are tucked in back by the storage rooms, and behind those are the tiny break room and his office.

The first thing he wants to stress with this staff is that it is a joint responsibility to keep this place clean and inviting. Working together is also an excellent indicator of personalities. While most of his back-of-house employees take cleaning in stride, he's had too many waiters and bartenders who resent this type of work. He runs a small place; in all his years of restaurant work, as a waiter and manager and now owner, Asher's always found that when people can pick up each other's slack in all areas, the ship runs more smoothly.

And this is where Claudia shines; the most experienced of the wait-staff he's hired, she's a natural leader. She's patient and self-directed and, unlike some of the others, she can see what needs to be done, delegating tasks in a manner that doesn't grate on the others. It's reassuring for Asher, who knows that managing employees is similar to herding young cats.

Tyler needs the most direction—he's the least experienced person Asher's taken a chance on—but he does everything with grace and a good attitude.

"Up here?" Tyler asks Claudia. He's standing perched on the back of the bar, cleaning the corners of the ceiling and the lights while she holds his legs. "Of course I do the stunt work. I see how it's going to go. If I'm going to be up here, shouldn't I at least be strutting my stuff?" He turns to do a tiny mock vogue with exaggerated pursed lips.

Claudia slaps his leg, laughing. "Shut up and finish cleaning before you fall to your death, please."

Asher's at the other end of the bar, polishing liquor bottles with Joy and struggling not to laugh when Tyler takes a break to shake his butt and dance, all angles and awkward, hamming it up. Joy giggles helplessly, and Jared is snorting with laughter from the other end of the front where he's been stuck with cleaning the undersides of the table tops.

"All right, all right," Asher says after a particularly enthusiastic move sends Tyler wobbling. "I don't want to pay a worker's comp claim quite yet, thank you. We'll find a space for you to shake it out down here when you're done working. Or, worse comes to worst, I'll get my ancient butt up there."

Tyler hops down with an easy smile. "We should have some music. "Everyone works better with music."

"Whistle while you work?" Joy offers. Asher shudders.

"Oh, dear god, not that. Anything but that."

"Seconded," Tyler says fervently. From under a table somewhere they hear Jared giggling again.

"FOR WHAT IT'S WORTH," TYLER says later, when the two of them are at the touch-screen register while Asher gives him a quick rundown on the basics. His eyes slide down Asher's body and then back to his face. He blinks, bumping Asher's hip with his own. "I definitely don't think you're ancient."

Asher turns to him with wide eyes. *Was that flirting?* Tyler's smile is lopsided and sweet and bears no trace of flirtation, though. Asher clears his throat; heat rises to his cheeks. He has no idea what's going on or how to handle it, because Tyler is young and a new employee and yes, beautiful. He has no desire to mix any waters, even if they all run solely in the direction of admiration for him. Even at rest, Tyler is magnetic, the most charismatic person Asher's ever met. That's why Asher hired him despite his lack of experience.

"So, that's a rough go-through," he says after a silence that lasts two beats too long. "We'll do another training, and your first week you'll practice with whoever you're shadowing."

"No problem. I think I get the gist," Tyler says.

Asher gives him a fleeting smile and then pats his arm before walking away, unsure if he should be congratulating himself on acting like a normal human or beating his head on the nearest desk because he is *so* not a normal human. It's obviously been way too long since he's had a connection with another person.

He retreats to the tiny, windowless office crammed into the back of the kitchen and stares at the computer for five full minutes.

When he surfaces, he takes a good look around, then wishes he hadn't. If something needs a good cleaning, it's this room. It's not dirty, but it is dingy. Rather than a conventional desk, there is a counter that runs the length of one wall. It is absolutely buried under paperwork, folders and flotsam he cannot identify or find a home for. The safe, the filing cabinets, which should be holding the paperwork that's all over the desk, the computer towers and the chair are all jammed cheek-by-jowl. Organization—the kind that requires a detail-oriented and methodical person—isn't his strong suit. Asher's awesome at un-seeing things he's not sure how to approach and in so doing has created a mess of epic proportions. Finding employment forms for his new staff had been an adventure in horror.

He can hear chatter in the kitchen—they must be putting away supplies—and forces himself to stop his fruitless search for paper clips. Instead he sets the pile of completed forms on top of the papers already on the desk and goes out to see what's left to do and to set them all up to come for training he's staggering over the next three days.

"So how is your memory?" Asher asks.

"Uh, I don't know? Good?" Tyler responds. "Good enough to memorize tons of shit for my exams in school?"

"You did well in school, right?"

"Yeah, I did okay." Tyler doesn't offer any more information.

Asher's curious, but doesn't want to press. Instead, he hands Tyler a pad of paper, a plastic-covered book to hold his order pad, and another to hold the bill and take payment. "Here you go," he says.

"What's this?" Tyler flips one of the books open and sees with its two plastic pockets on the sides and a credit card pocket at the top. "Never mind, I got it."

"You'll want to get something to keep in your apron for your cash and receipts. Keep your order pad in there."

"I know that seems obvious, but when you're new to serving and are experiencing dinner rush for the first time in a loud bar, it can take a while to figure out how to keep a level head."

"Gotcha."

"I mean, that's assuming we'll have dinner rushes." Asher frowns. His stomach tightens. Tyler squeezes Asher's arm comfortingly. Asher blinks, surprised. The gesture is appreciated, if a bit personal. It reaches him in a way he's not sure how to handle.

"Claudia is going to go over more details, run you through some role play," Asher says. Tyler tucks the books into his serving apron. His smile seems mischievous.

"Mmm, role play? I didn't realize this was that kind of bar."

Asher laughs and rolls his eyes before retreating to his office.

ASHER SPENDS THE REST OF his evening taking notes: on what his new employees might need work on or training they might need as well as their personality traits and things he's learned about them. He wants to be sure he has a good sense of his employees this time around. Restaurants are a hotbed of drama and tension. Partying is a part of the culture, but Asher needs to keep that out of his restaurant. His last staff took to sneaking shots *while* working. This time he needs to keep his finger on the pulse. And do better liquor counts.

He can't make many notes; he's only had a day to spend with each group. He worries about Claudia's silence and unreadability when she's not on the floor and how it'll affect her relationship with the other staff members, and about George's family—his four kids and wife, his sick mother—all living in a small apartment, depending on George to keep them housed. Asher doesn't want to let him down. George is an excellent cook who is passionate about food—he'd come to his interview prepared with innovative menu ideas and ready to demonstrate them. He'd made Asher the most tender, delicious pork belly sliders he'd ever tasted, plated gorgeously, and a spin on a Michigan cherry salad with truffle oil vinaigrette. Asher knew they'd work well together, and had hired him on the spot.

Claudia knocks quietly when it's time to leave, and Asher does a final turn of the front house. The silence that falls when the building empties is both comforting and hollowing. He's used to the silence of living alone, and in this building it always seems heavier than when he lived in his apartment. Hoping for someone to help cushion the weight of silence is a tender wish, tied up in that "one day" on which he's pinned his future with this restaurant. One day, he'll have enough time to think about something besides this business, this burden. He's still young, despite how old his new, young staff might make him feel. There's time.

Chapter Four

"You know what you gonna do?" Malik asks one night. Tyler's got a night off and he's lounging in bed with a book while Malik hunches over his desk finishing an assignment.

"What?" Tyler closes his book but keeps his finger between the pages to mark his spot. "Right now I'm going to bed. Soon. Ish."

"No, I mean school." Malik gestures with a pen. He's not looking at Tyler.

"Do I need to?" Tyler asks lightly, narrowing his eyes. Malik often steps into places Tyler isn't ready to let anyone come near.

"What, you gonna work there the rest of your life? All that school and you gonna serve people forever?"

Tyler can feel his skin flush then buzz with anger. He holds it in carefully. This has been a hard adjustment for them. They're both driven. They both worked hard to make the men they are. Tyler's decision to take a break from school seemed as though he let down everyone who loves him. Tyler isn't sure how he's supposed to move forward when the knowledge that he might never please everyone else blocks his every move. Once he'd told them he wanted to be a doctor, the summer after his freshman year of college, they'd wanted that dream more than he did. The pressure of disappointing them is paralyzing.

Malik glances over when Tyler doesn't respond; despite the desperate attempt to hide his anger, Tyler can tell when Malik sees his misstep. He sits next to Tyler on the bed and takes the book from his hand. Tyler loses his spot, but he doesn't say anything.

"I've only started working there, Mal," Tyler says.

"I'm sorry. I know this is hard for you to hear."

"Do you?" Tyler's lips feel numb. He wants to cry. Sometimes Malik is right with him, the closest person in his life—or who is meant to be—but at other times he leaves Tyler feeling the most alone.

Malik touches Tyler's chin and meets his eyes. Tyler doesn't want to read them and he doesn't want the kiss Malik gives him. But he can't bear the thought of the distance he'll create if he pushes Malik away.

"I... I just want you to be happy. You worked so hard, Ty," Malik says. Tyler closes his eyes. "I want you to find what makes you happy too. I don't want you to get lost."

A year behind Tyler academically, Malik is in the difficult home stretch of school and feeling it; he came to college with more obstacles than Tyler, and it's been a very hard road. When Tyler studies him he has to wonder if Malik's anxieties are more about himself than about Tyler. Malik's too carefully guarded vulnerabilities, projected onto Tyler, create spaces he's not sure he wants to bridge. Sometimes Tyler wonders if Malik can read those thoughts in Tyler's fingertips on his skin, in the hesitation of his desire, in the space between Malik's touches and his responses. He doesn't think he can. But he doesn't trust, inside, that this version of himself, a closed off and careful and subdued Tyler, is a boy Malik will stay home for.

"Want to go home for dinner this weekend?" Tyler smiles when Malik looks up with his own smile. They have a history that spools behind them long before Idlewild, and it includes touchstones Tyler can use to guide them closer, to connect them.

"Yeah?" Malik. "You sure it'll be okay?'

Tyler shakes his head and smiles. "Of course, you know that. You're practically family." Malik does know, but sometimes he needs reminding that he has a place, that he has a place to land, too. Resentment shivers through the room and dissipates at Malik's smile.

* * *

TYLER MET MALIK THE SUMMER between his junior and senior year at Wayne State University at Hotter than July, Detroit's Black Pride. Potter Park was crowded and effervescent. July's heat was oppressive, what his Mama called August-hot: damp Michigan heat that wilts clothes, leaving everything soggy. Tyler was drunk and happy; there was so much glitter in his hair it drifted down whenever he shimmied hard. He was singing, dancing on a park bench, when a hand at his waist stopped him.

"You're gonna fall off of that thing, babe."

Tyler looked down and had to balance himself on the boy's shoulder. "I wasn't thinking of it just yet," he said.

"You plan these things?" the boy asked. He was cute as hell—not even cute, Tyler corrected himself. He was straight up gorgeous: dark, dark skin and wide eyes, built shoulders on display with muscled forearms and wide hands that were now wrapped around Tyler's waist. He wore a tight black tank top, low jeans and a very confident smirk.

Tyler blinked down at him coyly. He knew how he looked made up the way he was: white-glittered cheekbones and darkly lined eyes that made their green color glow in the party lights. "Just waiting for the right rescue," he said and laughed easily when lifted off of the bench as if he weighed nothing.

"I'm Malik," the boy said into his ear with his breath hot against Tyler's damp skin. He suppressed the deep shudder and desire that coursed through him. His hands curled over Malik's shoulders. The music was loud, and everyone was moving around them, dancing and grabbing, laughing and milling about. "Do you have a name, babe?"

Tyler smirked. "That one works for now." When Malik moved to step away he hooked a finger through the strap of Malik's tank top and glanced at him through his false eyelashes and shook his head. Malik ran one finger over Tyler's exposed collarbone; his white shirt was a very low scoop neck bearing multicolored hand prints.

Together with Tyler's friends Sasha and Dace and Malik's friend Craig, they made their way through the crowd, the revelry of Pride singing deep in Tyler's bones. They ended the night stumbling into Malik's apartment, laughter and desire making them clumsy. Tyler's tiny shorts were too tight at the start of the night; with Malik's mouth at his collarbone and big hands cupping his ass through the leather, they were downright painful. Together they barely got Tyler undressed before everything became a frantic mess of kisses and hands. Afterward, Tyler collapsed on Malik's unmade bed giggling through pulling his clothes back on.

"I'm surprised we didn't break the door," he whispered between afterglow kisses. Malik didn't bother pulling his clothes back on. His skin was warm and smooth against Tyler's palms.

"So, do I get your name now or what?" Malik asked.

Tyler couldn't stop running his fingers up and down the bulge of Malik's bicep. He bit his lip. "You think you'll need it?"

"Hmm, maybe next time," Malik mumbled.

Tyler smiled into the dark and half successfully wiggled under the covers.

"I'm Tyler."

* * *

TYLER IS TIRED THE NEXT morning after a night of restless sleep. It's his first real day of work, and Idlewild's soft open. All through training Asher's anxieties have radiated clearly to all of them. Each person hired embodies his hope and uncertainty; Asher doesn't have to ask for every one of them to understand that they are giving Asher a second, and maybe last, chance. Asher is likable, even when he doesn't seem easy or uncomplicated or accessible.

"You ready?" Claudia pats his arm. He nods.

"Of course. Just following today, right?" Tyler pulls his shoulders back and pastes on an easy smile.

IT'S DEFINITELY A SLOW START, but they opened at four, and very few people eat dinner at that time when there's nothing happening in the city. Asher had opted for what he called a "soft open"—a phrase that means nothing to Tyler—without fanfare or advertisement and with limited hours and menu.

"Once we have the hang of it, have ironed out some wrinkles that are bound to come up, we'll do a grand re-opening," Asher explained. Asher and George assured them that their menu is a rough draft and asked them to keep ears open for suggestions, complaints or praise for certain dishes.

Claudia is the picture of efficiency, and, despite her subdued and serious nature, she's all smiles and charm for the patrons they do have. Either she shines in this environment or she's a top-notch actress.

By seven they begin to fill and at seven thirty they experience a sudden wave of customers. Claudia has Tyler running food and drinks before long.

By ten he has a headache and his feet hurt; the heat from the kitchen is making him sweat, and his admiration for the experienced cooks and servers has gone up several notches.

Asher's on the floor more than Tyler expected, considering how withdrawn he usually seems. He's poised and friendly in a new way—he has definitely projected a nice guy persona from the start—but with patrons it's a completely different energy, calm and open and warm.

By the time the crush of dinner has passed, Tyler offers to cover their tables so that Claudia can take a small break; although Tyler's head is spinning, he feels competent enough to work alone for a bit. Their temporary menu features some designer cocktails with unique names Tyler isn't familiar with, so when a table begins to ask for suggestions he has to swallow discomfort and tell them he's training. He hates the feeling of admitting ignorance, the vulnerability of exposure, even if it's to a table of twenty-somethings out celebrating a birthday before a visit to the Greektown Casino.

"Claudia," he says as he pokes his head back into the small nook that serves as their breakroom. Claudia is eating fries, and Asher is breaking apart boxes and laying them in a pile.

"Sup? Need me out there?"

"Sorry, yeah. They are asking about gin fizzes? I have no idea."

She hops off the stool and pats his shoulder. "Sit for a minute and take your own break, honey."

Tyler sits. The silence is uncomfortable; Asher's still working on the boxes and Tyler, for once, has no idea what to say.

"You did ask if I have a good memory," he finally says. "I guess I've shown you now."

"No." Asher looks up from his work. "No, not at all. You're new to this. It's natural."

"So…" Tyler shifts on the high stool and begins to eat Claudia's fries. "How did tonight seem to you?"

"Good." Asher sighs, sits next to him and slides in the blade of the box cutter. "More people than I hoped for. There were snags, but we got hit all at once. You guys didn't fall apart too badly."

"Does it always go like that?" Tyler asks. "Everyone all at once?"

"Not always, but often. Weekends are downright insane sometimes, or when there are games or festivals. At least, they used to be. We'll see what happens when we open for full hours."

"It will again." It's a blind promise—Tyler has no authority of knowledge, and yet it seems to comfort Asher. He smiles hesitantly through a slow silence.

"All right," Asher says eventually. When the loud thump of Eminem's new song blaring from George's small stereo propped on the grill window filters back and the raucous laughter of the table he'd left comes past the swinging doors, Tyler realizes that it wasn't silence at all, but a moment they've both been lost in. He stands and brushes imaginary lint from his apron before rushing out onto the floor.

* * *

"YOU SMELL LIKE FOOD," MALIK mumbles against Tyler's shoulder once he's crawled into bed. It's dark; he's woken him.

"Sorry," Tyler whispers. "Want me to shower?"

Malik arranges his body around Tyler's. "No."

Tyler listens to the silence of late night and Malik's deep breathing. He feels too awake for the darkness, feels hemmed in by the weight of Malik's limbs around his. His feet bear the memory of too many steps.

Morning comes much too soon after an hour spent trying to fall asleep and an early rise with Malik, who has to get to classes.

"How'd it go?" Malik asks, swinging his foot so it bumps Tyler's. Tyler is working on prying his eyes open enough to see his coffee cup. Conversation is beyond him. Instead of answering he tips until his head is on Malik's shoulder. "That rough?" Laughter is clear in Malik's voice.

"Tired is all," Tyler mumbles. He feels the mug being taken from his hands, and Malik moves off the couch and helps him lie down. He kisses Tyler's cheek and covers him with a blanket. Malik is so sweet sometimes. He's dressed in a bright green shirt that makes his smooth dark skin shine.

"I love you," he says, hand on Malik's cheek. Malik's eyes widen. Tyler rarely says that anymore, not first, not plainly.

"I know." He kisses Tyler's palm, who is asleep before the door closes.

Chapter Five

"ALL RIGHT, EVERYONE," ASHER SAYS. He's got the whole front-of-house staff in the breakroom, crammed too close for comfort. "Yesterday went pretty well, and the week seems to be going okay. How do all of you feel it went?"

"I think there is room for improvement," Claudia offers. Asher suppresses a grin when he notices Tyler's eye roll.

"Is that a problem?" she asks, eyes cutting over to him.

"No, not at all," Tyler says, smile all sweetness. Asher narrows his eyes and makes a note to observe the two of them working together.

"Of course there is always room for improvement," Joy offers. "But I also think we're all doing well; this is new to all of us."

Now Claudia is rolling her eyes. Asher takes a deep breath and bites back the urge to call her out. "All right, so," he says, clearing his throat. "I want to sit down with everyone individually—we can do it after shift ends when you're counting out. If tonight doesn't work for you, tell me, and we can figure out when it will."

Everyone nods.

"Now, on to menu," he says. "Feedback on it from customers?"

"Lots of great feedback from mine, other than a few kitchen-issue complaints," Jared offers. He's slowly shredding an empty cigarette box someone left behind.

"Same," Tyler says.

"George, Santos and I are still keeping the menu fresh and flexible without letting go of things that are really popular. For now, I have these forms for you guys to fill out at the end of shift. Let us know what feedback you've gotten."

He sets his pad down on the long counter and claps Tyler on the shoulder. "You ready for this?" It's his first shift on his own.

Tyler shrugs. "I hope so."

"Don't worry too much," Asher says. "If you fuck up, win them over with your charm."

Tyler's face softens and brightens. "You think I'm charming?"

Asher bites his lip. Tyler has a naturally flirty way of speaking; it's almost saucy, and Asher has to remind himself it's not directed at him specifically. Asher wonders if he does it on purpose. "I think you know exactly what you can do."

Tyler winks before going to the kitchen. Asher is mostly successful at not staring at his ass.

THE SOUND OF CRASHING PLATES echoes through the clattering kitchen; even over the din Asher hears Tyler apologizing profusely. Perhaps he should have put Tyler on the floor alone on a lunch shift or weekday shift; it's the third mistake he's heard Tyler apologize for. The kitchen is soupy humid, full of too-loud voices calling orders and swearing. Asher works the food line in front of the windows, expediting orders. He and the servers are in each other's way; the rush seems to be disorganized tonight, and it's all Asher can do to keep them out of the weeds. The sweat along his temple brings memories of when Idlewild was one of the Woodward stretch hot-spots.

They somehow manage to limp through the rush with only minimal complaints and a few obvious errors. Once things slow down, Asher does a quick round. The bar is a wreck; lemon and lime wedges litter the floor along with ice. The bar rail is sticky, and the bottles are in the wrong order. Claudia is harassed enough that he doesn't say anything, just starts to clean, too. He keeps half an ear on the conversations behind the bar as Tyler recounts a mishap with a table. He's got Claudia and Jared cracking up over it, and from what Asher can tell, he'd managed the situation the best he could. He doesn't intrude on the conversation. He's strangely emotional tonight; his breath is tight in his chest, and something, he's not sure what, rises through him. He retreats to his office.

Asher almost regrets that. It's a relief to have some silence, but the office is a constant reminder of all the other things he's letting slide.

He sits down, pushes papers aside to clear a spot and examines the paper he'd made notes on at during the shifts. Their numbers haven't been staggering, but they've improved throughout the week. Asher has to think carefully about when to start expanding his staff. For now though, he'll have to get used to juggling.

Asher sits in the comforting press of silence when a soft knock interrupts.

"Hey, boss, can you check me out?" Tyler says when Asher lets him in. He pats his pockets and then searches for his keys.

"Yeah, I can," Asher jokes. He closes his eyes and shakes his head. *What's wrong with me?* "Can we forget I said that?"

Tyler only laughs. "No way! You made a joke. I'm putting it in the permanent memory bank."

Just that one? Asher almost says, barely biting it back. There's kidding, and then there's flirtation. Asher's not sure how to respond. He busies his hands, lifts piles of papers to make room, creates a small avalanche. Tyler takes it all in with wide eyes that Asher ignores. In the stark light of the office, they're greener contrasted with the darker tones of his skin. "Boss?"

Asher shakes himself. "Sorry." He takes the keys and then opens the door to let Tyler pass through. He bumps shoulders with him. "Don't call me boss."

Tyler laughs and goes to the bar register where Asher prints what he calls a read, a printout each server gets at the end of the night that breaks down sales by categories and also by payment types in order to establish if they owe the restaurant money or, if most of their transactions were via credit cards, what the restaurant owes them for their tips. Asher jokes with Claudia while Tyler sorts his checks, faces his money and lines up his credit card slips.

"Ready?" Asher asks. Tyler nods and follows him back to the office. His tips don't amount to anything grand, especially after he tips out to Claudia, who had been working at the bar, for which Asher apologizes.

"I'm on limited tables, boss, don't worry." Tyler tucks the folded bills into a wallet that he manages, somehow, to squeeze into the back pocket of his tight, tight, pants. "Any amount of money right now helps out."

"You did well," Asher says. It's not quite true; Tyler fell into the weeds midshift, but he didn't fall apart and he handled his mistakes with grace. Asher clears his throat. Sitting in his chair while Tyler stands by the door puts him at an awkward angle. "I promise you'll have more tables soon."

"Excellent." Tyler turns back, hand on the doorknob and smiles; there's some secret in the shape of his lips that Asher isn't sure how to read. "Have a good one, boss," Tyler says, a little breathy and all camp; Tyler throws him a wink over his shoulder as he exists to the sound of Asher's light laughter.

Now that Asher has seen him in action, he thinks that, once Tyler finds his footing, he could be invaluable to the restaurant. Tyler's natural charisma and magnetism can be stunning. He waits in the silence of the office for the tightening of his stomach to ease before going back and tells himself he's only noticed it because he's imagining a future for his business. Tyler definitely mentioned having a boyfriend and, although he hasn't spoken of him since, Asher doesn't read Tyler as the type of boy to flirt with intention while with someone else.

George stays late cleaning the kitchen. He's meticulous, which Asher appreciates. They don't talk much, just listen to the radio and work companionably. By the time Asher lets him out the back door it's past one, and his whole body is urgently asking him to take a rest. He won't get up again if he sits, though. He does a last check of the restaurant, thinks about the paperwork he has to do and then closes his tired eyes, shakes his head, and goes upstairs.

Without the radio, the building is quiet but for the settling language of old bricks and tired walls. Despite his exhaustion, Asher lies awake. His empty bed is lined with loneliness, and his skin aches for something he can't give it. It's been a long time since he's had sex, much less had a lover who would understand him well enough to calm the jittering energy of his muscles.

It's just as well. Asher hasn't energy for his own self-care, much less anyone else's. He contemplates his body: warring exhaustion and urgent desire. He tries to push the image of Tyler, coquette, from his head. Asher shakes his head, rolls onto his side and pushes his hands under his pillow, away from the temptation that will only muddy the working relationship he's trying to foster.

*   *   *

SUNDAY IS THEIR QUIETEST DAY. Asher commits himself to office work and to fleshing out a business plan. Sales, though limited due to hours, show a tiny positive trend. Any evidence of forward momentum is like a spark, a spark Asher knows he has to fan into flames, and that'll take more than sitting and waiting, more than hoping. He sifts through everything for bills and invoices and stacks them in the top rack of a letter tray he hasn't actually used in months. A cost/benefit plan breaking down projections for when to increase hours isn't getting Idlewild's name on the street in a fresh light.

The ring of the back doorbell lifts him from a haze hours later. His eyes burn; staring at the computer screen does that. He rubs them as he exits the room. Tyler is at the door, an hour early, which Asher is beginning to get used to.

"Sorry, I'm here really—"

"Don't worry about it."

"I won't get in your way, I promise." Tyler's smile is sincere but there's a shadow of something else. Asher swallows.

"I could probably use some company."

Tyler examines him. "You look like you've been up for hours."

"Is that a kind way of telling me I look like shit?"

Tyler rolls his eyes and bumps into him playfully. "You never look like shit and you know it." His eyes flit up to Asher's and away; warmth flickers under Asher's skin. He's unused to appreciation.

"Since I'm here anyway, want me to get the front of house set up?"

Asher hums an affirmative, but then blinks.

"Actually, wait. How do you feel about extra money?"

Tyler squints at him. "Is this a trick question?"

"You're a smart kid and you have time to kill. Maybe I could run some ideas by you?"

"I can definitely do that." He stashes his bag in his locker and slams the door shut.

Asher leads him into the office; it's a catastrophe of papers and coffee mugs and office flotsam. He winces.

"Actually, let me grab my notes and stuff and meet you out front. Would you mind making coffee, and we can sit out there?"

Tyler salutes; Asher hears him mutter something about the mess giving him hives. He's still chuckling when he juggles his way to the front of house with stacks of papers, a notepad, a laptop and his pens.

"Just how you like it." Tyler pushes a mug of coffee at him. Clean, early light filters in the windows behind him where Woodward is beginning to wake up. His eyes are cast in shadow; the sharp bones of his chin and those high, high cheekbones are even more striking than usual. *God, you are so pretty.* Asher barely bites the words back, covering them with a too big sip of coffee he almost spits onto his shirt. *Wow. Hot.*

Tyler smirks.

"Have you ever gone to Downtown Street Eats?" Asher decides to cut to the chase.

"No, I don't think so?"

"They do this thing down at Campus Martius during the week. Food trucks and other local restaurants hand out samples. There's always stuff going on down there, you know, concerts and fitness classes and shit."

"That's interesting," Tyler says. "I've not really spent a ton of time Downtown before."

"I was thinking maybe I should try to get us on the calendar, before we go into a grand reopen." He waves a weary hand at the papers. "I should research it. But…"

Tyler waits him out, lips pursed and wide eyed.

"Do you ever have so much to do that it all blends together and you get overwhelmed enough to avoid figuring out where to start?"

"Oh, honey, I coulda gotten a degree in that at Wayne." Tyler holds his hands out for Asher's laptop. "How about this. You do your numbery-restauranty thing—"

"Inventory?"

"And I'll look into this for you. Costs, times, logistics. How's that sound?"

Asher closes his eyes and yawns. "Amazing."

"Great." Tyler is already clicking away on the laptop. "Then you'll know if this is good idea. If you do decide to do this, you should totally take me." Tyler's confidence is refreshing. "People like me. I am good at that, making people like me, disarming them. Then I can go in for the kill." He winks and laughs. "The sell, I mean!"

"I've borne witness," Asher attests. "Tyler," he says, then lowers his voice. "Thank you. Really."

Tyler smiles; it lights the room and it punches straight through Asher's gut. "Anytime, boss."

"So, you don't seem to be close to done here," Tyler says forty-five minutes later when Claudia's arrived and he's finally tracked Asher down in the dry storage room.

"No, I'm doing inventory, which is a long, soul-crushing job." Asher hops off of the stool he's been standing on. "Please tell me you have some exciting news or ideas for me?"

"Definitely." Tyler holds out a paper he's taken notes on. Asher sticks it on the clipboard without glancing at it.

"Don't think I'm offering because you need to pay me or anything," Tyler says. "But would you like me to help put this together so you can focus on finishing your thing?"

Asher bites his lip. Lunch is starting already, and Tyler is shadowing Claudia at the bar today. "I'd like that, but...would you mind doing it after your shift? Or early tomorrow? I'd definitely pay you."

"I can stay late, no problem. I'll just text Malik to tell him; he had a thing anyway."

"Malik?"

"My boyfriend. Um... yeah." Tyler twists his shoulders in a gesture Asher can't read.

"Okay," Asher says. Startled, he realizes he has no idea what Tyler's life is like outside of Idlewild. He'll have to add enigma to the list of words he's using to try to figure Tyler out.

Chapter Six

"IT'S EARLY." MALIK ROLLS OVER and grabs at him, sleepy and uncoordinated.

"Yes," Tyler says, rubbing his palm, fond and soft, over the barely there roughness of Malik's hair. "Today is Downtown Street Eats. I promised Asher I would help him and George, remember?"

"Ugh." Malik rubs his eyes and sits. "When'll you be home?"

"This is gonna be an all-day thing," Tyler says. Dawn is breaking but their curtains hold most of the early light out. He fumbles for his clothes. Malik lies down, making sleepy, not-so-happy noises. Once dressed, Tyler sits carefully and kisses his cheek and jaw. He hates when people are annoyed with him. "I love you," he whispers into the safe bowl of Malik's neck.

"Mm." Malik kisses him back, fleeting, soft. "You too."

Brandon is still sleeping, so Tyler tries his hardest to be quiet as he grabs a toaster pastry and his work bag with serving clothes. He walks down the hall to the stairs, pressed forward by an unsettling silence from the other residents; everyone else has the good sense to still be sleeping.

He devours the pastry, cold and sugary, as he waits for the bus. The sparse beginning of morning rush hour trundles past along Woodward. Tyler begins to sweat despite his thin shirt and imagines the sun resurrecting the dew, imagines the August humidity coming up from the ground, wilting and thick. It's probably not how humidity works, but he's always loved the image; thinking of the dew drops lining all the leaves like zombies ready for rebirth.

The bus is a loud interloper, startling him out of his thoughts. He swings up, yawns through paying his fare and lets himself doze. Asher doesn't come to the door when he rings; the dumpster they share in the alley with the other storefronts is almost full; he waves to Demitri, the cook from *The Black Swan,* and resorts to calling Asher.

"Sorry about that," Asher says, opening to door. He locks it behind Tyler. Inside it's warm—over-warm—and the breakroom is a mess. Asher's hair is a thick riot. It's unfair how Asher makes rumpled seem so sexy.

"Did I wake you?"

"Yeah," Asher admits. "I think I hit the snooze button about twenty times."

"I understand that, honey." Tyler smiles. "Usually because I've had a great night the night before, though."

Asher shrugs, but it's good-natured. "Nothing thrilling in my life right now."

Did I overstep? Tyler follows Asher to the kitchen where George is singing and prepping food to go.

"Don't worry so much," Asher says, reading him perfectly. His genuine and bright smile, a rare and lovely thing, diffuses Tyler's apprehension. "It was a bad joke."

"Okay." Tyler traces the shape of a floor tile with the toe of his shoe. He looks up and into Asher's steady gaze.

"Ready to work?" Asher asks. Tyler nods and shelves the moment for thought later.

THE MORNING'S WILTING HUMIDITY HAS nothing on the afternoon. Despite the shade of the pop-up tent, they're all sweating.

"It's like breathing through a sponge," Tyler complains. George hands him a napkin he's dampened with water to wipe his face.

"Hi!" A little girl and her mother come up to the table.

"Hi there." Tyler bends down so he's on eye level with her. She's adorable with her hair in two snowball buns on the sides of her head and a sweet, bashful smile and chocolate smudges on her face. "How are you doing today, sweetie?"

"I got ice cream," she says proudly. "Before lunch even." She widens her eyes; next to him both Asher and George chuckle.

"This must be a special day, then," Tyler says. He glances up at her mother. She looks worn, sweaty, but fond.

"Not so special we shouldn't try to eat some lunch, right, Abigail? And maybe some vegetables." Abigail makes a face, and Tyler winks, leans forward, and stage-whispers. "Don't worry, we put magic on our vegetables."

George has already put together a small offering—their pulled pork sliders and, on the side, fried Brussels sprouts with a balsamic glaze.

"What's 'at?" She points at the Brussels sprouts.

"How about I'll eat one if you do?" Tyler offers her one and solemnly takes his own. He senses Asher next to him. He doesn't mind being watched; he glances back and offers a teasing smile. He turns back to Abigail, toasts her with his Brussels sprout, which makes her giggle, and encourages her to eat hers at the same time. Her eyes widen and a big smile breaks out on her face. By the time she's finished chewing, Tyler has fist-bumped her and handed her mother a card.

"You should come over," he says. "Our Grand Reopen is next week." He winks at Abigail. "Lots of magic veggies there, too."

They've gathered a small crowd: some people looking to see what's going on and others on tiptoes to see what they're offering.

"Give me some cards," Tyler says over his shoulder to Asher. "And smile!"

He skirts around and out of the booth. Without the shade, the heat ramps up; he barely notices. He wanders a little; happiness fizzes through him. Surrounded by community, with music on a stage to the left and so many people happy who have come together share this experience—this is one of many things he's always wanted for Detroit.

Tyler loves people and he knows how to make them love him. He mills around introducing himself to people. He's a boy from a different world in the same city, and today he gets to be a part of bridge-building. Every now and then he catches Asher's eyes on him through the crowd. Tyler convinces people to go taste their food. He hands out cards, and when the park thins, Asher comes out to walk with him.

"You're so good at this." Asher is direct, and his admiration is clear and Tyler is so, so grateful.

"Thank *you*," Tyler says by way of acknowledgment for everything. "This was so much fun. Can we do it again?"

"It was. Plus I could probably use more fun." Asher falls in step with him. "Confession? Time for fun is a distant memory."

"Well then, you definitely need to try it more," Tyler says.

Asher looks up into the sky, squinting against the bright sun and unending blue of the cloudless day. "Should I ever manage to get Idlewild floating again, maybe. It's been so long, I think I've forgotten how to have fun."

Tyler touches Asher's shoulder.

"When we're done here, we should go get a drink."

Asher blinks and smiles. "That sounds…yeah. How about I take you and George out, as a thanks? I don't know why I don't think of these things."

Because you're fucking exhausted. The food trucks are shutting down, but people are still gathered at tables, talking and drinking. At their tent, George is packing up.

"We should probably go help George," he says to Asher. He puts a hand on Asher's back to guide him to their stand. Even through the shirt his skin is warm. Tyler tucks his hands into his pockets and takes a breath. Asher is quiet; Tyler can tell he's contented. They share a sweet smile and affection curls in Tyler's stomach.

GEORGE DEMURS WHEN ASHER OFFERS to take them for a drink. Tyler hugs him before he leaves. "Give your family kisses from me." Tyler winks, and George laughs. He's never met George's family, but knows they could all use some laughter. He hopes when he makes George laugh it's a lightness he carries home with him.

Asher decides to walk down Monroe toward Greektown, where there's a cluster of restaurants. "Some of these have changed, and I haven't checked them out in ages," he confesses. Tyler is happy to follow. It's been a long day, but he's the best kind of tired, the kind that comes with doing rewarding work. This is how he feels when he does volunteer work.

"Oh, my god, Flood's!" Tyler exclaims. "Dace told me I should come here some time. Can we go?" He's aware that he's hopped up onto his toes.

"Sure," Asher says. He leads them into the restaurant, which is dark and, since it's relatively early, only about half full.

"Soul food," Tyler moans theatrically. The slight drama is totally worth it when he's rewarded with Asher's laugh. They make small talk until their food comes. Asher's more intent on playing with his side of macaroni and cheese than eating it.

"Asher, can I ask you something?"

"I'd normally say no," Asher teases, "but since that's the first time you've used my name instead of 'boss,' I will."

Tyler ducks his head. "All the heat wrung the professionalism out of me."

"*Boss* makes me feel a million years old. I'm older than you, but not that old. You have got to stop."

"You aren't that much older than me, are you?"

"That's your big question?" Asher smiles in a way Tyler hasn't seen; his eyes brighten. He seems more unguarded.

"No," Tyler laughs. "Though I am curious."

"I'm thirty-two," Asher says. "Ancient to you."

Tyler bites his lip. "Haven't you heard? Thirty is the new twenty."

Something fleeting crosses Asher's face before he smiles again. Tyler swallows a flutter of worry.

"I would do that again in a second," Asher says.

"What? Your twenties?" Tyler asks.

"Yeah. They were good."

Tyler knows about Asher's husband—well, that he had one and he died a while back.

"I'm sorry—"

"Don't be; it's fine." Asher spins his beer. "Maybe one day things will be settled and I can kick things up like I'm young again."

Tyler rolls his eyes. "Like I said, you are young."

"Young and stupid then," Asher says, and smiles brighter when Tyler giggles. "So what was your real question?"

Are you lonely? Tyler bites it back. "Have you ever done karaoke? Because I hear they start at seven."

"Oh, my god. Not for a long time. My karaoke days are over."

Tyler just lifts one shoulder. "Don't underestimate my powers of persuasion."

After a long pause, Asher smiles, and the moment passes. "I won't."

Tyler stays late to help Asher with the inventory he abandoned to do Eats. Asher didn't ask him to, but Tyler can tell he's grateful. They're both tired and clumsy.

Tyler pants as he grips the metal shelf. "Why do you keep paper plates back here when you have room in other spots?"

"Fuck, I have no idea," Asher says. "I didn't even realize I had them."

"Well then." Tyler wiggles forward, grabs the commercial packages of paper plates and passes them back. He can't reach them all and he can't climb onto the shelf so he wiggles back slowly. When his feet are close enough, he feels Asher's hand on his leg, guiding it back to the step stool, and when he wobbles, on his thigh to steady him. He winces as his shirt pulls against the shelves and his stomach scrapes against the metal. It's impossible to ignore the heat of Asher's hand, which doesn't move even when he's safely landed. Their eyes connect. It's not only the heat of that palm Tyler feels but Asher's eyes steady on his, dark in the dusty storeroom. The heat curls into Tyler's core and flushes over his skin. He exhales, trying to ignore recognition of that feeling; its flavor is like the one earlier, the moment of honest connection over dinner. Only now it's sharper and so, so much easier to define. Asher snatches his hand away.

"God, sorry," Asher says, almost inaudibly. He's turned away. From Tyler's perch on the stool, an extended hand is meant to comfort Asher. Tyler tries to ignore the power imbalance of the position, to calm him without condescension or false words.

"It's fine," he says. He steps down and moves the stool over when Asher takes a step back. Asher inhales, harsh and sudden, and turns back with his face neutral and blank. Tyler smiles, and Asher does as well; if he wants to act as if nothing happened, Tyler is willing to play along.

TYLER COMES IN THE NEXT morning dead on his feet. He was close to dead on his feel when he got home last night, but Malik was feeling frisky and he kept Tyler up even later. Asher lets him in, and rather than start opening, they sit in the office, make small talk and eventually doze off.

The ringing of the back doorbell startles Tyler. Asher snorts and wakes with a jerk, accidentally kicking Tyler in the shin.

"Fuck, time 'izit?" Asher scrubs his hands over his face. The bell rings insistently.

"Too early," Tyler says over the shrill noise. "God, shut up. I'm here." Tyler opens the door and lets in Claudia and Santos.

"What the fuck were you doing? You look like crap," she says. He smiles, the bitchiest one he can muster. "No, really," she insists.

"I fell asleep on the desk," he admits. He tries to crack his neck, because he can feel the crick in it. "We were here late after Eats."

"God, you're so much more devoted than I am." She cracks open an energy drink and slumps on the stool with a sigh. Tyler roots around in his bag for his serving shirt. Halfway out of the shirt he's wearing, he hears someone clear his throat.

"Undressing in the breakroom?" Asher says. Tyler pulls on his work shirt.

"Sorry," he says. "That's probably not a good idea, is it?"

Asher's lips do that *thing*, the quarter-quirk that's close to a smile. His cheeks are a little red. Tyler holds his own smirk in. It might not be professional or right, but it's flattering when someone finds you attractive. "Perhaps not."

Tyler salutes him. "Duly noted, boss." He and Claudia laugh when Asher rolls his eyes. Tyler tucks his shirt in and stuffs the other one in his bag.

"Can I have the keys back?" Asher asks.

"Oh yeah, sorry." Tyler fishes them out of his pocket, wiggling a little. Claudia snorts and slaps his ass.

"Can you even breathe with those on?" she asks.

Tyler winks at Claudia and tosses the keys to Asher. "The point is to make it hard for the other boys to breathe, honey."

"Ooh, now you're a player?"

Tyler shrugs. "Hardly. You know me." He looks at Asher and explains. "I'm hopelessly monogamous. I might be the last man standing on that island."

"No, definitely not," Asher says. He's swinging the keys in jerky circles over his finger.

"Aw, this is so sweet. Sharing circle at the crack of dawn." Claudia mimes throwing up.

"Shush." Tyler covers her mouth and doesn't meet Asher's eyes. He's flustered and at the sound of the office door swinging shut he breathes a sigh of relief.

"What is up with you?" Claudia demands.

"I have no idea," Tyler admits. "Come on, let's go get everything set up."

"Ignoring thin—"

He cuts her off. "Yes. Please."

She pauses. "Okay. I'm here. If you need an ear."

"Thanks, honey." He beginning to learn that Claudia is genuinely caring under her gruff exterior. Maybe with time, she'll become a true friend.

Chapter Seven

ASHER IS AWARE THAT HIS employees know he's a widower. He's not sure *how* they know, and they've never said anything to him, but it's one of those open secrets Asher's unsure how to address. He's not sure he *wants* to. He's often tempted to tell them the bar's history. Not the building's history in the city, which is printed on the back of every menu and on their website. But *his* history, his and John's. As people have begun to come back to Idlewild, so have his hopes, and with them, some of the joy he used to take in this place. That surfacing echoes and sometimes aches; he wishes he had someone to celebrate these steps with who carries the same stake and investment and heart as he does.

The thing is, Asher can't tell his staff about Idlewild. And that's not only because it would invite an intimacy he's not sure would be good for his dynamic with them, but because the history and his and John's are intertwined. Idlewild's story is a beautiful mess.

Asher could tell them of their first blockbuster night. He could tell them how amazing it felt despite the rush and intensity and errors. But he could never capture how it felt to lock the doors at the end of the night and have John catch him from behind into a swinging hug. How they laughed into a kiss and made love on the floor. How they knew as they moved together that they had made something incredible, utterly theirs.

How could Asher explain why he kept Idlewild despite it all? He reopened a week after John's funeral under the misguided hope that it would establish some normalcy in his life. He reopened and then fell apart not even a week later. John haunted him in every corner, in every draft and crashing pan, in the shouts of the staff through a rush and the crushing silence in the office.

John's family and Asher's brother Eli took turns driving in to help him. Telling his new staff this story means that he'd have to explain why his family hasn't been here to help since. He's not sure he could answer that—or that he wants to.

Morning is tight in his bones, and he hurts with exhaustion. In the office Asher ignores the mess, as he always does. On the set of hooks by the door hangs a single, useless key. He always forgets to hang his own keys; rather he tosses them on the desk as soon as he's in the door, which necessitates a search and rescue effort whenever he needs them again.

But this key doesn't move. It's the color of darkened silver, on a simple chain. Asher has changed the locks a few times in Idlewild's history, but this key was *theirs*. Their first key to the restaurant. Asher found it in John's nightstand a few months after his death, when he'd started packing things away and getting ready to move. He'll never understand why John kept it; John wasn't a sentimental man. But Asher was. He'd hung that key, and for the first few years its presence was both a comfort and a source of pain.

Owning a restaurant had been John's dream since he was a little kid. When they were dating it was always a "what if" dream John would talk about when they were curled around each other, lazing into sleep. Asher can't pinpoint when it became his dream too; after a few years it must have soaked into his bones until it became the sort of wish they had semi-serious conversations about, a "what if" that became a "maybe one day."

They both enjoyed relatively stable jobs, Asher in insurance sales and John doing freelance IT work for chain restaurants. They were great at saving, choosing to live in small apartments with cheap furniture.

They both knew that somewhere in the future they'd need money for something: children, a house in the suburbs. They had lots of dreams together.

But when John's grandfather died suddenly, he left behind a large trust no one had known about and they suddenly came into *a lot* of money.

"What if" and "maybe when" became, "oh my god, now."

"Are you sure this is something you want?" John asked him. They were at the tiny table they'd wedged into the breakfast nook of their galley kitchen. Although their big, drafty picture window was covered in plastic wrap to try to keep the apartment warmer, Asher was shivering.

"Well, no," Asher remembers saying. "But it's like having a kid, I think. When people ask if you're ready, and you realize you'll never be ready exactly, but you still want a kid."

"Do you?" John said. His smile was sweet; his hair was sticking up in all directions. His hands were wrapped around his coffee mug. Asher did the same, hoping to retain the warmth. Sunday stretched before them with the promise of no responsibilities for the day woven throughout. Sunday mornings with John had been one of his favorite parts of living with him.

"Of course," Asher said. He wormed his toes under John's stockinged feet. "One day. But do I want this, too, even if I question it or worry sometimes."

John's face then, bright with a smile, is something Asher will always hold in his heart. He pulled Asher onto his lap and kissed him, and kissed and kissed, keeping his arms tight around his waist. This memory is one of the things that's kept Asher hanging on to Idlewild.

Asher's first choice was always Detroit. It was a gamble, and an expensive one, too. He had to convince John, who understood the desire to be a part of change in the city. But he didn't understand why it was so personally important to Asher. It was hard to quantify and hard to articulate because it came from the smallest wisp of a memory, from when he was thirteen. He remembered his parents talking about

Detroit with someone else—he's not sure who—and his mother told them she would never go into that city again, that it was hopeless. Asher had begun to struggle with understanding his sexuality, waking every day with dread and anxiety. Admitting it to himself had been hard enough, but the idea of telling his conservative parents, in their conservative town, of disrupting their lives and beliefs and changing utterly whom they thought he was—that seemed hopeless too. Her words lit the smallest fire in him, which burned low but constant over the years. Hopelessness, he taught himself, wasn't an option. Fight was, and hard work, and changing a world that gave up on things, on people.

When Idlewild was a nascent but tangible dream, finally Asher understood what he could do with that fire: create change in a city so many people had given up on.

IDLEWILD HAD BEEN MANY THINGS in its previous life. They were told it was originally a dry goods store built in 1890. After the Great Depression, when Detroit was shaping itself into part of Roosevelt's Arsenal of Democracy and auto factories were turning out tanks and Jeeps, airplanes, bombs and so much more, a man named Gerald Heimer bought the three-story building and made it the bar of the new Ponchartrain Inn. By the time John and Asher saw it for the first time, it had been several bars, worn many faces and, over the years, become more and more neglected.

It needed a lot of work but had beautiful bones. Everything was in some state of disrepair, although the kitchens in the back were set up well enough. Everywhere paint was peeling, revealing plaster that needed repair, and the front-of-house probably had once been a cream color that had grayed over the years. It would all need updating and care. The third floor, which must have been used as an apartment or living space at some time, was a disaster, but they both agreed that was a project that could wait. Despite the mess and scope of work ahead of them, they both fell hard for the space; its history and future seemed clear, laid out before and ahead with their hopes and hard work the nexus of that potential.

* * *

"Can I ask you a question?" Tyler says, startling Asher out of his thoughts. They're in a lull between lunch and dinner shifts. Tyler and Jared are finishing the late lunches; Jared has gone out to the alley to smoke. Asher rarely has much to say when his staff sits to socialize or chat during their breaks or after shift. Mostly he enjoys listening and being with other people.

"Sure," Asher says. He shifts on the stool he's sitting on and faces Tyler more fully.

"How long have you been here?"

"Since morning?" Asher responds.

"No, I mean at Idlewild. Someone said that your—" Tyler looks down.

Asher bites his lip and looks at the ceiling. "We bought the restaurant, um… eight years ago? So yeah, um… we didn't have it that long before John died." He clears his throat.

"John was your husband, right?" Tyler's voice is soft, as if he might startle Asher with his questions.

"Yes."

"You must have married very young," Tyler says. His smile is sweet—almost wistful. Asher tries to understand what's in Tyler's eyes.

"Yeah, we were very young." Sometimes Asher feels ages older than he is. Youth is a dream, even though he is still young. "No one gets married that young nowadays, do they?"

"Oh, I'm sure some people do. People who are sure. Who trust each other and want to do the marriage thing." Tyler fiddles with his apron strings, tying them into a series of knots and then untying them. Asher is dying to ask more questions. He wants to ask about Tyler's boyfriend. They must have an up and down relationship because Tyler's moods are unpredictable when he comes into the restaurant, confused winds blowing in surprising gusts. On the floor when he's working, Tyler's always lovely and lively with customers. He charms them easily and naturally. He holds on to that with everyone, but some mornings when they're both exhausted and working in the pressing silence of the empty restaurant, Tyler is still wearing worries he slowly shuts away as the day breaks.

"The marriage thing?" Asher finally settles on asking. He and John were lectured by some of their gay friends about buying into a heteronormative narrative and institution. Asher always rolled his eyes at it. What others did was their business, but he meant every promise he made to John and he wanted their marriage. It wasn't technically legal in Michigan back then, but in their hearts and intentions it was as powerful and true.

"Yeah. Lots of people I know aren't into it," Tyler explained.

"You?" Asher tries to keep his voice light, conversational.

"No, I think I'd want to, one day. But Malik is in camp 'marriage is for the straights.'" Asher snorts and Tyler laughs.

"Malik is your boyfriend, right?"

"Yeah." Tyler's eyes light up. "He's an amazing guy. Goes to UDM. Whenever I think about how hard things have been for me, I have to remind myself of what he's done."

"Oh?" Asher sits again, curiosity winning over his feigned-casual questioning.

"He grew up down in the city too, but in Delray. You familiar?"

"Yeah," Asher says. It's one of the worse areas of Detroit.

"Takes a lot to get out the places we grew up in, you know? Him especially." Tyler squares his shoulders. "But that's not really my story to tell."

Asher can tell that Tyler isn't comfortable with the subject. Despite his curiosity, both about Tyler's story and his boyfriend's, he won't push.

"He works so hard; wants to change the world," Tyler says, then stands, brushing his apron off.

"They offer degrees in that?" Asher says and is rewarded by another laugh. "Maybe I should have studied that."

"I know, right?"

The back doorbell buzzes, and Tyler lets Jared in. Asher doesn't offer more, and Tyler doesn't ask; instead Asher goes into the office and shuffles papers into new piles, thinking all the while of questions unasked and unanswered.

Chapter Eight

"WHERE WERE YOU?" TYLER ROLLS onto his side and then sleepily sits. He peeks at the clock, and it's past two. "You said you'd be home in a little bit, two hours ago." Tyler tugs down his shirt. He fell asleep waiting for Malik.

"Man, don't nag," Malik says. He's stripping off his clothes. His tone stings.

"I was worried is all," Tyler says, as neutrally as he can.

Malik climbs into bed, boxers only, and pulls the covers up—or tries; Tyler is on them. "I'm fine. Don't be." Malik lays down, turned away from Tyler. His words are dismissive. The sheer rudeness of his actions makes Tyler so mad his fingers feel numb. But he can tell Malik has been drinking, so he doesn't say anything. Instead he strips off his own clothes and climbs under the covers. He pulls them over Malik, who is already almost asleep.

Tyler's not dumb. This isn't the first time Malik has done this. He can only hope it isn't what it seems to be. Last time this resentment settled between them, Malik left. When Tyler remembers, his stomach hollows, his heart beats faster and anxiety builds slowly in his chest.

In the morning, Tyler still feels that space between them. Malik says good morning carefully. Before he can get out of bed, Tyler rolls over and puts his hand on Malik's stomach. He kisses Malik's chest and closes his eyes. This is the language he knows best to keep them connected.

With Tyler's work hours and Malik's school, they are often ships in the night with a common disconnect but not the urge to bridge it. Now he thinks maybe he was too complacent, trusting Malik's commitment more than he should have.

"Tyler—" Malik starts. Tyler rolls on top of him and kisses him before he can say anything else. Malik runs his hands up Tyler's back, and they both pretend that nothing is wrong. Tyler doesn't like doing that, but he'll take whatever he can get right now, because today everything might be slipping through his fingers.

* * *

"OH MY GOD, JONES AND Company fucking raised the prices of almost everything," Asher says the next morning, slapping an invoice on the counter. Overtired and trying to hide his anxieties, Tyler's just stumbled in. Asher's worries are radiating so clearly though that it is easy for Tyler to push his aside.

Tyler picks up the invoice. "They didn't tell you this was going to happen?"

Asher paces—as much as one can in a postage-stamp-sized room. "No. Well. I don't know." He gestures at the desk, where a pile of mail and papers spills from Asher's half of the desk to what has become Tyler's since Tyler started helping with inventory more often. After the last time Asher got tense about Tyler messing with his papers during inventory, Tyler had stopped touching them. Tyler resists the urge to point out that if Asher wasn't so fucking sensitive about being bad at organizing, this might not have happened. Of course, he can't do that since he doesn't have confirmation that there is a notice. And it's not his place, or his business.

Asher's pawing through the papers. Some scatter to the floor. Tyler closes his eyes.

"I suck at this," Asher mutters, so quietly Tyler almost misses it.

"What, paperwork?" Tyler is surprised Asher's acknowledged it.

Asher thumps into his chair, then folds his arms on the desk and puts his head down. He mumbles into his arms.

"Did you just say *at life?*" Tyler asks cautiously.

Asher's shoulders are slumped. He looks so defeated Tyler has to control the urge to hug him.

"Yes."

"Asher," Tyler starts, then stops. He doesn't want to overstep, but he's terrible at *not* comforting people. "You don't suck at life."

"I do, though." Asher ticks items off his fingers. "My restaurant is failing. My employees hate me. I am a total hermit—"

"Okay, whoa, whoa, *whoa*—" Tyler holds up his hands, gesturing for Asher to stop. "First, your employees in no way hate you. Second, if your restaurant was failing, we wouldn't be here. Third…"

Asher cocks an eyebrow, and Tyler shrugs. "Okay, I don't know, some people prefer solitude? Being workaholics?"

"I never did before. Do you know how long—" Asher cuts himself off. "Anyway, the point is, look at this." He points at the mess. Tyler takes a breath—he's not sure if he should point out that he's tried helping and that Asher has resisted, or offer to help again.

"Does it bother you when I help?"

"Yes. No," Asher says. "Both?"

"Oh." Tyler wasn't expecting the honesty. "Can I ask why? To the yes?"

Asher swivels in his chair, back and forth; the chair clicks like a metronome. Tyler presses his lips together, determined to wait out Asher's silence without prompting him. Something crashes in the kitchen, and George swears.

"I've always sucked at asking for help," he says eventually. "John hated that. I guess I was raised to think that asking for help means you're failing."

"Please don't take this to mean I think you're failing," Tyler starts. "But you just told me *you* think you are."

Asher's lips move in a way that could almost, perhaps, be considered a part of a near-smile territory. "You make a valid point."

"Listen," Tyler says. "Seriously. Everyone is good at something. They're okay at a lot of other things, and they suck at some too."

"This is encouraging," Asher says. Tyler resists the urge to swat at him the way his mother would at the tone and interruption: part playful and part serious.

"My point is that it's okay not to be good at some things and need help for them," Tyler says. "You're great at lots of things."

Asher is quiet again. The clock ticks, and the sound of voices draws closer to the office. A quiet knock disrupts them. Tyler rolls his eyes. Of course. Maybe he was about to get somewhere—if only permission to get his hands on Asher's messy desk. Asher offers him a half smile—it's forced—and opens the door.

* * *

THE NEXT DAY ASHER ANSWERS the bell promptly. He's dressed carefully, pressed and put together. He smiles when he sees Tyler, and, for once, it's completely genuine. Tyler's struck again by how handsome Asher is, and how much that expression transforms his face.

"Will you come into the office?" Asher asks, almost formally.

"Uh, yeah?" Tyler wonders what's up.

"I thought a lot about our conversation yesterday," Asher starts almost as soon as the door is closed. He leans against the counter across from the door, which leaves little room for Tyler to maneuver past him, so he hovers by the door. Asher doesn't seem to notice that it's awkward.

"Okay..."

"And I have no idea what I'm good at anymore," Asher says. He's way too cheerful for what he's saying, and Tyler is caught completely off guard. "But you're right, everyone sucks at something. Or things," he corrects himself. "And I suck at this—" he sweeps his hand out, gesturing at the whole desk, which seems to be in worse condition than it was yesterday.

"Asher—" Tyler starts.

"And whenever you've helped me organize, it's been helpful." Asher talks so fast he trips over his words. Tyler wonders if he's slept; he seems jittery and way too happy for someone admitting that he can only see weaknesses about. "I feel as though maybe when you have helped I've been a little edgy about it?" Asher looks at Tyler.

"Well... I mean—" Tyler stammers.

"I'd forgotten," Asher says. "John told me once that I get really uptight about that kind of stuff. I think..."

Tyler waits. And waits.

"I think I'm always so stressed out I can't tell when I'm being even *more* of a jerk."

"Well, I'd never say it like that," Tyler says.

"Whatever," Asher waves it off. "The point is... the point is that I need help. And—" for the first time, his chipper demeanor wavers. "Maybe if I had help with the stuff I'm not good at, I could figure out what I *am* good at. And that probably will help the restaurant."

"Asher," Tyler starts, soft-voiced and honest, "You're good at—"

"No, no," Asher interrupts. His voice is quiet too, although he still smiles. It's not as unsettling a smile, though. "We'll get to that later. Right now I'm hoping we can find a letter from Jones and Company about the produce so that I can figure out who to yell at and what to do next."

Tyler swallows his protests. Asher's admitted he needs help, and that it's hard for him to do so; Tyler doesn't want to push his luck or Asher's limits.

"So, while we're talking about out what comes next..."

"Hm?" Tyler snaps out of his thoughts to find Asher looking at him hopefully and gripping his hands.

"Do you think you'd be able to take some time this morning? I know you're on the floor, but it should be slow today, and you'd make more back here. Or if not, maybe tomorrow—"

"Of course," Tyler interrupts. "Of course. Will you guys be okay out there?"

"I'll go behind the bar and send Claudia onto the floor," Asher says. "I'm not going to test all this new 'ability to ask for help' stuff by hovering in here and getting upset. Or backseat driving. Because then I might make suggestions for how to organize things that make no sense."

Tyler smiles. He's seen Asher's attempts at organization; this is totally true.

"Okay. But the second you need me—"

"Believe it or not, I have worked in a restaurant before."

Tyler widens his eyes. "Did you… make… a *joke?*" He has a split second to wonder if Asher is beyond teasing just now, but he chuckles. Tyler offers him a smile that's meant to disarm. He hopes it sets Asher at ease. Judging from the jagged energy that vibrates from him, it doesn't. He seems to have burned through all of his bravado. "All right," Tyler says, imitating his mama's no-nonsense, time to get to the business of it, voice. "You go set up the bar and get out of my hair. I can bring the drawer out in a bit."

Technically it could go out now—it's not as though Asher is going to steal from himself—but he needs to get Asher out and busy and also have an excuse to check on him in a bit. And that way he can ask Asher questions before they're completely full.

TYLER IS ABOUT HALFWAY THROUGH when Asher comes back. It's mid-shift.

"Hey, everything okay out there? You need me?" Tyler can't imagine it's busy enough that he's needed at one on a Tuesday afternoon, but crazier things have happened.

"No, I could no longer resist the need to hover," Asher says. Tyler is surprised into a laugh, and then Asher is too. "It looks great in here," he says. His eyes wander around the room. Tyler grimaces.

"Not quite. There are a couple of things—"

"Oh no, bad things?"

"No! Well, no, not really. I mean your produce bill *is* going up. I found the letter. Also Fairway Meat."

"Fuck." Asher swears and stretches out his hand for the papers. Tyler shakes his head.

"You'll get stuck in here. I want to get more done."

Asher examines the room. The desk is completely clear. "What's left—"

"Oh *god*, so much, Asher," Tyler says. It's perhaps too honest and hearty an answer, judging by the face Asher makes. "I mean, once I needed to file things, I found that the files are a little out of order." The truth is the files are a fucking *mess*. He can tell that at some time, Asher started sticking papers into the files to get them out of the way. It doesn't seem they're things that would make or break the restaurant if filed out of order, but they're going to complicate the fuck out of Asher's life should he need them.

"Okay," Asher says at length. "What can I do?"

Tyler wants to say that Asher's help might be a hindrance, but then thinks better. Anxiety pours from Asher in waves.

"Clear out for a bit. Can I come in early in the morning or stay late?"

"Sure, if you need." Asher shakes his head, "I mean whichever you need. Both. All. Any—"

"Okay, okay, I get it, boss. If I make a list, do you think we could get a few office supplies to help keep things in order?"

Asher takes another look around the room, "Um, yeah. What—"

"Don't worry about it yet. I'm not sure. I'll know more once I've done a little more and have a good system in mind."

Asher clears his throat and turns to leave. With his hand on the handle, he speaks. "You're really good at this."

"One of *my* few things," Tyler says lightly.

Asher's laugh is halfhearted. "Tyler, I doubt there are many things you're not good at."

It's a compliment. Still, when the door swings shut, Tyler realizes he's gripping the pen. Other than small things, most of what he's good at is just Tyler faking it.

Chapter Nine

"What are these?" Tyler asks. Asher turns from the box of Coke syrup he is struggling to hook up. Tyler's in the back corner of the storeroom where he'd put the old pictures that decorated Idlewild's walls before he gave it a rough makeover. Tyler pulls one out.

It's weird, the visceral reaction Asher has—the picture has only been in storage for a few months. It's not as if he didn't see it every day for years before that.

But maybe that's the problem. These pictures are a part of a larger picture, of a larger story, with details Asher has chosen to ignore, to see without seeing. *Isn't that how I got into this mess?*

"Those used to be up," Asher explains.

Tyler pulls another one out. He doesn't speak. He's very still while he looks them over. Asher fidgets and wonders what's going on in Tyler's head.

Tyler doesn't take his eyes off the pictures when he asks, "Where'd they come from?"

"Um." Asher licks his lips. "John took them."

This gets Tyler's attention. "I'm sorry. Do you want me to put them back?"

Asher shakes his head. "No. I mean. Um, whatever." He's still holding the syrup box, and his arms hurt. He manhandles it onto the shelf and looks dumbly at the bucket of hot, soapy water they brought to wash the lines.

"Can I ask you something?" Tyler leaves one of the pictures out; it's of the Ambassador Bridge. John took a ton of shots of the city that day: Those shots were particularly good. He walked Fort Street all the way under the bridge.

"Yeah. Do I have to answer?" Asher tries to lighten the heaviness in the room.

"No." Tyler smiles, his rare one, the one Asher only sees when it's just the two of them. "Why did you put them away?"

Asher thinks of the answers he could give. Restarting Idlewild with the pictures, reminders of the hopes and successes he and John had together, was too hard. He's not sure why he didn't re-hang them later, though.

"To paint," he says simply.

Tyler opens his mouth, maybe to ask another question, but then seems to think better of it. Instead, he wrings out one of the rags and gets to work. Beyond the door, Asher can hear chatter in the kitchen as staff trickles in. He notices small and now familiar details: Tyler's cologne; the way he hums, so low and in little snatches they're almost imperceptible; the line his slim body makes when he stretches to wipe the Sprite nozzle over their heads. They're so close that if Asher moved an inch their bodies would be touching, shoulder to hip.

"So John was a photographer?" Tyler asks in a rush, then bites his lip and turns away. When he bends to rinse out his rag, his shirt rides up and exposes a strip of his underwear and his smooth back. Asher swallows and turns away.

There are days when Asher wishes he could know this boy better, when he wants to ask for his secrets. Asher has no name for what happens when he's with Tyler, but his wide open eyes and carefully held mouth, focused on Asher alone, make him want to spill secrets at his feet, to feel the lightest touch of care in human contact. That Tyler wants to know his secrets is both comforting and bracing.

Asher clears his throat and steps away, tries to make it appear as though he's merely moved to clean the shelf where syrup has dripped. They're almost finished. *What happens when we leave?*

"No, he dabbled," he says finally.

"It's hard for you to talk about him," Tyler states. Asher rolls his eyes. "I mean, of course." Tyler turns away with an awkward shrug.

"No, hey," Asher touches Tyler's shoulder. "Sorry. Yes. You'd think after years it would be easier. It's not…" He puts his rag down and leans against the shelf, searching for honesty, for the courage for honesty. "It's not about not being over him, I don't think. I haven't had anyone to talk to about John in a very long time."

"What about your family?"

Asher's smile is wry. "We're not close." He drops his own rag into the bucket and squats to grab it. The spell breaks apart. "Come on, everyone will be here by now."

IN BED THAT NIGHT, ASHER spreads his arms side to side in the mattress and sags against its give. It's not as comfortable as his old bed, but he's tired to the bone. The restaurant was busy, at capacity at the height of the rush. It was a rare smooth night, with no kitchen squabbles. There've been so few staff dramas, he's been waiting for the other shoe to drop. It happens in this line of work, in their culture. But he doesn't fear what seems a matter of course. His people seem capable of pulling themselves together.

Asher groans and wonders if he can ever do the same for himself.

He's tired—so incredibly tired—but his body, a lonely, starved thing, aches. It has ached since this morning with Tyler. Tyler left before the dinner rush. Asher's never sure where he might be off to, because Tyler's not often specific, and one of their unspoken rules seems to be to respect a non-intrusive friendship.

This morning popped that bubble. Going back to the way they were, reconstructing their boundaries, won't be easy. That bright moment was quicksilver and unspoken. Tyler is attractive—beautiful even—and

Asher noticed from the start. Tyler's charisma draws him; something intangibly compelling radiates from him. Until today, Asher's not let himself think too deeply about what he feels when he's with Tyler. But he's so very alone. His skin is starving for human touch, and the memory of that tiny patch of Tyler's skin burns bright. Letting himself want Tyler is fire Asher must not play with.

Maybe he needs to go out some night, slipping into familiar haunts he hasn't had time for in much too long, lose himself in dark and music, in bodies moving in a familiar rhythm of desire. Easy comfort and relief wouldn't be hard to come by and might work this distracting need from his body. He's much too tired for it now; he can't see when he won't be.

Maybe, once Idlewild takes flight, Asher can start on his own life, to define himself beyond the walls of his restaurant.

He rolls over and pushes his hand below his boxers and bites back a groan. For now, this will have to do.

* * *

"Do you think you'll hang them back up?" Tyler asks a week later. Asher pauses in the act of counting the coins from the bar register.

"Pardon?"

"Those pictures. That's how the restaurant was decorated right? John took them, they must be important to—I mean I don't want to assu—I, just—" Tyler spins in his chair away from him. He tapes the money Asher's counted and puts the tip outs together for him. "*Fuck,*" he whispers.

"Don't worry so much," Asher says. Tyler's curiosity is endearing— or at least, nice. It's nice to have someone interested in his former life. Sometimes his staff treat him as though his life began when they arrived. Maybe they're afraid to ask questions. Maybe they don't care. Asher's used to loneliness. "It's okay if you ask questions. You're not going to break me. It really has been a long time, and I don't mind talking about it. I'm out of practice."

"You said you're not close to your family. After I left that night I was thinking—about friends. About what you do when you're not here. You're always here."

"Well, I do live here," Asher points out.

"But you have to leave sometime. Unless you're allergic to the sun," Tyler jokes.

"Nope, I do love it." He does wish he got more of it. It's early fall. The city is lovely, but the city can't capture the stunning trees when on the west side and beyond. "I know I should do more of it. I do miss a lot stuck in here."

"Do you go out and see your friends?"

"I don't. . . a lot of people slipped away over the years," Asher admits. It's hard, saying the words, letting go of that small hurt.

"You did or they did?"

Asher thinks over the words as carefully as he can, tries not to raise his defenses. "I don't know. Maybe both. So much has happened and I haven't realized until so much time has passed. I've given up a lot of myself for this place." He does turn away then, because he's said too much.

Tyler is quiet, and Asher resumes counting out the coins, then marks the total. He separates out Claudia's tips and puts them in the tip envelope.

"I'm sorry. I always seem to ask the wrong questions," Tyler says gently.

"No. No you're fine," Asher says at length. "They're not questions I'm used to. I. . ."

"You need more people," Tyler says when Asher trails off.

"Oh?" Asher tries not to laugh. "Should I take out an ad?"

"No." Tyler turns to him. "But I'll offer myself if you want."

It's innocuous. It's an offer of friendship. But when their eyes meet, it feels like more. It feels electric; it takes Asher's breath away. They hang suspended in the moment long enough that Asher thinks something must happen—he has no idea what—when they're suddenly startled by a knock at the door. Asher feels the heat in his face. Tyler looks away and stares down at the counter in front of him. Asher runs his fingers through already disheveled hair. He opens the door to find Joy, book in hand, ready to check out. It feels too hot in the cramped office. He wonders if she can feel it too: the seismic shock, the charged air.

Chapter Ten

IT'S ONLY SEVEN ON A Thursday night—the bar is half full, but most
of the patrons are sitting at the bar and not at tables. Claudia is taking
the back half and Tyler the front. He's got his eye on two girls who are
out together for the night, dressed up and lovely, and the guy who's
come to sit by them.

"You think it's all good?" He asks Claudia when they meet at the
liquor shelves. He gestures with a lifted shoulder toward the girls. They
all try to keep an eye on girls who come into the bar to be sure they
aren't being harassed.

"Seems fine for now. Want to trade spots?" Claudia hands him the
tequila.

"No, I got this." Tyler pours efficiently and offers her a smile.

"So, ladies." He sets their drinks down, one Hurricane and a Tequila
Sunrise, and turns a smile on the guy as well, who is nursing a Two-
Hearted Ale. He's wearing a Captain America T-shirt, which Tyler
approves of. "And gent. I have a burning question that needs answering."

"All right." The girl on the left smiles and folds her arms on the bar.
Her long dark hair is shot through with bright blue, illuminated by the
lamp above them.

"What did Captain American's original shield look like?"

"Like, in the movies?" The girl on the right asks.

"No, the cartoons." A patron a few seats down holds up an empty beer glass; Tyler fills a new one, and by the time he's come back, their three heads are bent together.

"Well?"

"We decided that Matt here is the expert. He says it's a weird shape. Do you have a pen he can use to draw it?"

"Sure. I'm Tyler, by the way."

"Nancy." The blond girl smiles and points to her friend. "This is Olivia. And Matt, of course."

"Well, it's lovely to meet you all." Tyler scans the bar, but everyone seems content. When Matt tries to sketch on a bar napkin, he leans forward to watch. Matt looks up, brown eyes meeting Tyler's. Matt's eyes seem kind and mischievous. Tyler winks. Matt is halfway finished when the man next to him, who has been eavesdropping, shakes his head.

"Not a triangle," he says.

"No, it totally was," Matt says. Without speaking, Tyler rips a page from his serving pad and offers it to the guy.

"What's going on?" Claudia's come over to see what they're all doing.

"Having a small Captain America trivia moment," Tyler explains. "I have some experts here." The guys are sketching on the page together. Olivia is on her phone now, looking up Captain America and giggling. "I totally have the best half of the bar, don't I?"

"Aw, hell no," Claudia says. "Hey," she raises her voice to address her half of the bar. "Anyone here like superheroes?" A couple of men at the end whoop and raise their glasses. "Tyler here thinks he's got the smartest half of the bar." That gets some good-natured boos.

"He totally does," Nancy calls, making everyone laugh.

"All right, kids, I think this calls for a little *super* trivia," Tyler calls from the middle of the bar with his hands cupped around his mouth. He doesn't quite have the volume Claudia does.

Claudia pulls out her phone to find questions. At Tyler's end of the bar several of his patrons have started a conversation, and Tyler knows the competition is on.

By the end of the night, Tyler's sides hurt from laughing. Several of their patrons stay much later than usual, and thank both of them for a great night. Tyler thinks they've made several new regulars, and, when they start to empty he and Claudia share a high five, he's rewarded with one of her bright smiles.

"Let me," he says, bumping Claudia away from the ice well she's been emptying. She comes back with hot water and perches on the back of the bar while he cleans it out.

"Good night, huh?" She's counting their tips and sorting them into two piles.

"The best," Tyler replies. He doesn't count the money she gives him, because what he feels has nothing to do with money, but with fun: the happiness of bringing people together, of being a part of their great night.

*   *   *

"Asher, tell me what you used to do," Tyler says one night.

Work is done; they're sitting in the breakroom and eating, *finally*. Tyler is starving. While it's encouraging, from a business standpoint, that he had no chance to take a break and eat because they were busy, he does need food. Asher took one look at his face and made him dinner. Claudia wandered out as soon as she'd finished her work, which is not unusual. Tyler usually thinks he'll go too as soon as work is done, but often he finds himself lingering. Lately, even with his friends, Tyler feels lonely. He's not able to put his finger on a reason, other than that he feels changed. He's still the driven boy who worked his way through college, but he's now driven in a different direction. He gets the impression that his work in a restaurant seems transient and directionless to those who've known him all along.

"Um…" Asher puts his fork down and thinks. "We used to go to the cider mill."

"Seriously?" Tyler struggles not to laugh. Sometimes it's crazy, the reminders of how different their worlds are. They've lived in the same area for their whole lives, and yet Tyler is amazed at how different their experiences are. The culture gap between the city and the suburbs is absurd sometimes.

"Yeah." Asher lifts a shoulder. He rolls his eyes playfully. "It was fun. We'd pick apples. John loved making apple spice muffins." Asher looks down.

"What?" Tyler prompts.

Asher shakes his head. "I don't know. I haven't eaten those muffins in years. They were my favorite. He'd..." Tyler stays still. "He used to wake me up with them. He'd bring a plate into the room to me."

Tyler bites his lip. He's never experienced the loss Asher has. By the time Tyler's father left them it was a relief. He'd felt heartbroken over the pain he'd put Tyler's family through, yes, but not the loss. Tyler is by no means unfeeling, but he'd never realized how long the sharp ache of grief might last.

"You don't have to talk to me about this if you aren't comfortable," Tyler says when the silence carries, "but I hope you know I want to be here to hear you."

"Thank you." Asher's eyes are everywhere but on Tyler. He takes a deep breath. "It's not... I don't know. Missing John isn't like it used to be. I don't want to say I'm used to it, but I do feel as though I've moved past it. Or I did think so."

"Did?"

"I've been remembering him more lately." Asher picks up his fork and pushes his food around, then puts it down. "I guess I was so busy or lost in work I didn't let myself think about things."

"I'm sorry. I'm always asking questions."

"No." Asher looks at him. "I should... I should want to let myself remember the good things, right?"

"Yeah. I think so," Tyler says. In Asher's eyes is an honest sadness; so much was laid open. "Thank you."

"For what?"

Asher is one of the most closed off people Tyler's ever known; the way he's slowly unfolding is revelatory. "For trusting me enough to talk to me about this."

"I wonder if I have that recipe."

"Why? You gonna make them?" Tyler asks.

"I don't know. Maybe." This time Asher does take a bite of his food. "Maybe I'll go pick some apples. Get some real cider and bring it back. We can all have some spiced cider."

"Real cider?" Tyler asks.

"You know, the unpasteurized kind that doesn't taste like cloudy apple juice."

"I've never had cider," Tyler admits. Asher looks at him. "Never done any of that shit."

"Want to?" Asher asks, then looks as if he wishes he hadn't. Tyler wants to touch his hand but doesn't.

"Yeah." Tyler wants to get Asher out of Idlewild. Wants to coax those smiles and enjoy the sense of waking he sees come over Asher from time to time. "I'm down."

* * *

"You're *what*?" Malik says.

"Oh god, don't be weird," Tyler says, still half in the closet. "You can come, too."

"Babe, I ain't apple picking. You kidding?"

"A bunch of us are going. We can pretend we're from the West Side."

"Ty, why the fuck would I want to pretend to be some spoiled kid from the 'burbs picking apples?"

"Mal." Tyler sits down on the bed.

"It's okay," Malik says at length. "You do what you want to do. There's a game on right now. I'll stay here for that."

Tyler kisses his cheek and is grateful to feel the tension leave Malik's body. "I'll bring you some apples," he says. Malik side-eyes him and Tyler giggles helplessly.

IT'S A BEAUTIFUL DAY, TYLER can give Asher that. And it is fun, despite the bees. *So many bees.* Joy and Asher and Tyler get into the tractor to go out to the apple fields. Across from them sits a family with a little girl; she can't be more than two. Her blonde hair is in little pigtails, and she claps the whole way. Tyler's always loved little kids.

Joy makes it a contest. Asher bought a bag for the apples, and they all race to see who can get the most. Tyler trips over fallen and discarded apples, but, as the lightest and smallest of them, he can actually climb into the trees to get the ones at the top where the unpicked apples are cluttered.

"Is that allowed?" Joy asks when Tyler almost falls out of one.

"Probably not, but it's never stopped people from doing it," Asher says.

They buy donuts and eat them on the grass. There's a maze of hay bales next to a pen with goats and a pony. At least twenty children—more and more as the day goes on—shriek and toss hay into the air. They chase each other, jumping from bale to bale and their laughter rings through the air. It's one of those stunning October days, with a wide blue sky and sunshine Tyler wants to soak into his bones. He's rarely had a reason to come this far out on the west side of the Metro Detroit area—they're almost beyond it—and on the drive he'd taken in the gold and yellow, deep red and some stubborn green foliage. It's beautiful, but he can't imagine driving up north to watch the leaves change as Asher said his parents used to do.

"So what do you think?" Joy plops down next to him. They're far from the tents with picnic tables—still *so many bees*—and Tyler leans back on his elbows and takes it all in.

"This is the weirdest thing. People really do this. Outside of like, school field trips and stuff."

"Oh, come on, it's fun." She nudges him. "We're doing it right now."

"No, you're right; it is. Different strokes for different folks and all that."

Joy rolls her eyes and hands him a donut. "It is beautiful, though."

"Isn't it?" Asher comes to sit with them. Speaking of culture shock: Asher outside of Idlewild in a place that was a part of his life and which he's cautiously re-entering is surreal. "I love Michigan in the fall."

"You ever live anywhere else?" Tyler asks.

Asher shakes his head. "Never wanted to."

"I did," Joy says. "Wanted to get out so bad when I was in high school."

"Where'd you want to go?" Tyler asks.

"Anywhere but here," she says.

Asher crosses his legs; he watches the children play but listens as well. "But you're here now."

"Ugh. Fucking homesickness," she says. "Went down to Georgia for college. My mom's sister lives down there. Even with family, I still only lasted a year before I came home. God, I was homesick." She sounds somewhere between bitter and playful. The conversation peters out, but it's not uncomfortable. Tyler watches Asher watching the children play. If Joy weren't with them, he'd ask Asher more personal questions. Did Asher and John want kids? To live out here in the suburbs and raise a family? Tyler realizes that he and Asher have two relationships: the work one everyone sees and the one that seems to only exist in private spaces when it's just them.

Asher glances over before Tyler has a chance to change his own expression. Asher's body tightens a little, the way he carries himself when he's closed off. "We should head back," he says. Joy stands and gives Tyler a hand.

"So, cider and rum tomorrow?" she asks. Asher smiles and nods.

"WHAT ARE YOU GONNA DO with all these apples?" With a grunt, Tyler sets the bag down. He hands Asher his car keys.

"Send some home with you?"

"No, thank you. I do not need a bag of apples; there's got to be at least thirty in there. We'd eat like, five."

"I guess I can share them out to everyone tomorrow." Asher moves around the kitchen.

"Making sure no one burned the place to the ground?" Tyler asks. Leaving the restaurant in Claudia's hands had made Asher antsy all day.

Asher is crouched behind the line, counting the pans George set up before leaving. "I think someone would have told me by now if it burned down," he says absently. Tyler rolls his eyes. He drags Asher out by his arm.

"Enough. George and Santos are more than competent enough to do their jobs. Everything is fine."

Asher sighs and runs his hand through his hair. It had been adorably mussed by the winds in the apple orchard; it's positively wild right now. Tyler resists the urge to smooth it.

"So…" Tyler clears his throat. Ever since his talk with Asher about John he's wondered how Asher's managed all these years without processing his grief. He doesn't want to push him, but he'd love to help Asher recall good memories and learn to carry them from his past into his life. He steps closer. "I was thinking… maybe you could teach me."

"Teach you?" Asher repeats. A momentary quiet hangs heavy and loaded between them. Tyler blinks and takes a step back. That too much-feeling curls in his stomach. It feels dangerous and unintentional and heady, and a shade wrong when Malik is waiting at home for him— or could be. He never knows anymore.

"How to make the muffins," Tyler says carefully.

"Oh. I think that would be nice." Asher's smile is sad.

"Are you sure? I'm sorry; I didn't mean—"

"No," Asher interrupts, "I think I'd enjoy that."

"It's not a hard recipe," Asher says when he comes down. He went upstairs to search for it. Tyler waited for what seemed like ages.

"Oh?" Tyler says. This is a very strange moment. John's ghost resurrected has been by his questions; he doesn't want to fuck up.

"How many are we making anyway?" Asher asks.

"I don't know. We're having an employee appreciation night tomorrow, right?"

"Yeah."

"Want to make the muffins to go with the cider?"

Asher props the recipe card against the container of flour he's retrieved. "That sounds great."

"Awesome," Tyler says. Asher smiles, and it's not sad this time, or hopeful or anything to make this whole exercise hard. It's normal, it's level. Tyler loves that smile and the natural camaraderie.

"All right, boss, tell me what needs doing."

But for the directions Asher gives him, it's quiet in the kitchen. Tyler washes and peels and chops the apples while Asher collects and lines up ingredients. Despite the hours he logs here, Tyler's not very competent in the kitchen.

"You're going to chop a finger off," Asher says. "Here." He takes Tyler's hands carefully. "Curl the tips of your fingers under." Asher's fingers are gentle, warm and bigger than his. A tingle shivers down Tyler's spine. His breath comes out harder than it should, giving him away. Asher pauses—it's barely perceptible—and takes a breath of his own. But he doesn't move away. Tyler can smell him and feel the height difference. Asher's not overly tall, but he is bigger than Tyler. Most men are.

"How's that?" Tyler manages. He mimics the movement Asher's shown him, and places his fingers more carefully on the apple.

"Perfect," Asher says, and then moves away. Tyler goes back to chopping.

Once they're finished, Asher tilts the recipe card so that Tyler can see it. He mixes the dry ingredients while Asher does the wet. The air is so charged Tyler almost can't take it. He looks at Asher often, averting his eyes when Asher glances back. He wants to speak, but there's nothing to say. This is John's recipe. Tyler intended this moment to be cathartic for Asher. This isn't catharsis.

But when Asher glances over at him while he mixes and catches Tyler's eye, Tyler is sure his feelings are not one-sided.

Once the batter is in the tins and then into the oven, Tyler takes his apron off, grabs some water and follows Asher into the breakroom. He hands Asher the glass and perches on a stool. Instinct—or maybe cowardice—tells him he needs to wait for Asher to break the silence.

"Thank you, Tyler," Asher finally says. He twists the glass round and round in his hands with his gaze focused on it. "I… I've needed this."

"Anytime," Tyler says softly, and means it.

A MONTH AGO ASHER DECIDED he should host an employee appreciation night. He and John used to do that, and his employees— those they'd had then—had always seemed to enjoy them. Tyler's such a help; Asher has time now to be out on the floor and in the kitchen. It's been good for him, and for his relationship with his staff. But still there is a divide. He hopes this will help bridge it.

When Tyler leaves, he takes with him that beautiful, confusing tension that buzzed through Asher's bones. Half the lights are off and the kitchen is so still it's unsettling. Asher doesn't want to go upstairs; rest won't come to his body any time soon. He pulls a stool up to the high steel prep table where the muffins are cooling, waiting to be put away. Asher touches one to test how warm it is. He picks it up and when he breaks it open a wisp of steam curls out.

When he takes a bite, nostalgia floods him. It lies heavy in his chest, too heavy—perhaps it's not nostalgia at all.

Unable to sit still in the cavernous half-dark of the kitchen, Asher decides he wants to make something else for tomorrow to busy his hands and clear his mind. He remembers seeing a recipe for miniature caramel apples on Pinterest—and really, what speaks of fall like spiked cider, caramel apples and apple spice muffins?

He and George have been testing out making sea salt caramel brownies, so there's caramel on hand. Using the smallest melon baller he can find, Asher scoops out apple. It's a slow job. It takes a few tries to get the hang of it, but once he's started he falls into an easy rhythm, easy enough that his busy hands can no longer quiet his mind.

When Asher lets himself remember John, he often thinks how the best thing about being with John was that John was his best friend. Because they'd been friends before falling in love, because falling in love had come with time and with growth, it wasn't a struggle. It was a lovely awakening: reciprocal and tender and right.

They met their freshman year of college through a mutual network of friends that made it surprising they'd not met in high school. They'd grown up a few miles from each other, he from West Bloomfield and John from Farmington Hills. They had the easy shared experiences of growing up with the security of wealth, but the constant knowledge that being gay set them apart, that there was no inherent safety, that they lived in the Midwest where homophobia was a subtext almost everywhere, even under the words of many people who declared themselves allies.

Asher shakes his head; he picks up an apple ball and bites into it; it's tart and juicy. It'll pair well with caramel, which will be a counterpoint to the sharpness of a slightly too-new apple. He flicks on the lights in the front kitchen and melts the caramel.

John taught Asher to cook; before then, cooking had been a chore to get through. Above all, John loved to bake. They'd spent many Sunday afternoons together in their tiny kitchen, experimenting with altered and new recipes with various degrees of success.

Asher has never been able to pinpoint when he knew with certainty that he had fallen for John. He remembers dinner with friends over winter break their junior year: how he'd met John's eyes from across the table, flushed with laughter and so comfortable in his body, and felt a connection down to his bones. John had smiled; had continued to sip his beer and converse with their friend Sandy.

And after that came moments of shared energy, of knowing they were in the same place: perhaps waiting on the edge of the precipice to prolong the sweet anticipation; perhaps testing the edges of their different lives and potential different futures to understand how they might fit together.

Asher had no plan other than desire. There was a certainty to it that they both reveled in. Taking their time was a shared pleasure, a buildup they both wanted without discussing it.

Their first kiss, sweet lips and excited exhalations of finally, finally, *finally*, on the doorstep of John's parents' house, is a memory that Asher still carries viscerally.

Once the caramel is melted Asher closes his eyes and takes a breath to clear his mind; he doesn't want to burn his fingers. It takes a long time to dip the apples just right. When he finally has them finished and lined up in jagged rows on wax-papered cookie sheets, it's late, but not too late, and he's not ready for sleep. Asher studies them. They look plain, uniform and unexceptional. If John were here, what would he do next? Asher roots around in the pantry until he finds pecans, toffee and chocolate he can drizzle over them. By the time Asher is crushing the pecans and trying to think through how he'll make them look pretty, he's remembering Tyler's hands, the closeness of his body in the kitchen and how Tyler is so calming to Asher's anxieties. He's a dazzling boy who makes Asher laugh unexpectedly and who has been beside him day by day while he's rekindled what was left of Idlewild.

It's been more than five years since he was widowed and twelve since his and John's first kiss. It's been time enough for him to think of how young they'd been, how sure they had been—of their maturity, of their future—and wonder at his luck, both the good and the heartbreaking. It's been more than long enough for Asher to move past the debilitating stages of grief, past the longing and loneliness, past knowing he'd never be able to love someone else that way and past the moment he realized that though he'd never have that again, he could have *something*.

Somehow, that realization required its own grief.

But it's been five years, and although Asher's told himself that he's moved on, he sees that he's been stagnant—not just in trying to bridge his loneliness and reach out to someone, but in letting anyone else reach out to him.

* * *

ONCE EVERYTHING IS PRETTY WELL closed down the next night, Asher gets everyone up front. Jared and George have come in on their day off. He's already made a pitcher of warm spiced cider with rum. He's pouring when Claudia comes up.

"Thanks, boss," she says.

"You don't have to call me that," he points out for the ten-millionth time.

"Naw, by now it's stuck. Might as well get used to it." She picks up the mugs. He's used what Jared calls the ugly hipster mugs—mason jars with handles and inlaid glass designs.

"Wait," Asher says. He drops a cinnamon stick into each drink. She raises an eyebrow, then turns to deliver the drinks.

When she comes back he says, "Thanks."

"We're a thankful pair, aren't we?" she says. He finishes the drinks and then ducks into the kitchen while she delivers them. In one of the walk-in fridges he's hidden the mini caramel apples.

He plates them attractively and then grabs the basket of muffins Tyler prepared. He's excited to thank his employees for their hard work and what they've finished—saving his restaurant and, he's realized, saving him.

"Treats," he says, when he comes through the swinging door. Jared and Joy's eyes light up, and Joy claps lightly.

"I'll get some plates," Tyler offers. It's the first time he's spoken today.

Asher shakes his head. He has his own feelings to deal with after last night, which had been many, many things: intense, encouraging, fraught with his own vulnerability. Asher feels Tyler's silence keenly but he doesn't think it would do any good to bring up the electricity that lit the air between them—

"Thanks," Asher says quietly as Tyler passes. Tyler's eyes flicker to his, unreadable and uncharacteristically dim.

"Of course."

They sit on the bar, at the stools, spread around the tables. People sort themselves into groups. Claudia is teasing Jared; he blushes and shrugs but also laughs. Asher knows so little about them. He wonders what they do after work, whom they go home to, *if* they have anyone to go home to. *Where does Claudia go every night, when she leaves the minute her shift is over? Do they socialize outside of work?* Santos asks George how his mother is doing and Asher's stomach tightens. He works with George almost every night closing the kitchen and hasn't asked about his mother in months.

"Want help with those?" Tyler asks. Asher clutches the basket of muffins.

"Oh, um, yeah. I mean. I'm fine. Um…" He feels fragile. Asher's never been shy, but he is unpracticed. *How on earth can he approach these people?* He wants camaraderie. He wants to make jokes and feel the warmth of easy knowledge of other people. He cares for and admires his employees but he has no idea how to do this. He remembers the way it felt to be disliked by his former employees, to go home alone, their resentment clinging like residue on his skin.

In his hands he holds more than just some muffins. These are some of his best memories. These are a gift—to himself and to them. No one in this room, save for Tyler, understands what this moment represents. Maybe that's okay. Asher used his hands to make these, shaping a memory with each step, deciphering the scribbled directions John had written in his recipe book connected him to those memories. That moment in the dark silence of his kitchen, warm muffin in hand and fingers tracing the ink on the recipe, was a circuit complete.

Tyler takes the basket from him. "Go sit," he instructs. Asher goes behind the bar and gets himself a drink.

"How did you make these? They are amazing," Joy asks around a mouthful of caramel apple. She licks the stick where caramel has dripped.

"These have Pinterest all over them," Jared says.

"You are not necessarily wrong," Asher says. He smiles carefully. "You take one of those melon ballers and make little balls of the apples. Put them on the skewers and dip. The rest was just fooling around with what we have on hand. Pretty easy."

"Just time-consuming," Tyler says. He hands everyone a muffin on a napkin. Claudia looks at the two of them, and Asher's cheeks heat. He's wondered what the staff makes of how much time he and Tyler spend together. Tyler hadn't been with him when he made these; he had told Claudia they made the muffins together. If Asher were one of them, he'd think they were sleeping together. He's never worked at a restaurant that wasn't ripe with tension, gossip and drama.

There's no way to dispel any rumors, and having a new friend—albeit a very young friend whom he occasionally doesn't understand at all, a young man with changeable eyes and personas—is something he's been starved for. Not that it doesn't throw him for a loop sometimes.

Asher hops onto the bar next to Jared and plucks an uneaten caramel apple from his plate. Jared doesn't object. Instead he shoulder bumps Asher and hands him a napkin. Happiness so full rises in Asher he actually tears up.

Chapter Eleven

"You look like you're on your deathbed," Tyler observes the moment he walks in the door. He hasn't worked in two days, and it's his first of six days on.

"Thank you," Asher says hoarsely, then coughs.

"No really, why are you up?" Tyler unwinds his scarf and rubs his hands together. The weather has been wildly unpredictable. It was beautiful and sunny, with wide high blue skies two days ago.

Asher doesn't respond; instead he gives Tyler a look that might be annoyed or sardonic. Tyler follows Asher into the office. When Asher turns to give Tyler a questioning look, Tyler puts a hand on his forehead. Asher startles then closes his eyes.

"Your hands are so cold," he says.

Tyler's mouth twists. "Probably too cold to tell if you have a fever." He's pretty sure Asher does. He seems to enjoy the coolness of Tyler's palm though, so he puts both hands on Asher's cheeks, then flips them so the backs of his fingers can cool the sides of his neck. Asher makes a little noise.

"You need to go to bed," Tyler says.

"Tyler, I have to run a restaurant," Asher counters, mimicking Tyler's tone.

"Okay." Tyler takes a fortifying breath. What he's about to say is uncomfortable, but it has to be said. "I don't want you to think that this is because I think you should give this to me, okay?"

"Hrm?" Asher looks at him with bleary eyes. His nose is red and his hair is ridiculous.

"You need a manager. You *cannot* do all of this work alone."

Asher moves Tyler's hands away slowly and then turns his back to go to the computer, which hums awake. His shoulders shake when he coughs.

"I'll be fine."

Usually Tyler isn't one to press an issue, especially with Asher, who can be closed off and who closes off even more when pushed. But he's being ludicrous.

"Asher, I mean it."

Asher turns, surprised. Tyler rarely uses his name.

"You've been doing this alone for a while now, which is admirable, but also kind of insane. We've been here for ages now. I already have keys, so you trust me to a certain point. I know how to do all the back-of-house dailies. Claudia is on bar today; she can help with the front-of-house. You let her run a shift already. You'll be in the building."

Asher looks as though he's considering it, so Tyler presses a little harder. "I'll come up and give you updates. And soup, because you sound terrible. I promise not to make it."

Asher chuckles at that, but it's weak. He's painfully congested, Tyler can tell, and his skin a sickly pale.

"You don't have to commit to having us help in the future if it doesn't work out."

Asher sighs and puts his head down. Tentatively, Tyler brushes his fingers through Asher's hair. It's a strange intimacy to initiate, but maybe not. Tyler never could resist taking care of people when they're down or sick. Maybe that's why he thought he should be a doctor, why everyone was so excited about it.

Well, one reason.

"Fine," Asher says into his folded arms. Tyler almost misses it.

"All right then." He tugs on Asher's arm, gets him standing. "I'll need the keys to the safe so I can get the drawers."

Asher hesitates, but Tyler weathers it patiently. Finally, he hands over the keys, then lets himself be led upstairs.

"Fucking hell, man, it's *cold* in here," Tyler says.

"There's a draft somewhere, and I haven't figured out where." Asher collapses on his messy bed.

Despite the draft, the air is stale, the way it is when someone's been sick. Tyler wonders how long Asher's not been feeling well. He leaves Asher on the bed and hunts around to see where the cold is coming from. The loft is an absolute mess. The tiny sink in the kitchenette is stacked with glasses and mugs. Asher has stacked milk crates next to the bed to use as a night stand; tissues litter the top and the floor around them. Tyler kicks piles of clothes into one big pile as unobtrusively as possible. When he glances over at the bed though, Asher has buried himself in the covers. Tyler checks the windows until he finds one where the caulking needs to be fixed. The wind blows in around the frame. Tyler sighs and checks the time, and then looks around the loft for anything he might be able to use to fix it. He's seen old plastic downstairs in the storage closet, but it's close to open, and if Asher is ever going to trust Claudia or Tyler to run Idlewild for him, he needs to do a damn perfect job.

He settles on getting more blankets from the rickety crate setup Asher is using for linen storage. He covers Asher, who is sleeping. He'll come back when he has a break.

THE MORNING GOES WELL, AND the lunch crowd is easy. They don't hear a peep from Asher, which is a little shocking. The day warms, so Tyler worries less about the window. When everything seems to be running easily, he leaves Claudia in charge. He'd asked Santos if he'd throw together a soup; he gathers it and crackers and hot tea.

Asher is awake, curled on an old futon in front of his wall-mount television. He seems to be absorbed by infomercials.

"Hey," Tyler says. He comes in quietly, not wanting to startle him. Asher grunts and wiggles farther into his blankets. Tyler sets the soup down on a side table and touches the back of his neck: definitely a fever.

"I brought you soup. Do you think you're up for eating?" Asher shakes his head. "Do you have any Tylenol?"

"Maybe in the bathroom cabinet," Asher rasps. Tyler holds back a smile. Asher's "bathroom" is barely more than a couple of walls blocking off a tiny area that could be described as a bathroom. Like the rest of the loft, Tyler can tell it was put together fast. Asher's loft could be charming, with its exposed brick and large gothic windows; instead it's dusty, with window frames splintering with age and deeply scarred wood floors. It doesn't help that Asher's furniture amounts to a sofa, a small table and a mattress and box spring on the floor, accented with milk crates being used as shelves. Tyler roots through the bathroom and finds some Tylenol, which he makes Asher take.

"I think your window needs caulking. Well, replacing, really. But for now," he says, then hands Asher the bowl to remind him to eat. He refrains from adding that the apartment could use cleaning and that he desperately wants to change Asher's sheets, not because he presumes they're dirty (although given the mess it wouldn't be a far jump to assume that), but because clean sheets are always a lovely luxury when he's sick. Tyler looks at Asher's bed, then at Asher, who is sweating lightly but shivering. He makes a judgment call.

He doesn't bother to ask, just searches for clean sheets; Asher does have some. Enough clothes are strewn on the floor for Tyler to wonder when and how and where Asher does his laundry.

"What are you—" Asher starts when Tyler begins stripping his bed.

"Taking care of you."

"Tyler, come on." Asher starts to stand but struggles with the blanket he's tangled in.

"Asher, sit down." Tyler uses his authoritative voice. It's quiet, but people rarely argue with it, perhaps because he rarely uses it. Tyler's chameleon nature is quite the tool, and when he wants to act stern he can. Asher sits back.

"You don't have too, that's…"

Tyler lets Asher trail off and smooths the sheets with efficient hands. The bedspread could probably use a good wash, but he can't do that now. He plumps the pillows, then comes back to check on Asher, who's slumped over, staring at the TV.

"Need a magic bullet?"

"Not that kind," Asher jokes weakly. It surprises a laugh out of Tyler, though.

"Asher, did you just make a sex joke?" Asher smiles with his eyes closed. Little moments like these, unguarded—though because of illness, which is not preferable—endear him to Tyler.

"Wanna get in bed?" Tyler invites.

"Are *you* making a sex joke now?"

"Oh yeah, baby. Sick men really get me hot," Tyler says back. He smooths Asher's hair and Asher sighs into the touch. Tyler scratches his fingers through Asher's hair, whose body loosens and lets go. He wonders when Asher last received any affection. The thought makes Tyler's chest hurt.

"I can totally see why you'd want to be a doctor." Asher's eyes slip closed. "You're very good at caring for people."

Tyler's hand pauses, and he takes a deep breath. Even half asleep, Asher senses Tyler's tension. He rolls onto his back and, through puffy, reddened eyes, peers up at him.

"What?" Asher's voice, coaxing and kind, and the quiet of the apartment, disarm Tyler.

"I don't want to be one," he confesses. "I know everyone thinks I'm saving money to go to med school, but I'm not. At least, not anymore."

Asher struggles to sit, and Tyler shushes him and eases him back down.

"Have you told anyone else?"

"Just you and Malik," Tyler says. He tries to force the anxiety out in a long breath, but a sick shakiness courses through him; his heart pounds hard and fast. "Malik keeps telling me it's all right—once I really explained it all. He keeps telling me I haven't let everyone down. My family, I mean."

"He's right, you know."

Tyler shakes his head. Not with either of these men has he been able to express how keenly he feels his own failure or the crush of guilt and the weight of disappointment he knows his family will feel. "Malik has been trying to help me figure out what I want to do next." Tyler puts his fingers back into Asher's hair.

"There's no rush, you know." Asher rolls over and snuggles into his pillow. It's adorable and Tyler is glad Asher's eyes are closed so he can't see Tyler's wide smile. "You're still young."

Maybe. But Tyler's not sure he wants to find something else. In Idlewild he's found a space he fits, a place he loves, where he knows the shape of tangible change and success.

He stays with Asher until he's asleep again and checks his phone. Claudia said she'd text if she needed him, and so far everything seems fine.

Asher snuffles in his sleep; he must be miserable. Once he's sure he won't wake Asher, Tyler begins to clean. The hamper he finds in a corner is filled with clean clothes. He's not sure how Asher organizes them, but he puts them away, then fills the hamper with dirty clothes. He picks up the tissues scattered by the bed and couch and then washes his hands six times. He cleans the kitchenette and dusts. He wonders how far he's overstepped and how annoyed Asher will be.

Tyler never could stand mess.

By the time he leaves, Asher seems to be waking. Tyler tiptoes to the bedside table with a fresh glass of water, takes the soup bowl and makes his way downstairs.

Chapter Twelve

"You'll never guess who is here," Joy whispers as soon as she comes into the kitchen. Asher is helping expedite orders at the window. The shift is slowing down; he's put Jared and Claudia on break.

"Who?" he whispers back.

"Malik!"

"No way," Asher says. He leans toward her, well aware that he's slipping into gossip mode. "Why is he here?"

"Fuck, I don't know, boss. It's not as though I questioned him."

"Well, did you meet him?"

"Meet who?" Claudia says, startling Asher.

"Jeez, sneak up on people much?"

She doesn't dignify that with a response other than rolling her eyes. He knows her well enough now to know that that's affectionate, even if it looks annoyed.

"Who are we gossiping about?" she asks. They all stand close, a tiny trio blocking the line; it's obvious they're whispering about something. Behind the line George leans across the window to listen in.

"Tyler's boyfriend is here," Asher explains.

"Does he seem upset?" Claudia asks. Tyler was supposed to go home a few hours ago but stayed to help when they had a sudden rush. It's no secret that Malik isn't crazy about how much time Tyler gives Idlewild.

"I don't know," Joy says. "Like I said, I didn't grill the guy. I sat him at the two-top by the window. He's with a friend."

"I'm gonna go out there," Claudia says. "Tyler was supposed to be behind the bar; at least I can relieve him so he can talk to Malik."

"Is it weird if I go out and introduce myself?" Asher asks.

"I don't know," Joy says. She turns to George, who shrugs. The sound of a ticket printing intrudes; George disappears from the window to get it.

"I'm gonna do it," Asher says, squaring his shoulders. Yes, he's doing it because he's dying to meet the guy, but he owns the restaurant Tyler works in. It would be strange if he didn't go meet him. Right?

Tyler's still behind the bar when Asher comes out. He's composed; he smiles at Asher when he goes behind the bar with Claudia.

"I'll take over from here," she says. She nudges Tyler. "Go sit with your guy."

"Joy went right back to gossip, didn't she?" Tyler says. Asher can't help but smile.

"Well, we're curious," Claudia says. Asher appreciates her straightforward nature more and more. Asher glances over at the table and does a double-take.

"He's the one on the side by the wall," Tyler says when he sees Claudia scanning the room.

"Oh my god, he's huge," Asher says, then presses his lips together. Tyler's laugh is like light bells.

"I know, right?"

Asher is flat-out staring now. "He must work out every day," he says. Apparently his filter has been completely obliterated.

Malik wears a casual green button-down shirt that's rolled to his biceps, which strain against the fabric. He's strikingly handsome, a guy no one could help checking out twice. He has a sudden image of Tyler and Malik together, and heat curls in his belly.

"He does work out a lot," Tyler says.

"Can I meet him?" Asher says. He winces. Filter. Yes. Must try to employ.

Tyler hesitates; it's a tiny, almost imperceptible hesitation. Asher catches it, although Tyler doesn't think Claudia does. "Of course." He grabs Asher's arm and steers him out from behind the bar. When Malik looks over, he drops it. Something about his body, or the way Tyler moves, shifts as they approach the table. Asher finds himself completely fascinated by this—he almost misses Tyler's introduction.

"Honey, this is Asher. Asher, this is our friend Brandon, and this is Malik," Tyler says brightly.

"Hey," Malik says. His smile seems genuine and his handshake natural. He doesn't do that extra-strong handshake guys sometimes do. Asher hates it when guys do that. Posturing annoys him.

"It's nice to meet you," Asher says and means it. He shakes Brandon's hand and remembers that this is Tyler's other roommate. He doesn't talk about him much, other than to complain about the mess he leaves behind in the apartment. Sometimes Asher has a degree of sympathy for Malik and Brandon. He doesn't think of himself as a terribly messy person, but he doesn't have Tyler's constant need to put things in order.

"So what brings you out tonight?" Asher asks. Apparently everything he says tonight is going to be clumsy.

"Just wanted to see what the fuss is about," Malik says. He tugs on Tyler's hand to get him to sit. Tyler darts his eyes over at Asher to be sure it's okay.

"I'd give you a tour, but this is pretty much it," Asher offers. Luckily they seem to get that he's joking. Sometimes people don't.

"You picked a great time," Tyler says. "The rush is over, finally."

"Why don't you take your break now," Asher offers. Technically Tyler should be off, but he knows Tyler won't leave without helping with the closing work the other servers have to do.

"Take one with us," Tyler says. Asher can't read what's in his eyes, but he can read the awkwardness that springs up between everyone when he does.

"Yeah, take a load off," Malik says. Asher glances back at Claudia, who is cleaning the bar rail. She catches his eye and nods, signaling that he should hang out there. He drags a couple of chairs from a nearby table and offers one to Tyler first. Tyler pulls it closer to Malik.

"Do you guys want another drink?" Asher asks before he sits. "Tyler?"

"I'm on the clock, boss," Tyler says. Asher smiles, then gestures Claudia over.

"I've officially clocked you out for a bit," he says.

"Do I get to un-clock you so you can drink?" Tyler says, then makes a face. "That sounded dirtier than I meant it to." Asher laughs but then straightens out to address the table so it doesn't seem as if he and Tyler are in their own world.

"No, someone has to steer this ship," he says.

"And of course it can only be you," Tyler teases.

"You're one to talk. Tyler has control issues." Asher points out.

"Oh man, tell us about it," Brandon says while Malik nudges Tyler playfully with his shoulder. Tyler makes an indignant huffy noise that's downright adorable. Asher bites the inside of his cheek to keep his smile disguised.

When Claudia comes, they all order drinks—except Asher who won't be swayed so long as the restaurant is open—and begin picking their way through awkward conversation. Asher worries that he knows too much: about Tyler, about Malik, about their relationship through guesswork and his tendency to observe Tyler and puzzle him out. He's hyper-aware that Malik has been told more about him than Asher is comfortable with. Asher is intensely protective of his own life, of the precarious balancing act between knowing too much and trying not to be too familiar with Tyler, that he's trying to execute.

Malik and Brandon are into their third beers, and Tyler his second drink, before things thaw enough for smoother conversation. Brandon's drawn Tyler into a side conversation and Malik has turned his full attention to Asher.

"I've been wondering, man," Malik says. He runs one finger over the menu, tracing the scripted font at the top. "Why Idlewild?"

"Why… the bar?" Asher asks.

"Well, that too, but no, the name."

"Nothing special, honestly," Asher says. "Before we knew this was really going to happen, we used to sit around dreaming things up."

"You and your husband?"

"John, yeah." Asher drags his finger through the puddled condensation on the tabletop, feathers it out into little designs. "You know, pipe dream-type things. What it would look like, colors. A lot of times it was just goofing off, making up the ugliest color schemes and worst menu items we could. Idlewild was a name that came up one night. Later, when this actually happened," he says as he gestures around them, "I remembered it."

What Asher doesn't tell him is the part that's closer to his heart. They'd been in bed, late at night. The windows were open with a box fan propped in one of them, which couldn't dispel the August humidity. Every time they stopped laughing, John would throw out something else, setting off another round of giggles. Asher's not sure why, of all the names John had tossed out over the years, Idlewild had stayed with him. But he remembers laughing until he cried that night, and kissing John's neck where it was damp with sweat, but refusing to cuddle because it was so damn hot.

"It's a good name for a bar," Malik says. Asher wants to thank him, only Malik's voice isn't quite genuine. Or maybe it is, but there's also an edge. Still Asher errs on the side of manners.

"Thanks."

"Did you always want to run a restaurant?" Malik's gaze is unwavering. Asher's a little surprised by the question; he and Tyler have talked about this a lot.

"No, not at all. John kind of talked me into it. The idea of doing it one day. So when the opportunity arose, it was my dream, too, by then."

"And you chose Detroit." There's definitely an edge to Malik's tone now, even if his body language and words and face seem perfectly fine. It's not aggression. Asher can't put a finger on what it is. He wants to ask Malik what answers he's really searching for.

"Feel free to ignore him," Tyler butts in. Asher wasn't aware that he'd been listening. "He's fishing to find out if you think you're singlehandedly going to save the city with one bar." Tyler smiles, bright and wide, in Malik's direction, though Asher can clearly see that he has a hand on Malik's knee, probably trying to squeeze it so he'll stop talking.

"Well, I wouldn't have put it like that," Malik says. Brandon chuckles and Tyler rolls his eyes.

How would you? Asher wants to ask; his hackles are up. He can't tell if it's because he wants to defend their choices or because there's something about Malik that seems so at odds with the Tyler he knows. Putting them together creates an unsettling dissonance.

"No solo city-saving here," Asher says, forcing himself to speak lightly.

"I'm sorry, man," Malik says, and this time his smile is more sincere. "Tyler knows me. I can be an ass about some things. I have a hard time sometimes, with all these folks coming from all over the place, acting as if this here's empty land waiting for someone to rescue. Like some of us haven't been here all along doing our best."

Asher remembers Tyler telling him about Malik growing up in Delray; that, like Tyler, he's worked hard to get himself through school.

"We never thought we were saving anything," Asher explains. He doesn't want to admit it, but Malik's words give him pause. He doesn't think that's what he and John intended or felt, but it's hard to articulate the difference between intention and action. "A lot of people believe in this city. Have believed. I wanted to be a part of that. Maybe that sounds the same, but it's not." He wishes he could find the right words to explain; he never could lay them out plainly for John in a way that made sense. He's not sure he can for a boy who sees Asher as an interloper.

"All right," Malik says. He finishes his beer, and it's obvious the topic has been shelved.

Asher's got at least eight years on Malik, enough to understand when he's been dismissed and definitely enough to wonder if this kid thinks that was subtle. When he glances at Tyler, Tyler twitches a shoulder in apology. Asher smiles and hopes Tyler won't worry about it. He's not sure he likes Malik, but it's not Tyler's problem. Malik is certainly admirable with his fierce determination and grit. From what little Asher can see, there's a softness in the energy he directs toward Tyler. His hand is on Tyler's. He'd taken it off of his knee and threaded their fingers together on top of the table.

ASHER CATCHES TYLER BY THE back office just before he leaves.

"Going home?"

"Going out, I guess." Tyler folds his tips into his wallet. He doesn't look at Asher. His shoulders are tense.

Asher hesitates, but can't help himself. "Everything okay?"

"Yeah." Tyler's smile is lopsided; not quite wry, but not completely honest, touched with exhaustion maybe. *Are you happy?* Asher fists his hands and, following a series of impulses he's been unable to contain all night, rests his hand on Tyler's shoulder. At a loss for appropriate words, he simply tells Tyler to have a good night and lets his touch linger a beat longer than he should.

Chapter Thirteen

MALIK AND BRANDON WANT TO go to a house party down by Mexican Town when Tyler gets off work. He's tired, and his feet hurt, but he's also wound up; work at the restaurant often has this effect on him.

"I want to; I've just been on my feet so long," Tyler says to Malik.

"Come on, babe, we never get to hang out. It'll be fun." Malik has Tyler's waist in his hands; he kisses behind Tyler's ear and it's nice but they are at work now, even if the only one in the room with them is Claudia. "We can leave whenever you want," Malik promises.

By the time they get there, Tyler knows it was a bad idea. He's dead on his feet, and the first thing Malik does is a round of shots with Brandon and a couple of their friends from school. They press drinks on him. He's tired enough that the alcohol seems to hit him very fast and, for a bit, that almost works. He's loose and unselfconscious on the dance floor when Malik drags him out, but after another round of drinks he has to sit down.

"Malik, I need to go home," Tyler says. He has to shout to be heard. Malik's mouth twists in disappointment.

"In a minute," Malik says. "I gotta go talk to Caleb about an assignment."

It seems strange to Tyler, but he's drunk and tired, and so he finds some water and a place to sit. After a while he dozes off, but wakes when someone trips in the dark and spills his water all over him. Whoever it is doesn't notice. Annoyed and so past ready for his own bed, Tyler searches for Malik. His watch informs him that it's been over a half hour, but when he does find him, he almost wishes he hadn't. Malik is deep in conversation with a pretty—gorgeous—girl Tyler's never seen before. Nothing is wrong with the situation per se—Malik isn't touching her, but Tyler knows Malik is definitely flirting; it's what he does. Tyler should be more used to it, but it's hard to ignore it when he's tired, drunk and already deeply insecure about the state of their relationship.

Wobbling a little, Tyler makes his way over to them to collect Malik. Nausea and anxiety wash through him. Malik has the grace to look a little sheepish when Tyler comes over.

"Honey," Tyler says it loud enough for the girl to hear, "I don't feel good. Can we please go home?"

"Of course. Sorry." Malik kisses his cheek. "I got distracted, babe. Let's go."

"Do we have to find Brandon?" Tyler asks.

"No, he went home a bit ago," Malik says. Tyler bites his lip, annoyed. Why the hell wouldn't Malik just have told him to go home with Brandon? Not because he wanted to keep Tyler at the party; it's not as if he's interacted with Tyler at all. Malik can be so dense and thoughtless sometimes.

Tyler bites his tongue for as long as he can; they're almost home before his annoyance wins out over his common sense.

"Do you have to do that?" It's more peevish than he wants it to be.

"What?" Malik doesn't look at him.

Tyler inhales sharply. "Flirt with everything that moves?"

Malik turns to look at him, but doesn't speak immediately. Anyone else might read his face as neutral. Disinterested even. Tyler knows him so much better than that.

"That's rich, Ty," Malik says. His chuckle is anything but amused. Tyler bristles but holds his tongue, waiting. But Malik doesn't say anything else. No spoken accusations follow, only distance and the unspoken knowledge that this is about Asher too. Tyler's worked so hard, kept palms cupped, trying to hold this all in, to shape the love they've felt—that at the very least *he* has been sure of for the last few years—into something steady and solid. The flirtation, the distance, the edges between them – it would be so easy to blame Malik for it all.

"Is there anything you want to say, Mal?" Malik doesn't respond. *What do I want from this?* Tyler twists his hands in his lap. Accusations? A reason to apologize? When Tyler is with Asher, it's as if everything comes alive in ways they haven't in so long. Tyler yearns for simple connections that aren't a struggle.

"Malik, listen," Tyler starts. He puts a hand on Malik's thigh. "I don't want us to be like this. You're so far away." Malik sighs, and when their eyes meet, his are sad. Guilt is a stone in Tyler's stomach. "Maybe," Tyler swallows and shuts his eyes, "Maybe I feel far away too? To you?"

"You do," Malik says, so quietly Tyler hardly hears him over the rumble of the bus. Tyler could say, *I'm sorry I'm more connected to him than you.* Or he could reassure both of them that he's doing nothing wrong—that his and Asher's friendship isn't wrong. It would be true, too.

Malik doesn't need his excuses, though.

They don't talk the rest of the way home.

When Malik is asleep, Tyler traces the shape of his face and lips with his own eyes. He's constantly reminded of the reasons he's here, of the moments that make their lives together, and refuses to give up easily. Maybe he's seeking with Asher a connection he and Malik are struggling to maintain. It happens. Love is a constant practice and it's not always easy. When Malik left the first time, he knew this. He wasn't willing to give up, and they managed to work it out.

* * *

TYLER'S FIRST BOYFRIEND WAS A small, sweet boy he met at his first LGBT People in Medicine group at Wayne State University. The meeting was held in a half-filled amphitheater-style classroom and was not quite what Tyler was expecting: mostly white guys filling the room with a sense of uncertainty. His friend Sasha wandered away and so he sat carefully where she'd parked him, next to a boy with cute glasses and a nervous smile.

Tyler gave back, his friendliest, most non-threatening smile. "I'm Tyler," he stated right off the bat.

"I'm Joe," the boy said. He didn't offer more, but he did shake Tyler's proffered hand, and when it slipped away, the pads of his fingers slid all the way down his palm to Tyler's fingertips, sending a small shiver all the way up his spine. No one had touched him like that. Tyler was an excellent secret-keeper, and his body, and his body's desires, had always been his deepest secret. He is aware that everyone within a five-mile radius of him assumed, rightly, that he was gay. But there was a difference—at least he's always thought there was—between words that defined him and the things his body ached for. Even with his family, whom he'd come out to as a teenager, his sexuality was more about personality quirks than desires.

But it wasn't long before he shared those secrets with Joe, who was disarmingly kind and serious, who was careful with Tyler as soon as he realized how much of Tyler's bravado covered uncertainty and inexperience. The first time they slept together, Joe paused halfway.

"Haven't you ever done this before?"

Lit up from Joe's touch, vibrating on the edge of what their bodies might bring them to, heart pounding from nerves and anticipation, the question left Tyler feeling more naked than he actually was. Being seen at this moment, vulnerable and needy, made it harder for Tyler to smile reassuringly.

He settled for words instead, pulling Joe in with shaky arms. "Don't worry about it." Their bodies, restless and touching, continued moving. Joe gasped, and Tyler bit his lip. "Just please don't stop."

And so they didn't. Joe never brought it up again. But it wasn't long before he began to observe Tyler with more care. And soon after, Tyler knew he was really being *seen*. Under that gaze he was unsure, off-footed, and that made it harder for him to figure out what to say and when. His jokes were flat; he couldn't find his usual false confidence. He tried hard, then harder, to figure out what Joe wanted. But the harder he tried, the less his attempts worked.

It didn't fall apart bright and hard, leaving Tyler broken. But it hurt enough to confirm Tyler's fears—that, just as he was, someone would always be leaving him behind. In the wake of this first heartbreak, Tyler learned he must always guard his self and heart and be careful with how he let himself be touched.

* * *

THE FIRST TIME TYLER SAW Malik outside of a planned date was at a house party near the University of Detroit Mercy that Sasha's friend Dace had convinced them to go to. Tyler was a quarter into his final year and coming hard up against the realization that he was no longer sure he wanted to be a doctor. Sasha was the only person he'd confided in. She assured him over and over that it was anxiety speaking, so Tyler never articulated the complexity of his worries. He had so much to worry about: lack of money, imperfect grades, uncertainty whether he was suited for medicine, longing for something else, wondering if he'd simply chosen something unattainable, the highest degree of success Tyler could imagine.

Tyler's friend Mary convinced them to pre-game and served lukewarm beer while she and Sasha raided Tyler's closet for him. Amused, he stood patiently, arms outstretched, allowing himself to be dressed. The result had been a little over the top but also cute. Mary topped off the outfit with a silvery scarf of her own. In the bathroom he snapped a ridiculous selfie, all vogue and duckface and sent it to Malik. They hadn't seen each other often in the last few weeks; they were both caught between school commitments and exams. They had different schedules at different schools in different programs. They both worked to support themselves; the lack of time to connect didn't seem unusual.

By the time they got to the party the house was dark with throbbing lights and bass pounding so hard it vibrated through his shoes as they walked to the open door. Mary grabbed his hand, and they worked their way through the crowd, stopping occasionally to greet people.

"Yo, Tyler!" Malik's friend Brandon appeared, grabbed his hand and pulled Tyler into a half-hug, pounded on his back with a closed fist. "What are you doing here?"

"Sasha wanted us to come," Tyler shouted. Sasha stumbled over with some beer.

"Hi!" She waved at Brandon then winked at Tyler. He rolled his eyes. She probably thought she was being subtle. "Is Malik here?"

Someone bumped Tyler hard from behind, and he had to catch his beer fast. He didn't hear Brandon's answer, but before he could ask again, Brandon was caught from behind by a guy Tyler had never seen. Brandon waved a hand in their direction and then disappeared into the crowd. Tyler looked at Sasha, but she only shrugged and pointed to her ear. She couldn't hear either. He checked his phone, but there was no answer to his text.

Tyler shook off momentary disappointment. It would be nice to see Malik, or to hear from him, but that wasn't why he was here. He pocketed his phone, and when Sasha raised her cup in a toast, he met it with a smile and twinkled at her, shimmying his shoulders. She laughed, and they stumbled into the next room where the lights were low and dancing bodies pressed close in the dark. With his drink held high, Tyler closed his eyes and lost himself in the music.

Eventually it was too hot for him—the outfit the girls had dressed him in was too warm for the whole "packed like sardines into a dancing environment," thing, so they went outside for fresh air. October winds rattled through the night, shaking leaves from the one scraggly tree between houses. The wind was bracing and smelled of rain. The stars were obscured by clouds.

"Better hope we don't get rained on goin' home," he murmured. Sasha laughed. Dace uncovered an old football, grimy and damp, by the corner of the house. He wiped it off and lobbed it toward Tyler, who shrieked and put his hands up. He managed to catch it. Still, the girls howled with laugher, and he had to hold his own in.

"Oh, you think you're funny, girl?" He pretended to frown and threw it to Sasha—too high but she jumped to catch it. She almost fell and so she kicked her heeled shoes off before she tossed it back to Dace. Tyler set her shoes on the step next to him. They spent a half hour playing. Tyler dropped the ball more often than he caught it. Despite the chill, they kept warm with laughter.

"I gotta go home," Mary said eventually. She was sitting on the porch step, squashed to the side to avoid foot traffic. "Tyler, boo, can you grab my coat? It's in the bedroom." Mary yawned, leaned her head against the rail and closed her eyes. He patted her head and went back into the party. It had definitely thinned, and the lights were low. Cups were everywhere, and someone had passed out with their arm dragging on the floor and face squashed against the couch cushions. Tyler steadied himself against the wall. In the damp and close air he could feel how drunk he was. He was wondering which bedroom Mary meant and where the bedrooms were when he saw Malik.

Malik was definitely not alone. He was leaning against a wall in the corner, showing all the flirting and open body language Tyler was so familiar with, playing with some girl's fingers and making her laugh. Their bodies were close enough that the suggestion of where they were going or had been was clear.

Tyler didn't wait to see more. Instead he found the stairs and searched bedrooms without knocking, regardless of who was in them, searching for Mary's coat.

It wasn't as if they'd made commitments to one another. Malik had never made promises, and they didn't see each other regularly. And he knew that Malik was bi; it was strange though, to see him with a girl. Tyler's stomach still insisted on twisting painfully, and he had to take several deep breaths before going out to face his friends. He slipped through the living room, hoping Malik wouldn't see him, but he wasn't there anymore.

"Tyler, baby, what's wrong?" Sasha asked. He straightened his face and gave her a smile. Tyler didn't wear his pain for those closest to him, much less for friends he'd only known for a couple of years.

"Honey, you done got me way too drunk for a weeknight, that's what."

She rolled her eyes.

TYLER NEVER ASKED MALIK ABOUT it. He woke hungover and anxious; it took him a minute to place the origin of that anxiety. He groaned and pulled his covers over his head to block out the morning light. He couldn't fault Malik. They weren't in a relationship; they hooked up. It was light and fun. But Tyler was falling for him, hoping that soon things might go in a more committed direction. He hadn't been with anyone since he met Malik. He didn't mind casual, but he wasn't one to split focus. Over the last few months, casual encounters with Malik had revealed a good man as driven as to success as Tyler, if not more. He was steadier than Tyler, who was often flighty. Grounded in his body, he held himself proudly. Malik was good man, serious and never silly. They foiled each other interestingly actually, but it worked. When they were alone, Malik was very soft with Tyler, careful with his hands, with his eyes always on Tyler's. Tyler knew Malik was attracted to his confidence; it's what he saw the first time they met.

But Tyler at Pride wasn't a common side to him and that was the first side to Tyler Malik ever saw. Tyler wasn't always that performative, that confident in his own body. Pride was magical that way. Possibility and freedom in the air. Tyler loved the way it soaked into his bones.

Tyler was made for love and he desperately wanted it, so the next time Malik called him, Tyler dressed for confidence in a dark vee neck wrap top that showed off his slim figure. If Malik liked that version of Tyler better, the confident and assertive one, Tyler could definitely pretend to be that boy. His pants were tight; comparatively, his boots—unlaced Doc Martin knock-offs, were downright butch. He gave himself pep talks and when Malik came back to his room after their night out, Tyler pulled him in without hesitation, kissed him without observable reserve, and pushed him down onto the bed with confidence. He rode him that night without breaking eye contact, slowly, all rolling hips and breathy moans. When Malik came he squeezed Tyler's hips so hard he carried the bruises for days. He didn't enjoy pain by any means, but when he touched them the next day and the day after, it was with a smile. They were a reminder that he could have this; that he was doing it right.

* * *

"What's wrong?" Asher asks the moment Tyler comes into the office. His color is blotchy and his eyes are still puffy. He's not a neat crier and it's always all over his face. He hates that he can't hide it.

He doesn't want to talk, and he doesn't want to work. He doesn't want to be at home; he's adrift and angry and so desperately hurt.

But Asher's face is nothing but concern, and Tyler trusts him completely. He sits in the extra chair but can't meet his eyes.

"Malik left."

"Again?" Asher asks, then sucks in a breath. "I'm sorry, I shouldn't have said that."

"It's okay. Yeah, again." Tyler picks at his cuticles. "He said he needs another break, or to try being with other people. I mean, I..." he sighs. "I make this sound as if it's all his fault. It's not. We sort of had a fight last night and then again this morning, and it just fell apart from there."

"You had a fight about him coming here?"

"No, we went out after that." Tyler doesn't want to talk about it, because the truth is that Malik drew Asher into the argument. The things Tyler brought up—Malik flirting with that girl; how he was always gone partying when not at school; the distance between them—Malik deflected and brought back to Tyler, to Idlewild and Asher. Tyler knew that Idlewild was a sore spot and that Malik was uncomfortable with his friendship with Asher, but he had no idea how deep that insecurity went. Seeing Tyler with Asher though—their comfortable relationship and ease of interaction—had sent Malik over the edge. Asher's face is drawn with anger. Tyler shakes his head. "You don't have to be mad about it. In the end, he tried to be kind."

Because once they'd calmed a little, Malik came back into their bedroom, which he'd stormed out of. He was calm, and Tyler could tell he'd been crying, which made Tyler cry because Malik *never* cried.

"This isn't working right now," he said. He sat next to Tyler on the bed and took his hands. "And I really do love you, Tyler. But I don't know what I want. And at least I know it."

"What does that mean?"

"It means that you *don't*, and you can't even see it," Malik said. The compassion hurt more than his anger. Despite the truth in his words, Tyler's panic reverberated deep, like bass drums thumping through him and drowning out everything else. He wouldn't beg Malik to stay the way he had last time. He wouldn't.

"I need to take a break, Tyler." Malik's words were soft, and his eyes were very, very kind. "Before I do something that hurts us both."

"This hurts," Tyler managed through his tears.

"Before we hurt ourselves, babe. I know you; if you ever cheated, you'd never forgive yourself."

"Cheated! What?" Tyler tried to pull his hands away. Malik didn't fight him and didn't say anything more about it. He kissed Tyler's cheek—a lingering kiss—and when he pulled back, Tyler's cheek was wet from Malik's tears.

"Tyler," Asher says, pulling him back into the conversation. His tone is full of careful compassion Tyler doesn't want. Not here, when he has to work and figure out what his feelings are because he's so conflicted. "What do you think—"

"I don't know," Tyler interrupts. "I just. I can't—I have to pull myself together right now. Shift is in twenty."

"Honey, you don't have to work right now," Asher says quietly. Tyler closes his eyes because such bounty of care from Asher is too much.

"I can't go home," he admits. "Not now."

"Is he—"

"Packing his stuff? Yeah."

Asher sighs. "Go upstairs if you need to. We can handle a night without you."

"But—"

"Please," Asher says. "You do so much for this place, for me. For everyone. Just take this for yourself okay? Pick a cheesy movie on Netflix; lay down. Stay as long as you need."

"That's... I don't want to impose," Tyler says.

Asher scoots closer on his rolling chair. Carefully, he puts one hand on Tyler's shoulder, and when Tyler sags into the touch, pulls him into a hug. "This is what friends are for, right?" Asher asks. Tyler nods, although the roiling conflict of emotions makes him a little sick.

Asher walks him upstairs and finds the TV remote. He pulls out a blanket out and sets it on his lap. "Do you want a drink?"

"No. Thank you," Tyler says. He's thankful for the kindness and care, even if right now what he wants most is to be alone. Asher gives him a lingering look Tyler can't figure out and then leaves. He wants Asher's kindness at the same time as he wants to shy away from it, and wanting it only confirms the truth in Malik's observations. He's too raw for any of this.

The blanket smells of Asher, of his detergent maybe. Tyler wraps it around himself and puts on an old episode of *Gilmore Girls*. Halfway through the episode his eyes droop and his body gives into the exhaustion that follows a late night and emotional day.

Before Tyler left for work, Malik held his hands and told him he loved him again, even if being together isn't for them right now.

"We're young and figuring out who we are. You have to figure out who you are, Ty," he said. "I feel like I've signed my life away. I want to live it. You want to live it."

Can't you live it with me? Tyler thought. He didn't say it. *What was there to say that would change Malik's mind?* He'd tried everything he could think of. Over the years Tyler has perfected being the person Malik wants: casual and undemanding, confident and desirable, desiring.

The never-enough settles in Tyler's stomach. The last few years of his life have been shaped only by that. By the never-enough. It's terrible, but it's easier to acknowledge than Malik's observations about what Tyler wants or needs.

Eventually he must slip into sleep, because when he comes back to awareness, Asher is there. He walks in quietly and tries not to wake him. Tyler sits and rubs his eyes.

"Hey."

"Sorry, I didn't mean to wake you," Asher says.

"No, it's fine. I didn't mean to fall asleep."

"You can go back to sleep if you want. I can lend you something more comfortable to wear."

Tyler is tempted to say no. He hates the idea of being an imposition.

"Tyler, come on," Asher cajoles. "You can't be comfortable in those jeans."

"You're right," Tyler says with a sigh. He's not going home tonight anyway; he planned to go to his mama's, but it's late, and if he shows up at this hour he'll have a lot of questions to answer.

He changes in Asher's bathroom and when he pads back out, Asher is on the couch watching TV.

"Here." Asher stands.

"No, sit." Tyler gestures nervously. "Want to watch with me?" Asher must be tired, but after his nap Tyler is too awake, and with that alertness has come the rush of hurt he'd carried with him today. A distraction would be welcome.

"Of course."

They settle into a slightly strained silence and watch the movie. It's hard to focus, because now his brain is going a million miles an hour, causing all of those thoughts hurt and then crest. He gasps and bites his lip hard.

"Oh, Tyler," Asher says, and the tenderness hurts, "come here." He lifts his arm and tugs Tyler close. Tyler has known he must be careful in their closeness, but right now, it's so, so needed. No one else in his life is only his; everyone else is shared with Malik. In some sense, Asher is purely his, and that's exactly what he needs.

Chapter Fourteen

TYLER'S IN A MOOD. ASHER can tell from the moment he comes in. He's late for work; Asher wants to talk to him about that but it's the first time it's ever happened, and Tyler's energy is all weird. Not angry or upset—other than from tardiness, for which he apologizes—but vibrating and projecting intensity. Asher wonders if he should have Tyler on the floor.

He retreats to his office to see if he can swing a shift without him when Tyler lets himself in.

"Got any work for me, boss?" Tyler asks.

"Sure," Asher says. "George and I drafted a new winter menu yesterday. Think you could call our vendors and price stuff so we can make final decisions? I'll have to pull you off the floor. Is that okay?"

"Of course." Tyler cocks his head. "This is my job too, right?"

"Yeah." Asher examines him. Tyler's shirt is wrinkled. His clothes are never wrinkled. "Is something up?"

"Nope," Tyler says. He pops the "P" at the end and when he looks at Asher it's almost challenging, too direct and raw.

That crackle, that tension that sometimes comes over them, cuts through the air. Tyler's body is taut, held together too carefully. Asher turns away and reminds himself to breathe. It was always one thing to feel attraction when there was no danger that it would go anywhere.

One minute Tyler is sure it's over with Malik, and the next Malik calls or texts and Tyler's not sure if Malik wants to come back. Asher is not sure if Tyler would go back, but regardless, a door *has* opened between them. It's dangerous, but tempting. Whenever this happens, Asher doesn't see Tyler's age or worries or his often confusing changeability. He sees a man whose skin looks inviting to touch, whose full lips are shaped like temptation and whose eyes burn bright when brought to life, who has a beautiful core self he only sees in intriguing glimpses.

There's a moment of silence again. When he's no longer sure he can bear the weight of the tension surrounding them Asher stands, ready to make an excuse to get out of this room. Tyler seems to have decided to do the same. There's not room in here for them to do much more than shuffle in that awkward, "no, you go ahead," dance. Tyler's hand brushes his, and the touch punches the breath right out of Asher. Before he realizes he's going to do it, Asher threads their fingers together and then crowds his body closer. Tyler inhales in a small gasp, then exhales with a shaky breath.

"Oh god, is this—" Asher starts, lips already so close to Tyler's.

"Yes," Tyler grips Asher's waist, hard, and pulls him in. Asher's hands are at the small of Tyler's back, and when their lips meet Tyler sways into the touch; his body curves in a lovely arc and melts into his hands. Asher curls one palm behind Tyler's neck to keep him there, tilts his head and then gets to work on those lovely lips: tiny tasting licks and nips and breathing in Tyler's little whimpers. He crowds closer, then lifts him so that Tyler is on the counter with his knees hugging Asher's waist. Tyler shifts and the kiss turns from a teasing, a little testing, to scorching.

Asher pulls away slowly. He swims up and out of the moment enough to realize that Tyler's hands are inside his shirt. Tyler's eyes open slowly; his long lashes flutter. The beautiful green irises are dark; his pupils are wide. He bites his lip. Asher cradles Tyler's knees with his palms carefully and, when Tyler doesn't stop him, runs them up the length of his thighs, feeling the flex of them as they're still squeezed tight around his hips. He presses his thumbs along the inside seam of Tyler's pants and thrills at the way Tyler's breath hitches and his hands come up around Asher's neck.

"Is this okay?" Asher asks. He stills his fingers and watches, fascinated, when Tyler squirms. This is so fast and out of control, but it's delicious.

"Oh, my god," Tyler says. His voice is breathy and high. "*Please.*"

Asher kisses below Tyler's ear and runs his thumbs inside the juncture of Tyler's thighs. Tyler spreads them a little more, then turns his face to give Asher access to his neck. Asher runs one finger, too lightly, up the length of Tyler's cock. Tyler makes another one of those beautifully needy noises. They're heady; they make Asher's blood sing. He bites Tyler's neck lightly and cups him, feels how big and hard Tyler is.

"Asher, please, oh *fuck*—"

It's been so long, too long, since Asher's touched someone, since he's had the contact of someone's skin and lips. And he's wanted Tyler for much longer than he's let himself admit. Drunk on this closeness, on being able to touch him, Asher's fingers fumble with the button of Tyler's pants. Tyler lets go of him long enough to try to help, and everything is a mess of fingers, and then Tyler leans back and lifts his hips enough for Asher to push his pants down. It's all awkward angles, and Tyler isn't as close as Asher wants, but that's okay because he's so beautiful. Asher pushes Tyler's shirt up, touches the taut skin over his belly, grips Tyler's cock and squeezes lightly.

"What do you like?" Tyler asks, biting his lip and obviously trying to keep still.

"Right now, I think that's what I'm supposed to ask you." Asher says with a light laugh. He holds his hand to Tyler's mouth. "Lick," he says. He keeps his eyes on Tyler's, holds his gaze. Tyler shivers. When Asher presses one finger against Tyler's beautiful lips, he opens his mouth and sucks lightly and moans. Asher doesn't let go of his cock.

He strokes it lightly and, when Tyler has gotten his fingers wet enough, he switches hands.

"Fast? Hard?" he prompts. His fingers close over the head of Tyler's cock as he strokes it. His other thumb is on his balls. Tyler is shaking.

"I don't—I, *oh fuck*—what?" Tyler is struggling to keep his eyes open, arching his back and tilting his pelvis. He tries to spread his legs farther but they are constricted by his pants.

"Keep your eyes on me," Asher instructs. Tyler's eyes open; its hypnotic. He's mesmerizing, and the confidence of his own desire courses through his own body. Asher loves this. He's good at this.

"I can't," Tyler whimpers. Asher wonders if he's asking too much.

"Kiss me then," Asher says quietly. Tyler hauls himself up and does. Asher works him over fast and hard. Tyler pants against his lips; his hands are around Asher's neck. Asher can feel the tension in Tyler's body as it works toward orgasm.

"Look down," he says. Tyler does. "Does this feel good?" Tyler's vulnerability and hesitations are sweet, unintentional seduction.

"Yes," Tyler says helplessly.

"You want this? Do you want to come?"

"*Please*," he sounds undone.

"It's okay," Asher whispers against Tyler's temple. "I've got you."

"Asher," Tyler says, voice laced with disbelief and pleasure. "Oh god, *Asher*," Tyler moans. His body grows tight; his forehead is against Asher's and his dick pulses as he comes all over them both.

IT TAKES TYLER A LONG time to pull himself together. Asher's smooths his shirt down and rubs his back, even though his hand is a mess. Tyler keeps his face tucked into Asher's neck and tries to calm his breathing. Tyler smells so good; his sweat has made a once familiar scent more concentrated.

"I—Asher..." Tyler finally looks into Asher's eyes. They're steady and focused. He puts his hand under Asher's shirt. His skin is hot to the touch. "Let me," Tyler whispers, hooking one finger under the waistband of Asher's pants.

The ring of the back bell, loud and shocking, startles them both badly.

"That's the produce," Asher whispers. He closes his eyes and takes a breath, kisses between Tyler's brows and backs away, then finds a rag to wipe his hand with.

"Wait—" Tyler pushes himself to stand.

Asher smiles. "We'll pause."

"Are you sure?" Tyler asks.

"Of course, don't worry," Asher says. He isn't upset or frustrated. Anticipation is a lovely, intoxicating presence. He kisses Tyler, then leaves the office.

It *is* the produce, with their regular delivery man, Marcus, at the door. Asher fakes calm. It's all he can do not to rush Marcus out of the door. He attends to small talk and wonders what's going on with Tyler, who hasn't left the office.

After what seems like hours, Marcus finally leaves. In the office Tyler is in Asher's chair, staring off into space. His pants are done up but his shirt is off. Asher leans against the door and appreciates Tyler's body; uncertainty edges Tyler's smile. "I… I didn't know what to do with my shirt," he says and crosses his arms, one hand cupping his shoulder.

"You can borrow one of mine," Asher says. He checks the clock. "You have some time before George gets in."

"Is that—"

"Stop asking if it's okay," Asher says and laughs. He pulls Tyler out of the chair. His skin is soft and lovely, and his waist is small in Asher's hands. He kisses Tyler slowly, giving him time to move away if he wants. Tyler doesn't. He kisses Asher back with increasing heat and confidence and when Asher pulls away he delights in Tyler's little noise of protest. "You'd better go," he whispers.

"All right," Tyler says. He makes no move to leave. His eyes are wide, jade bright and wondering.

"We'll come back to this later," Asher promises. "If that's what you want."

"Yeah," Tyler says, breathlessly. "Yes, please."

Chapter Fifteen

TYLER SPENDS THE REST OF his shift vacillating between confusion and anticipation. Working in the office instead of on the floor helps because it gives him time to pull himself together. The work keeps his mind busy; he makes calls and organizes information, which gives him a sense of control.

Sometimes he has to go out on the floor or into the kitchen to confer with Asher after a conversation with a vendor. He worries that he's obvious because just being close to him makes him dizzy with desire, but Asher never gives anything away. Either he's a better actor than Tyler or he's not as affected.

When the lunch shift is over, Tyler carries the bar drawer back to the office to count out, while Asher stays in the kitchen with Santos to prep for dinner. Tyler sits in the quiet of the office and closes his eyes. His imagination runs haywire; the air in the room is charged, as if the intensity of the moment they shared lingers in the air. Tyler lays his palms on the counter and tries to breathe. Now that he has time to reflect, all he can think about is how easily Asher gave, how easily he undid all of Tyler's control, took him apart and held him through the aftermath.

He tells himself that if they had not been interrupted he could have pulled himself together enough to give Asher exactly what he wanted. Or at least to *find out* what Asher wants and to try to take him apart as equally as he had done Tyler. He's going a little crazy wondering what will happen when things get "unpaused."

Tyler isn't working the night shift; once he's finished with the administrative tasks for the lunch shift he had planned on going home. He spends so much time at Idlewild he hasn't had an opportunity to volunteer at Affirmations or the rec center in his old neighborhood as much as he used to. That's okay because he enjoys his work; he loves Idlewild. Since Malik left, Tyler's had a lot of time to examine what he's doing and where he's going. He can see how Idlewild has drawn him in; he loves this work so much. But he's let other things in his life slide and let many things that balance him fall by the wayside.

Suddenly he hears the clatter Asher's keys unlocking the door. Tyler turns blindly to the counter and grabs the clipboard.

"Hey," Asher says quietly.

"Hi."

They stare at each other. Tyler fidgets then drops his gaze. He turns back to the drawer and begins counting the money. He startles at the touch of a finger on the back of his neck.

"Is this—" Asher starts.

"*Yes*," Tyler says immediately. Asher's fingers trace the skin on the back of his neck tenderly, a gentle reminder of this morning, or perhaps the promise of what's to come. When Asher kisses the nape of his neck, Tyler closes his eyes. He grips the edge of the counter and lets himself exhale. Chills course through his body. Asher's hands come to rest on his shoulders, then slide down his chest. Nothing is uncertain about his touch. With Tyler's permission, Asher doesn't hesitate.

Tyler reaches out to grab one of his hands as if in a trance; not to stop him, but because Tyler needs to connect. He doesn't naturally have the same confidence that Asher exudes, and he's off balance enough that he's struggling to find his ability to pretend he does. Tyler turns the chair around and puts his hands around Asher's waist, squares his shoulders and tilts his head with a small smile on his face. He keeps his eyes on Asher's and rucks the hem of his shirt and then of his undershirt. Above his belly button, Tyler can revel in the soft texture of Asher's skin and the hair leading down toward his waistband. His body is nothing like Malik's, and this, lovely and soft, is a novelty. The newness of it and the strangeness of it is exciting.

"We can't right now," Asher whispers.

"I know," Tyler says. His thumb grazes the edge of Asher's ribs; a fleeting smile and twitch ripple through Asher. Tyler runs his hands from Asher's waist down over his hips and the outsides of his thighs.

"Will you come back later?" Asher asks.

"If you want me to. If you're sure." Tyler stands and tucks his face into Asher's neck, certain his uncertainty is written plainly across his features. Asher pulls back and kisses him.

"Of course."

Tyler smiles and kisses him again. Asher's confidence is so soothing.

"What time?" Tyler asks. "Should I stay for the shift?"

"No. It's your night off, go enjoy it. I'll text you when we're slowing down and closing. It'll be late. Is that okay?"

Tyler looks Asher in the eye. "Absolutely."

He wants to say, *I'd stay up all night.* He wants to say, *Can I give you as much as you gave me?* Instead he steps away and says, "I have to count the drawer."

"Of course," Asher says. He chuckles and turns to grab whatever he needed from the office. He doesn't touch Tyler again; he leaves the office without another word. It's only been a few hours since the morning; the excitement in his body, the vibration of longing throughout Tyler's limbs hasn't abated at all.

Tyler gets home exhausted. The bus was an ordeal. Brandon is home when he gets there. They've done their best to avoid each other; he can't make eye contact and flits to his room as quickly as he can. In the last few years that Brandon has become his friend, but they're not as close as Brandon and Malik were. He imagines that Brandon would rather Tyler had left. But it was Malik's choice to leave.

Is it temporary? Whenever Tyler opens the bedroom door he half expects to find Malik at the desk lost in his books, or on their bed. The room doesn't smell of his cologne, and the floor is neat and clean. Malik stays in contact with him all the time now and Tyler wonders if that's an extension of friendship or Malik trying to keep him on the line.

The pang he expected to carry for a long time is absent. After they broke up the first time, Tyler suffered for months. This time what lingers is anxiety. He's worked so hard to be what Malik wanted, to keep him home with him. He's not sure where he failed. If he can pinpoint it, find what he's done wrong, he can fix it.

He drifts around the room, touches things, haunts the spaces Malik had filled.

Tyler half expects his own body to seem haunted when he lies on his bed. He's tired, but the exhaustion isn't the bad kind. He's loose, sated. He's still wearing Asher's shirt. He pulls up the collar and inhales. It no longer smells of Asher, but instead of the restaurant. Tyler wonders how brave he has to be to get dressed and meet Asher at Idlewild. He wonders if he'll come home with his hands knowing the shape of Asher's pleasure and body, carrying smell of him too.

He wants that, badly. But to make that happen, he'll have to learn how to keep a straight face around the other employees. He doesn't want to broadcast this affair, and he's sure Asher doesn't either. Tyler is adaptable and can be many versions of himself, but he's got a terrible poker face. Maybe it'll be just this one time, or a friends-with-benefits thing. Whatever it is, he cannot let it affect their work. So long as he knows that's what Asher wants, he can adjust.

That's another thing. He's going to have to figure out what Asher likes. Of course, they've only been together this one morning. What happened seems like a dream; it's hard to pinpoint how things escalated so quickly. The tension they've danced around was by turns delicious, confusing and frustrating. Guilt so often followed him. But there's been no guilt today.

On paper, Asher is far from his type. He's taller than Tyler, but smaller than Malik, who works so hard to maintain a body with rippling muscles. Tyler loved how much smaller he was than Malik. Malik could lift him easily and manhandle him in a way Tyler loved. He doubts Asher could do that, yet Tyler could not care less.

And then there's age. It's not that Tyler objects to older men at all. He's definitely felt the ten years between them in hearing about and seeing Asher's experience and at times when he's sure Asher doesn't *mean* to condescend. Now, thinking about the night to come, Tyler wonders at what Asher's learned in ten years and how experienced he is, how much more he might bring to a lover.

He doesn't want to shower this morning off of his skin, but he smells of food and definitely should shower; despite perfunctory clean up, he's still a little messy.

He grooms his body; his chest hair is so sparse that he's always waxed it, and it's been a while. He's got hours, so he exfoliates and trims and smooths.

After his shower he's too antsy to read. He doesn't want to go into the living room with Brandon, who is watching TV. He cleans his already clean room. He changes his sheets. He emails his mother. He organizes his calendar to schedule time to for the volunteer work he's let slide. He e-mails Emily at Affirmations to be sure they have tasks for him when he is available.

By nine, Tyler cannot stand sitting at home any more. He runs down to the store and buys lube and condoms. It never hurts to be prepared.

His bus comes early, and Tyler rolls his eyes. Of course.

In one of December's warm snaps, he's warm enough that he can tuck his hands in his coat pockets and wander Campus Martius for a while. He stops at the ice rink and watches the ice skaters. There's always one person, that one girl who is practicing spins and simple jumps, weaving between the inexperienced ones who laugh and fall, who play tag and enjoy each other. It starts to snow: tiny, almost invisible flakes. Between the soft lights of Christmas and the horse-drawn carriages, the too-bright light of the Hard Rock Café and Texas de Brazil signs down the Woodward corridor to the changing lights of the Renaissance Center, downtown sparkles with life.

Whenever he takes the time to explore this part of Downtown, Tyler reflects at the conflicting sadness and hope that crowd him. No one is bringing a high-end tapas and wine restaurant down Trumbull and West Grand Boulevard or into Brightmoor. Downtown is the shiny dream magazines write about, contrasting it with blight and crime statistics in worse neighborhoods of the city. No one sees the in-between or hears the stories of people working hard every day, filling spaces others deem empty.

But, businesses and restaurants sprung in Midtown, through parts of Cork Town and Mexican Town; Potter Park, a neighborhood often spoken of at Hotter than July, where people dream of making an ideal gayborhood: All of these changes make Tyler hopeful that positive change will spread and that with it, all of the stories and faces of the city will too. Wherever he goes, he sees people coming together. They farm in empty lots to turn things around. They take safety into their own hands and patrol neighborhoods; they take down blighted homes on their own. Men like Tyree Guyton, who created the Heidelburg project, taking found, everyday objects to turn dejected buildings into living art, have turned their lives and communities around. Men like Malik who are determined to make change, even if his view was so much more unbending than Tyler's. For Tyler, this city's story isn't *us vs. them*, no matter what others might think. It's a place with lots of hope and potential and heart in all of its spaces.

These opinions always made Malik mad. In this city there's no guarantee that corruption won't line the shit out of pockets of people that don't care the way they should, and Tyler understands that. What Malik saw was a rhetoric of white, young newcomers saving the city from itself, of people who lived out in the suburbs shaking their heads and passing judgment rooted in apologetic—and sometimes not—racism. Rhetoric from outsiders who choose to ignore Detroit's heartbreaking and complex history, one that goes back farther than the riots of the 60s, back to the birth of the auto industry, to a time when many black families fled the south to cities like Detroit with hopes for better lives and more freedoms. Rhetoric from those who ignore the reality of white flight and how it systematically changed the landscape of the city left behind.

But Tyler sees more people coming to his city. More will see the phoenix rising. Change is on the news and in the air and, while many aspects of change are rough and unready, to Tyler, this all spells hope.

When Tyler checks his watch again it's almost eleven—no wonder his ears are freezing and he's shivering. His coat is warm but not that warm. He wanders back down Woodward. The streets are crowded: women dressed for a night on the town; groups debating the merits of Greektown Casino over MGM or Motorcity; people wondering where to eat. Butting in and telling them to go to Idlewild might not go over well, but he's tempted.

Tyler knows of the middleness of his body. He is self-consciousness about the lightness of his skin and worries that he might be too light to fit into spaces at home, in college, with Malik's friends. And he's too dark to pass as white, which he'd never want anyway. He hides the things that make him genderqueer from many, many people. They slip out in ways he can't always control, but not many people get to see that side of him in full effect. He doesn't plan to tell those secrets any time soon.

In this stream of people coming to Downtown from the safety of the suburbs, Tyler is definitely the other, and he's not up for it tonight. Tonight is for new with Asher. His heart beats too fast; he loves this moment, the one where you slide against and then into the fireworks of first touches.

He slips through Idlewild's back door using his key. He doesn't want to be seen; he hopes everyone is up front, busy with the pre-gaming crowd getting ready for the casino, or the ones trickling out from whatever show is at the Fox Theater tonight. Last week it had been The Monkeys. Tyler's not even sure who The Monkeys are. But people came to see them.

He makes his way up the stairs, light-footed and fast. Once in the loft, he has no idea what to do with himself. Sit on the bed? Make himself at home and turn on the TV? Wait around in the nude?

Tyler laughs at himself. Never.

He texts Asher.

I'm a little early. I'll wait upstairs?

It's a while before he gets a response. Tyler's tidying the loft. He's been here a few times—when Asher was sick and the days after Malik left, eating ice cream and leaning heavily on Asher's shoulder while watching movies—and each time he's tried to resist making order in Asher's chaos. Other than when Asher was sick, he's succeeded. He's doesn't know if Asher will mind, but Tyler's got to do something to keep himself busy.

That's fine. I'll come up as soon as I can. Make yourself at home.

So he does.

BY THE TIME ASHER COMES, Tyler's on the couch, drowsily watching TV. Asher's footsteps announce his arrival. Tyler smooths his shirt and sits up. He turns to look over the back of the couch. Asher's eyes seek him out, and that thrill of anticipation that faded while he waited comes back like a hurricane.

"I'm…" Asher gestures at himself. His shirt is stained, and his hair is messy, which means he's been running his hands through it. Tyler wants to put his own fingers in Asher's hair, to tangle them in it, to pull on it and see what response he'll get. He bites his lip, unsure what Asher wants. Should he get up and coax him out of his clothes? Does Asher want to shower? Because Tyler really, really wants to make a mess of them both.

He swallows his indecision and stands. Asher stays still. He looks at Tyler without flinching. Tyler tugs on one button of his shirt. Beneath,

Asher wears an undershirt. Tyler must make a face or noise because Asher smiles. "It's a habit," he says.

"It's a bad one," Tyler says with a smile. Asher frames Tyler' face in his hands. They're so warm, and Asher's eyes are so direct.

When Asher kisses him, it's like melting, as if in Asher's touch Tyler's body gives way. He's never been kissed the way Asher kisses him; as if his mouth is a feast, and he'd be happy to stay there for hours. He's deliberate and slow and careful, giving little nips and light licks. He tilts Tyler's head and deepens the kiss, and Tyler's breath comes short. He's dizzy and his hands grab Asher's shoulders.

Asher pulls away a bit. Tyler brushes his lips against Asher's—not a kiss, but a desire to have him stay. Their breath mingles. Asher's fingers run down the sides of his neck, and Tyler can't help the shiver that rolls down his body. He takes a breath and orders himself to pull himself together.

"Can I—?" Tyler tugs on the buttons of Asher's shirt.

"Yeah," Asher says. He keeps his hands at his sides; his eyes never leave Tyler while he lets Tyler work him out of his shirt.

"Lift your arms," Tyler says.

Asher's skin is so light Tyler would bet he hasn't been out in the sun in a very long time. He's by no means unfit, but he has the smallest rounding to his belly. He has only a little more chest hair than Tyler has naturally. Tyler runs a finger from Asher's belly button to the top of his pants.

"Yes," Asher says. But before he does, Tyler spreads his fingers and wraps them around Asher's waist. Tyler's skin is hungry for touch. Asher's hands cover his; he's so confident it's a little stunning. He leads Tyler's hands to his pants and together they work them off until Asher's in his boxer briefs and socks. He's not completely hard, but is getting there.

"What do you want?" Tyler asks. He pulls back and meets Asher's eyes.

"You in my bed," Asher says, laughter in his voice and a new smile on his face. He kisses Tyler again and pulls his shirt up with his palms. They break apart to take it off. Asher pulls Tyler toward his bed by tugging on a pant loop. His lips are on Tyler's neck, behind his ear, along his collarbone. While Asher undoes his pants, Tyler finally gets his hands in Asher's hair. It's soft and thick. Tugging it pulls a shocked breath from Asher. Tyler smiles.

He lets Asher lay him down. Asher straddles him and begins to kiss his belly. He runs his hands up and down Tyler's sides, then moves back a bit. He mouths, teasing and light, over Tyler's dick.

"Asher," Tyler starts, then moans when Asher slips a finger under a leg band of his underwear and strokes his balls. *This is all wrong,* he thinks, even as he spreads his legs for more of that touch. This was meant to be about Asher, whom he left unsatisfied this morning. "Come up here," he asks. Asher does, dragging kisses up his chest. "Stop making me ask what you want," Tyler says. Asher's eyes crinkle. This is a side of Asher he's never seen and could never have guessed lay under that veneer of distance.

"This, dummy," Asher presses against him, hard against his hip.

"How? What do you want me to do?"

"Why don't you let me show you?" Asher says. He moves to straddle Tyler again; lays his body against Tyler's; grinds against him with slow rolls. Tyler kisses his shoulder and neck. Asher makes a tiny noise that encourages, so he does it again, and then nips lightly. Tyler slides one hand under Asher's underwear, cups his ass and feels the flex and give of the muscle in his palm.

"Take these off," he says. Asher lifts his hips and helps wiggle them off; soon enough they're both naked and it's skin for miles, hot and close. The air in the loft is warm and quiet. Almost too quiet. Under his fingers, Asher's back flexes. Tyler wraps his leg around Asher's hip and tries to let go, to lose himself in what feels good right now.

"You still with me?"

Tyler averts his eyes. "Yeah, of course." He looks back at Asher. Touches his lips and smiles when Asher kisses them. "It's very quiet in here."

"Say no more," Asher says. He rolls off the bed and searches for his phone. He must have a Bluetooth speaker somewhere because soon enough low music fills the air. Tyler's rakes his eyes over Asher's body; he's stunned by the way he carries his nudity so easily. Asher catches Tyler's stare and his lips quirk. Slowly, his eyes travel down Tyler's body. Tyler is rolled on his side with his head propped on his hand. He fidgets.

"Shy?" Asher asks, crawling back onto the bed with him. He cradles Tyler's head in his palms. His other hand runs up the smooth inside of Tyler's thigh, then over his dick and up his stomach and his neck. It cups Tyler's cheek, and then they kiss. Tyler grabs his waist with one hand; Asher's skin is slightly damp. He seems calm but he's panting. Tyler thumbs one of Asher's nipples and feels the subterranean shiver, so he does it again, this time scraping lightly with his nail. Asher makes a tiny, broken noise.

"Can I blow you?" Asher asks. Tyler closes his eyes.

"Shouldn't I be asking you that? I think it's my turn to get you off," he jokes.

"We'll both get there, trust me."

Tyler cracks open an eye.

Asher looks down his body, fingers exploring. "You worry too much," he says and smiles. He glances up and must notice Tyler's confusion. He slides down, settling between Tyler's legs.

"Condom?" Tyler asks shyly. He'd never go without, but it can be uncomfortable to ask. He's walked away from men who refused to use one.

"Oh, yeah." Asher sits and runs a hand through his hair sheepishly. "It's been so long—crap!"

"Don't worry. I brought some. They're in my pants." Asher squeezes his thigh to get him to keep still and goes to get them. While Asher fumbles with the foil package, Tyler wonders how long it's been since he's been with someone. Surely he's been with people since John died. It's been years, after all, and Asher is so clearly a deeply sensual person.

Tyler startles when Asher touches him while he's rolling the condom on. Malik rarely wanted to blow him; he was always one for hands when they were too busy for anything else. Above all he loved to fuck Tyler, loved his light body and easy acquiescence and pleasure. They're far enough apart now that he feels disconnected from Asher. Asher moves to kiss him; deeply, dirty and confident with his hand moving and sliding over him. Tyler shudders into the touch and puts his hands on Asher's head.

"Stop thinking so much and let me make you feel good," Asher says.

That's my line. Tyler doesn't say it though, because Asher's mouth is on him and soon enough he's caught in a pleasure that's on the edge of unbearable.

Chapter Sixteen

It's not that Tyler, asleep in his bed, appears young, precisely. But there's an innocence in the way Tyler's legs curl toward his body. His hands are tucked under the pillow, and in stillness, there's something almost *other* about him. Tyler's charisma comes from his body and words, and from his bright and changeable eyes. His face, lost for its animation, displays his natural beauty differently than when he is awake.

Asher lets him sleep for a while longer, though. Wrapped in a blanket, he sits with a mug of tea on the couch and lets the lovely buzz of satisfaction linger. Down in Asher's bones is the relief of finally connecting with another human body, of giving touch where he's ached to for a long time. His body had starved for it, but he's been so busy. That he's had the privilege of doing so with Tyler, this bright, beautiful flame of a boy he's been lucky to have in his life, is an honor.

He has no idea what happens from here. Tyler's spent weeks caught in a back-and-forth with Malik. He's worked harder than anyone might expect, given Malik's obvious fears and inability to commit. He wonders if it is too much to let Tyler sleep here. But it's late, and he certainly doesn't want him to leave.

Asher is tired: the good kind of tired, but still tired. He gets into bed carefully, hoping not to startle Tyler awake. He pulls the covers up when Tyler's eyes open, hazy and hardly cognizant. He smiles and slides over, tucking his head onto Asher's shoulder and tangling their legs. He's asleep almost immediately, and then so is Asher.

* * *

MORNING COMES WITH THE BUZZ of his phone. It's too early for sunlight; it's that part of winter when sunlight becomes a rare commodity. Asher's always been lucky because he's never felt low when the days are short and the darkness presses.

He grabs the phone and swipes at the screen. He's got shipments coming this morning, but he has a little time. Usually he'd use this time to tidy the restaurant or to try to keep up with the office system Tyler set up.

But Tyler's sleeping body is still a warm presence in his bed; they'd shuffled apart in sleep, but under the covers is the delicious warmth of another body. Asher is still unsure of what happens when the day does truly break, and they have to have a conversation about what this means.

Right now though, there is a beautiful boy in his bed whose eyes melt, liquid and stunned, under his attention, who is reticent to let go but breathtaking when he gives in to his body's desire to take and take.

He turns on the bedside lamp and rolls over and puts one hand on Tyler's naked hip, then kisses the back of his neck. Tyler wakes with a sigh, then a long, arched stretch. He rolls onto his back and smiles at him.

"Good morning," Tyler whispers. Asher's eyes linger on his lips, but when he meets his eyes, he hopes that look communicates what he wants well enough. The loft is hushed in a fragile spell. He wants to lean into that silence with Tyler, to take as much of this night as possible. He mouths the words back. Tyler's hand strokes down his waist, then carefully, down over the curve of his ass. In his eyes are questions that Asher can answer by rolling on top of him and kissing him.

THEY'RE STILL IN BED, SLIGHTLY sweaty and tangled and facing each other. Somehow, through it all, that wonderful, safe and hushed space still envelops them. Asher watches Tyler's eyes as they come down. They both sigh when they hear the insistent high-pitched buzz of the back doorbell.

"That fucking bell," Tyler mutters when Asher jumps out of bed to throw on clothes. Asher shares his frustration. He hops into his pants, and Tyler sits up. "Need me right now?"

"No," Asher gives him a quick kiss. "Take your time." Tyler smiles at him, and something curls, warm and delicious, in Asher's belly.

Tyler doesn't come down until it's time for his shift, and then he's in his work clothes. When he comes into the office, Asher catches a whiff of his own bath products. He needs to shower himself.

Tyler is perceptive enough not to press him or ask questions. "I can handle things for now if you want to get dressed," he offers. Asher gives him a grateful look. They can talk later. He shuffles past Tyler and wonders if he should kiss him.

"Everything good?" He touches the back of Tyler's hand and smiles when Tyler takes it and squeezes his fingers.

"Very," he says, and sighs into the kiss Asher gives him.

Asher wants to linger in the shower, to take the time to enjoy that glowing lovely night in his muscles. But he's behind, the bar's about to open, and he's not sure if this is a memory he has to keep and tuck away, or if he can carry this happiness and hope for more.

Chapter Seventeen

TYLER'S BEEN SITTING QUIETLY IN the office with Asher when his phone rings. Beyond the door he can hear some of the employees taking a break, loud and rowdy. It's almost the end of a Friday night shift and their energy seems to be high.

"Hi, Mama," he says. He keeps his voice low, disconcerted by answering a personal call in front of Asher. Asher's taken him to bed every night for a week, so the shyness makes no sense. Other than Malik coming to the restaurant the night they broke up, Idlewild has always been completely Tyler's, and how people see him here has nothing to do with the rest of his life.

"Tyler," Mama says in her no-nonsense voice.

"Uh-oh, what have I done now?"

"Don't you sass me," she says. "Not when we haven't seen you in weeks. You haven't called me in over a week!"

"Sorry, Mama, I've been busy." Tyler bites back a completely inappropriate smile and glances back at Asher, who watches him unabashedly. Tyler makes a face.

"Tyler, all you do is work. I saw Margerie the other day and she said she hasn't seen you in weeks. Those kids miss you. You tell your boss that you need time for other things in your life. You've made commitments." Technically, he hadn't. He's worked with Margerie at his community rec center for years on a drop-in basis, with no commitment to volunteer, other than the relationships he'd formed and the kids he's worked with to help them have positive role models and make good choices.

She's totally right. "It's not my boss," he says, and Asher's eyes widen dramatically. Tyler covers his mouth and moves the phone away from it so she won't hear the giggle. He shakes his head. "I've been... it's hard to explain." And it is. His audience of Asher is awkward, but finding the words to explain why he'd rather lose himself here than go back to an empty apartment—he still hasn't told her he and Malik broke up—seems impossible.

"Well, we're having a family dinner Sunday night. We expect you to be there."

"Let me see if I have that day off first, Mama."

Which? Asher mouths at him.

Sunday, Tyler mouths back. Asher checks the calendar and gives him a thumbs up.

"All right, Mama, I'll see you there."

"And don't bring any food. I don't want you spending any of that money you're saving."

"Mama..." he protests.

"Nope. Not a thing. Please?"

He sighs. He can't resist when she uses that tone. "All right, Mama. I'll see you Sunday."

He hangs up the phone and looks at Asher. Asher's grinning. "Mama?" he asks.

"Shut up," Tyler mutters, trying not to smile.

"Oh my god, you are adorable." Asher hooks his feet around one of Tyler's and uses his leverage to roll him closer on his chair. Once he's close enough, Asher pulls Tyler up out of the chair and onto his lap.

"Adorable?" Tyler squints down at him.

"One of many adjectives," Asher says. He kisses down Tyler's neck; Tyler has to grip the armrests; his perch is precarious, even without

Asher doing delicious things to his body. His eyes slide shut and he nestles into him.

"I'd ask what they are, but I'm afraid you'd start complimenting me and end up fucking me on the counter." Asher is insatiable; Tyler's not sure if it's symptomatic of not having had sex in a while or if Asher's always been like this. He's certainly the most uninhibited man Tyler's ever taken to bed.

Or if he assesses the situation honestly, who's taken *him* to bed.

"Don't tempt me," Asher says. He's made his way to Tyler's mouth, which he captures and then takes. Tyler laces his hands around Asher's neck and holds on tight so he doesn't fall backward off of the chair. Asher's started to do that thing where he nibbles on Tyler's lower lip, when someone knocks on the door.

"Fuck!" Tyler pulls away so fast he almost falls off of the chair. "Christ." He rights himself and puts a hand to his chest where his heart thumps madly. They hear another knock.

"Coming." Asher straightens his shirt.

"Do I look like you've been kissing me?" Tyler hisses. Asher examines him; his gaze soon turns from assessing to soft.

"No, you're fine," he says. He gives Tyler a sweet kiss on the cheek when he slides past him to open the door, and Tyler's chest clenches. He turns and puts his hand over his heart; he's terrified and hopeful and completely unsure himself and this situation.

* * *

TYLER GOES TO MAMA'S HOUSE earlier than he'd planned. He'd been sitting at home, bored and still uncomfortable in Brandon's presence. He has to work something out. Rent with two of them was going to become a problem, and avoiding his own apartment all the time is stupid.

He's anticipating a good night with his family and is caught completely off guard when he sees Malik on the porch. "*Fuck,*" he says under his breath. Malik is smoking on one of the porch chairs. He's wearing the hideous hat Tyler gave him as a joke for Christmas last year. He looks good but, as Tyler comes closer and can see him better, tired.

"What are you doing here?" Tyler asks. He hates bad surprises and he can't manage more than a flat tone. "And why are you smoking?"

"Your Mama invited me," Malik says. "Stress." He doesn't make eye contact. Tyler swallows another swear word. No swearing in this house, ever, and that's a deeply ingrained habit.

"And you couldn't say no?" he says. He's got his arms crossed and he's definitely being unkind. Malik's been in contact with him regularly; sometimes it's been comforting because it seems like a gesture of friendship, and other times it's seemed like manipulation.

Malik's shoulders hunch, and he takes another drag off his cigarette before putting it out. Tyler wants to lecture him for taking up smoking again. He wants to ask why Malik is wearing exhaustion tight around his eyes. And he wants to kick himself for caring. Tyler can be pissed and concerned at the same time. Eventually one emotion will win out. He sighs.

"I wanted to be here," Malik says quietly. Tyler's shoulders drop. Malik has no family. He never knew his father and his mother had drug problems off and on from the time Malik was young. She'd died shortly after Malik went to college. Malik has no contact with his brother, and Tyler doesn't blame him. Malik loves Tyler's family: the dinners and laughter and camaraderie. Mama, who isn't given to hugs, always gathers Malik in and hugs him tight and long. She never asked him for his story; she always sensed he needed all the love he could get.

Tyler opens the door and gestures Malik in. He'd tried to give Malik as much love as possible, too. Malik not only needed love, but gave it when he could, which wasn't consistently. Tyler knew that Malik wanted to love him, but he couldn't figure out how, and Tyler couldn't crack the code to keeping that love. If Malik's inability to figure his shit out hadn't hurt Tyler so many times, Tyler would have been happy to keep Malik in his life.

IT TAKES ALL OF FIVE minutes for Tyler to understand why his mother insisted on dinner, and it starts and ends with his sister Hope's new boyfriend, Kevin. Tyler has an instant, visceral reaction to him from their first handshake, and he can tell that Malik experiences it as well. Still, he plays nice while he helps get dinner ready. He tries to get Hope alone because he has to ask her what is going on in her head. This guy is dressed like trouble. He has an air of self-indulgent swagger and hubris. He's wearing expensive brands and a pricey watch but is evasive when Gayle, not so subtly, tries to talk to him about his job.

God bless his mama, who does not suffer fools, something she's told them she learned from her disastrous marriage to their father.

"Hope, why don't you tell Tyler about your plans?" she says sweetly. Too sweetly. Hope narrows her eyes and sets her shoulders defiantly. Tyler can see her trying on youth and defiance at the same time. He doesn't remember acting that way at eighteen. But he'd had a hell of a lot more responsibilities. They've all spoiled her.

"Shawnee needs a girl at her shop," she says. "Cleaning up. She said she'll teach me how to do hair, too."

"Don't you need a license to do that?" Gayle asks. Hope rolls her eyes.

"How much money do you think you're going to be making?" Tyler asks. He has a sinking feeling that this conversation is really about her dropping out of school.

"I'll be okay," Hope says. "Kevin makes lots of money. He can take care of me, too."

"Oh hell—"

"What was it you do?" Malik interrupts Gayle smoothly. His voice is deceptively quiet, but his muscles are coiled. His gaze is confrontational, unflinching.

"What's it to you?" Kevin says.

"You think you're gonna take this little girl out of school? Promise her expensive things?"

"I take care of my women," Kevin says. He juts out his chin. Every head at the table turns toward him. Judging from Hope's defensive and closed body language, Tyler doesn't think direct confrontation will help them.

"Boy, you think making money in all the wrong ways makes you a big man?" Malik asks.

"What do you know about it?" Kevin asks. Tyler observes everyone, and sees that even Hope is uncomfortable, fidgeting in her chair and biting her lower lip.

"You want to be a real man? Want to walk tall, make something of yourself? The way you do it? It takes a chickenshit to walk out the door and start dealing. Fuck. Doing the *fucking* work." Malik throws his napkin on his uneaten food. Under the table Tyler lays his fingers on Malik's knee.

"Look at you, pretty boy in your church goin' clothes, acting like just 'cause you're in college you aren't a fag, too," Kevin says, nodding toward Tyler.

And then a whole lot of chaos breaks loose.

"You gonna let her talk to you?" Malik asks Tyler later that night. They're back on the porch. Tyler's been dead silent ever since Kevin left. He couldn't respond to Hope's tearful apology and not only because one apology won't fix things. Some guy calling him a fag isn't her responsibility and it isn't all she has to apologize for. All of his hard work and his Mama's, all that they did to give her opportunities means nothing if she's going in this direction, if she thinks that men like Kevin are a good choice, if she doesn't realize how hard she has—they all have—to work to help her get ahead.

Fuck.

"Eventually," Tyler says. He studies his hands and ignores the way Malik plays with his pack of cigarettes, tapping them against his palm. They'll be the best packed cigarettes in the city at this rate. "It's my fault."

"Ty, seriously?"

"Shoulda come home more. Spent more time with them. I've been gone so much—" he cuts himself off, aware that this isn't a great topic to bring up with Malik. It's quiet.

"I'm not gonna say you've been busy," Malik says carefully. "But I can say you've done your best. You all have. Girl just has to get her head on straight. We can all help her do that." Tyler catches Malik's wince. "You guys, I mean."

A softness settles in Tyler's heart. With space and time, Tyler's come to be thankful they broke up. It was right, even though failing at holding it together stings. Realizing that that's the loss, not Malik, brings him up short. But he does still love him. Tyler's not sure what Malik wants from or with him, but he doesn't want to take this family away from him.

"Malik…"

"Naw, you don't have to say anything," Malik says. He tears the cellophane sleeve on the box.

"I'm sorry things didn't work out," Tyler says. He tries to find a kind way to shut one door and open another. "But you don't have to walk away from this." He waves back at the house. "They love you. They still will when we tell them." Malik blinks hard and turns blind eyes toward the street. "If you want, they can still be your family. If you can. I mean… with us not—"

"I get it, Ty," Malik interrupts. His voice is rough. "You think your mama will forgive me this time?" After Malik left the first time it took her ages to forgive him.

"Well, it ain't like we're not on the same page this time," Tyler says. Then, because he needs to close the door for certain. "Right?"

Malik turns back to smile at Tyler. It's sad but honest. He kisses Tyler's cheek.

"Right."

Chapter Eighteen

"What's that?" Tyler asks, nodding toward the end table, where a gaudy blue and white Hanukkah card lies.

"A card from my brother," Asher says. He sits next to Tyler and grabs it. "My niece must have picked it out."

Tyler's eyebrows shoot up before he can stop them. "You have a brother?"

"Yep." Asher hands him the card. Inside are two tickets to a Red Wings game and a sloppy and crooked message which must be from his niece.

"Julie?"

"Yeah. She's five. She's named after my mother." Asher looks at the ceiling.

Tyler wants to ask why he's never heard that Asher has a brother or niece, if he has more siblings, where they live. He bites his lip and does the math. Julie would have been born right around the time John died.

Asher smiles and then turns to him. "They live in Montana."

"Montana? Who actually lives in Montana?"

Asher shrugs. "They do. Eli works there."

"Is he older?"

"Yeah, eight years."

"Oh wow." Tyler picks at the edges of the tickets.

"We were never too close. I don't know that we ever will be."

"How come?" Tyler shifts so that he's a little closer and his body faces Asher.

"Shit like this." Asher flicks the tickets.

Tyler frowns, trying to make sense of what Asher said. *What a cryptic answer.* Asher seems agitated and annoyed, so he doesn't press. "Do you like hockey?" he ventures.

Asher gives a little half laugh. "Of course? Who doesn't? Isn't that a Detroit staple?"

"Um." Tyler tilts his head. "No?"

"You don't?" Asher asks. Tyler wants to pretend it's not incredulity in Asher's voice.

"Asher, honey, your world and mine ain't hardly the same," Tyler drawls. He hands Asher the tickets.

"I've offended you," Asher says. He sits straighter.

"No."

Tyler thinks of all the things Malik said to him; about being an imposter in a different world. It was always easy to shrug off his words, but partly because that was the role he played in their dynamic. Tyler isn't half of that push and pull any more. It's hard to know what he's moving toward or losing when there's no compass north. He doesn't want Asher to think he's mad, so he snuggles closer and changes the subject. He thinks of Asher telling him he's not close to his family. But his parents came to give him a gift for Hanukkah. His brother's niece sent a card that's obviously from Eli. It's not as if he knows any of them; he can't even say he knows this side of Asher. But it seems to him that they're reaching out to Asher. He has to wonder if Asher knows how much he has isolated himself, and why he would still be doing so after all these years.

* * *

ALTHOUGH THEY BOTH SHELVED PERSONAL conversations that night, questions lingered in Tyler's mind. He didn't take offense at Asher's words. But Asher's assumption that his own experiences are the norm, rather than unique to him, sits wrong with Tyler.

And it's not just Asher who thinks this way. To so much of their world, particular experiences rooted in privilege are the norm, and those who live differently or who are different become the *other*.

Sunday Tyler goes for another family dinner, a habit he's getting back in to. He makes an effort to be more present for his family, especially to be more active in Hope's life. Sometimes Malik is there and sometimes not. His presence is still awkward and after each Tyler's not sure what in his life fits where. It disorients; Tyler's not sure where or to what he should be oriented. He's taking some time from Idlewild for his family, and he no longer has Malik to go home to. He's with Asher so much it's often all he can think about; but when he thinks too much he gets confused, because he's not sure what is happening or what they're doing. *It's supposed to be just sex, right?* If it were hookups, it wouldn't feel this way, would it?

After an early dinner he decides to walk down to the Conrad Center, the small community rec center by his neighborhood. He's stuffed from a good home cooked dinner that Hope made; she's trying to cook her way into forgiveness. The sun is setting. For once it's not cloudy, and in the crisp air the pinks and oranges are clear and sharp. The silhouetted houses lose their identities to the dark: those that are shabby, the ones that have been kept assiduously neat, the one on the corner that's been painted a variety of colors, they're all lost to the show put on by the sunset.

Tyler shivers and kicks at the litter in the gutter. He's been working hard and failing to get Asher off of his mind. It's a beautiful night, and he's alone in it. There's no better time for honest thoughts. When he was a kid, his mother encouraged him to see the world through other people's eyes. Malik used to tell him to open his eyes, too, but he meant it differently. He meant that Tyler needed to stop giving people the benefit of the doubt. He meant Tyler needed to see the world the way he did.

Tyler can see it that way. Other people see only what he gives them: the flighty brother at home, the boy who gave up on a dream of being a doctor when it got too hard, a man who won't see the way the world wants to hurt him and who resists others who try to unveil that for him.

He's not any of those things. And none of those are truths. But when he strips away all of the things he is for other people, even the things that perpetuate a negative persona, he's not sure who he is.

Even when it frustrated Malik, Tyler grounded him. That's what Malik needed: someone calm in the face of his fire. Malik fought and fought; he's fought for everything in his life. It's not as if Tyler hasn't struggled, but it will never compare to Malik's life. In Malik's shoes, who knows who Tyler would be. But he isn't in Malik's shoes, and he can't go into life that way, burning with fight to make insurmountable obstacles right. It wasn't Tyler not seeing things; it was Tyler not reacting to them.

But Malik was right about many things. For men like Asher, the world works in a particular way because he's never lived the press of racism in every part of his life. He's never had his skin written upon by other's eyes at a glance. All of Asher's world operates through his lived experience as a white man.

Unlike Malik, he doesn't believe that Asher thinks he's come to save Detroit from the hands of those who held it for years and years, even as it crumbled apart. Asher and John came to build something, to create something. And unlike Malik, Tyler knows that it's not just Asher who has things to learn.

* * *

"DIA, CAN I ASK YOU something?"

"Sure, honey." Claudia puts down the rag she's using to wipe the bar rail and perches on a stool.

"I was thinking about doing a fundraising drive for the Ruth Ellis Center."

"That sounds great. What brought that on, though? How many places do you work at, Tyler?" Claudia smiles, and it's her kindest version.

"Well, not there, though I've visited. But I was walking around the other day and thinking about how fucking cold I was. And I thought... what about kids who don't have this shit? Who are kicked out or homeless or whatever, who would be really fucking happy with the coat I was complaining about?"

Claudia examined Tyler. "Tyler, you are about the nicest person I've ever met."

He ducks his head; her praise makes him uncomfortable because he doesn't deserve it. He was one of the very lucky teens who didn't have to worry about getting kicked out for being gay. There's so much that he could or should be doing to help kids—the city—that he doesn't do.

"Hardly," he says. "I think I'm fucking things up here, because I've been taking so much time off."

"Tyler, you should have a life. We're all entitled. Spread yourself too thin and you'll have so much less to give people."

"Right now, I don't give enough and there are so many people I could—"

"Tyler, you gotta give to *you*. You won't be any good to anyone if you don't take care of yourself. Be kind to yourself. You are an amazing man. Don't forget that."

Tyler looks away and clears his throat. He does not want to cry at work. He can't let himself think through her words right now. She pats his arm, closing the topic for them both.

"But Ruth Ellis?" she prompts.

"Do you think Asher would be cool if I asked him if we could do a drive? Ask people to donate warm things? Some event or week or something?" He's not sure why he's nervous asking, and he's not sure why he's not taking this to Asher on his own.

"Of course," Claudia says. "Why wouldn't he be?"

Tyler shrugs.

"Okay, baby, no." Claudia turns to face him, lips pursed and face serious. "What's this really about? Now that he's got it bad for you, you can't talk to him anymore?"

"What?" Tyler's eyes about bug out. "What do you mean—"

"Do you actually think you aren't the most obvious men in the city?"

"Uh…" Tyler smooths his hands down his thighs. "No?"

"Well, you are," she states.

"*Fuck.*" He starts to stand.

"Where are you going?" She pulls him back down. "I am *so* not done with you yet."

"I don't know. I don't—crap."

"Ty, seriously, why are you so upset? If you wanted to hide it you should have been better about sneaking off upstairs at the end of your shifts." She says this with a smile and nudges his foot with hers.

"Does everyone know?" he asks.

"I don't know if everyone *knows*. But everyone definitely *thinks*."

"What should I do?"

"Do you need to do anything?"

"I don't want him to know that you guys know." Tyler says.

Her eyebrows shoot up. "He ashamed?"

"No! Of course not. I mean, I don't think… he's not that kind—" Tyler stutters and then takes a breath. "I don't know what's going with us. I'm all over the place. He is. It's complicated."

"Good complicated or bad?"

"I think good," he says. He looks at her and smiles. "I really like him. So I hope so. I don't know what he wants. Sometimes I don't know what I want."

"Have you asked him?"

"Ugh, stop being reasonable!" Tyler says. She grins at him.

Jared comes in from the kitchen, swinging through the doors carrying a couple of racks of glasses. Tyler stands abruptly. He doesn't mind Claudia knowing, exactly, but he's not sure how to talk about it, and he's definitely not going to talk in front of an audience. He likes

Claudia, but it's not as though they're close, and Tyler doesn't make a habit of trusting people with his stuff, particularly when he's so confused and uncertain.

* * *

"So I've been thinking," Tyler says.

"What about?" Asher asks.

"You know the other night when we were talking about the Red Wings tickets," Tyler says, "and I told you I wasn't upset?"

"But you were?"

"I don't know if I'd say upset, but it got me thinking." Tyler picks at the cuticle of his thumb.

"Thinking about what?"

"Just how different our lives are," Tyler says. "The ways that we see things being so different."

"Well, yeah," Asher says with a little eye roll.

"Okay, yeah, obviously. I mean you're like a million years older than me and you grew up someplace different and you wear those really ugly button-down shirts—"

He's snickering when Asher swats at his arm.

Tyler takes a deep breath and steels himself, reminding himself how to be brave and how to ask for the things that he wants, or even a little of what he wants.

"You love the city, don't you?" Tyler asks.

"Of course," Asher says.

"But you know the Detroit that you know and Detroit that I know are very different," Tyler says. He plays with the hem of his shirt and still refuses to look up. When the silence has dragged on for a moment too long, Asher clears his throat.

"I know that." Asher doesn't sound defensive, but leading and maybe confused.

Tylor tries to gather his thoughts because he's not sure he can put into words what he's trying to say to Asher. He's not sure that he can articulate them to himself. But he wants to share his city with Asher, and he wants Asher to share his city with him.

"This sounds stupid no matter what way I put it," Tyler says. "But I was thinking, if you wanted, I could show you my Detroit." He takes a deep breath and realizes that his heart is pounding. It's more than a trip to the Farmer's Market or stroll around his block that Tyler is offering. He's offering something very private.

Asher sucks in a breath, and Tyler glances up, risking a small smile. It takes a moment, but then Asher smiles back. "I would love that," he says.

Tyler's smile grows; he knows how goofy and young he must look, but he doesn't care. He swings around in his chair and then nudges Asher's with his own. Asher nudges back, and somehow before Tyler can prepare himself they are engaged in a playful but competitive game of footsie. Tyler happens to be in the more unstable chair and almost falls out when he's startled by a knock at the door. He's still laughing when he opens it.

"Hey, boss," Claudia says, sliding into the office.

"Not me," Tyler says.

"Why not?" She says with a sly smile, "You're practically—"

"What do you need?" Tyler interrupts. He hopes that Asher can't see the daggers he's shooting her with his eyes.

"Just getting ready to check out," Claudia says. She pulls her folder from her apron.

"Sit on down," Asher says and rolls the chair in her direction. She begins to sort out her checks, credit card slips and cash and to make a little pile of faced money. Tyler loves that she pays attention to these details, because Asher doesn't care but it still needs to be done before they take it to the bank. A little wave of fondness rushes through him. It's little things that hit home how much help they are here, and how important they are to this business. How important it is to him.

"Did y'all talk about that fundraiser yet?" Claudia says without looking up.

"What fundraiser?" Asher asks.

"Nothing!" Tyler hurries to say. Claudia glances at him, and he shakes his head minutely. Asher glances at him too. Tyler sighs. "I'll tell you about it later," he promises. He can ask Asher as his boss about work things, but right now, with the memory of their laughter in the room, it's not Asher the boss he's with. They're blurring so many lines; it's intoxicating but has the potential to burn so much down.

Chapter Nineteen

"Do you want to hang out tonight?" Asher says the next night. "I mean it doesn't have to be…" Asher takes a deep breath. "I mean hanging out you know, like, *just* hanging out. If you want."

"Just hanging out?" Tyler says teasingly.

"I don't want you to get the wrong impression. I don't want you to think that I *only* want to hang out with you because we're fooling around."

"Fooling around," Tyler says. "Is that what the kids call it these days?"

Asher scoffs. "I don't know, why don't you tell me, you're the kid." He regrets it as soon as he says it, because he doesn't want Tyler to think he's talking down to him. He stands, crosses to Tyler and kisses him, at first soft apology but followed with increasing heat. Tyler sinks into it; his hands creep around Asher's neck. He's craning up to reach more, then startles at a loud crash from the kitchen. Pink from being bitten, his lips are tempting and sweet, but he rolls away from Asher the tiniest bit and throws a glance at the door.

"Everything all right?"

Tyler exhales slowly, smiles and stands. He slides next to Asher and puts a hand on his arm. If Asher weren't watching so closely, so curious about every enigmatic move Tyler makes, he might miss the way Tyler seems to slide into a role, how he lowers his eyes in a particular way and moves his body just so. He slips his hand up Asher's arm, a tease perhaps, maybe a promise, but it reveals insecurity when he glances back at the door again. They've been together in this room before—incredibly intimately, teasingly, testingly—and yet tonight, Tyler's skittish. And he's trying to hide it.

"I'd love to hang out with you," Tyler says. His voice is breathy, and his eyes flit between Asher's mouth and his eyes. Asher is both wanting and wondering; he's also determined and understands wariness. Rather than push him—possibly push him away—Asher plays along. It doesn't help that Tyler's eyes have the power to connect, that his direct gaze, when focused, sends waves of heat through Asher, tightening his stomach and groin. It's only when they're in the loft and Asher's hands are on Tyler's body that Tyler's shields peel away and that gap between their experience becomes more clear. When Tyler submits himself to pleasure, Asher delights in taking him to delicious heights and getting off on how intensely he falls apart.

"We could watch a movie." Asher lowers his voice; his hand slides up to Tyler's neck until he touches his face, gently stroking the skin right behind Tyler's ear.

"I'd like that," Tyler says and bites his lip; he bends into the touch. Asher moves his hand away slowly and runs it down Tyler's arm, fingers barely pressing against him, until his hand grazes Tyler's pinky.

"Maybe not here, though?" Tyler asks.

"Of course." Asher goes out into the kitchen to make sure it's all clear. When he sees that it is, he texts Tyler. Together they climb the stairs. Tyler checks over his shoulder every now and then.

"Do you want a drink?" Asher asks. Tyler hovers at the top of the stairs as if he's never been here. Uncertainty is clear in his posture until he sees Asher examining him. He smiles and, like quicksilver, adjusts his body and expression into confidence and allure. Asher marvels at how good he is. He makes a note to ask him if he's ever considered acting. Hell, if he's ever done any. Of course, that wouldn't do now and not for a long time, not until they've reached some level where Tyler's confidence in vulnerability would come to them. Asher wants ask Tyler for his secrets and stories, but, for tonight, he'll settle for the honesty of touch.

"Why don't you make yourself comfortable on the couch? I'll get you a drink and we can pick something out."

"Okay," Tyler says softly. He fiddles with the remote. Asher pours them both ice water and then joins him on the couch. He is careful to leave some room between them. The air is thick and slow and heated. Anticipation tingles on his lips, which want to be on Tyler's, on the palms of his hands, which ache to caress Tyler's muscles and skin. He turns on the TV and the Xbox.

"Why don't you pick? We can watch some Netflix and chill." The corner of Asher's mouth curls when Tyler huffs a little laugh and clears his throat. Here Asher can make Tyler safe in wanting; in this room they've taken each other to places where outside worries haven't intruded. When Asher glances at Tyler, his lips shine, and his eyes are wide. His breathing has picked up, too. "You'll help me?" The question is so loaded it takes a lot of willpower for Asher not to close the distance between them right there. But it's clear Tyler wants to play.

"Of course," Asher says. He risks a small touch and relishes the gasp Tyler can't help.

They settle on *Midnight Cowboy*, and Asher stares at the screen as if he cares, when all of his attention is on Tyler, whose hands twitch toward him and away without landing, who crosses and uncrosses his legs and darts glances at Asher before breathing deep and slow.

"You seem a little tense," Asher says. "Why don't you come a little closer."

Tyler looks at him and takes a fortifying breath. "Okay." He scoots over. Asher puts his arm around Tyler's shoulders and pulls him in until Tyler rests against him more comfortably, with his head against Asher's shoulder. They continue to watch the movie in silence.

After a few minutes, Tyler's fingers, which are on Asher's chest, begin to move, making small circles against his shirt. As usual, Asher's clothes are layered, so he can't touch what he wants, but the awareness that it's there is more than enough. Asher puts his hand over Tyler's, and Tyler's whole body stiffens.

"I'm sorry—"

"Don't be." Asher flattens Tyler's hand against his chest. "I like it."

"Yeah?"

"Please," Asher says, eyes on Tyler's lips, "keep touching if you want." It's amazing, how Tyler's body seems to go liquid at that. For all of Tyler's put-on confidence, Asher has more confidence in his experience with men. Tyler wants direction. He asks so often what Asher wants; he craves direction as much as Asher aches to give.

Tyler plays with the button of his shirt, tentatively, then slips one finger under it. He makes a little noise of frustration when he encounters Asher's undershirt.

"Do you think—would you...?" Tyler asks, tugging on the button.

"Yeah, of course." Asher shifts to face Tyler and guides his fingers to one of the buttons. Slowly Tyler works the buttons loose, and Asher pulls the shirt off, getting stuck at the cuffs. Once he's extricated himself, he guides Tyler's hand to the hem of his undershirt, encouraging him to take it off. He does. Asher's skin prickles, and he shivers when Tyler's fingers and palms begin to explore his chest and stomach. Asher's under no delusions that his body is perfect, but he's never been self-conscious or worried about it.

"Could I kiss you?" Tyler asks. His eyes are everywhere: on Asher's face and chest and over to his bed.

"Of course. You can do anything you want." Asher runs one finger down Tyler's chest. Tyler nods and then shimmies out of his own shirt. Asher can't put his finger on where Tyler's true sensuality is, in his muscles or skin or lovely eyes, or how much of it is performance. Tonight is different from the other times, though. A softer Tyler, maybe a more vulnerable one, shines through. Asher takes Tyler's lips with his own and catches Tyler's gasp. Tyler's kisses are hesitant, but Asher's aren't. He pushes in, crowds Tyler's space until he tips back, hands gripping Asher's shoulders as he goes. It's not comfortable, and they don't quite fit on his narrow couch, but Asher still takes his time, feasting with nibbles and small licks and then deep, delicious kisses, until Tyler is panting, and they're both shaking.

"Here, honey," Asher finally says. He stands and pulls Tyler with him. "Come to bed with me?" He phrases it as a question, as if he's giving this Tyler, this new and uncertain one, a choice. Tyler nods his head, already wound around him again, kissing Asher's neck and exploring the skin and muscles of his back. The desperation in his touch moves Asher. He pushes Tyler gently toward the bed and lays him out on it. He kisses Tyler's flat stomach and runs his fingers along the waistband of his pants. His intentions are clear. Tyler's body can't seem to still; his hips tilt slightly, then roll back. Tyler puts his hand on Asher's head lightly, and when Asher looks up, says, "*Please.*"

Asher undoes his pants slowly, kisses each inch of skin revealed as he unzips them. He works them, and Tyler's underwear, down, kissing and kissing and licking as he goes, until Tyler's is exposed, *pleasepleaseplease* a constant, quiet chant. Asher strokes one finger up and around; affection and desire throb to the beat of his heart and sing in his blood.

"Did you bring a condom, baby?" he asks, inhaling the slightly sweaty but heady scent of Tyler's body.

"N-no—"

"That's okay. I have some in the drawer." Asher can tell that Tyler is hesitant to move away. Tyler hands him a condom with wide eyes and shaking fingers.

"Do you want this?" Asher asks. "Want to be in my mouth?"

"Do you—is that something *you* want?"

Asher wonders at that, recalls times in the past when Tyler's seemed awed by Asher going down on him.

"Of course," Asher says. He opens the condom and slides it onto him. "I can't wait to have you in my mouth."

"Okay. Can I pull your hair?" he asks, then gasps when Asher lowers his head. With his mouth against Tyler's skin, Asher murmurs.

"Yes. You can pull; you don't have to be gentle with me."

Tyler is very still at first. He grips Asher's hair more and more tightly as Asher works him torturously toward orgasm. Whenever he senses that Tyler is close, he pulls away and tries to gentle him with soft words and encouragement. Tyler devolves into a mess, all ragged breaths and moans, and, as he gets more desperate, he rolls up and into Asher's mouth, just a little. Asher is high on the pleasure of dragging out how good he's making Tyler feel.

When he does finally come, it's loud. He holds Asher's head in place and pushes and throbs and throbs. Asher gags a bit, but breathes through it.

"Oh my god, I'm so sor—" Tyler says.

"Don't worry, I like it," Asher admits. "I love that." Tyler is all loose and sleepy with awed eyes. His body is so new compared to Asher's. Tyler lifts a hand and traces Asher's collarbone. He lowers his eyelashes and bites his lip.

"What do you want?" he asks. His lilting voice, that sweet lisp and his soft body language make Asher a little crazy.

"What do *you* want to do most?" Asher counters. "I want this to be so good for you." He's not persuading anymore. He wanted to coax a truer Tyler out, he certainly wasn't planning to become so desperate himself. Tyler is magic, though all liquid in his bed and so naked undone, and Asher is so turned on it's hard to think.

"The same?" Tyler phrases it as a question. Asher settles next to him on the bed and kisses Tyler.

"If that's what you want."

In the morning, Asher's alarm is the worst thing ever. It's black outside, and waking is torture.

"Stay. I'll go," Asher whispers, easing Tyler back down against the pillow. He kisses Tyler's cheek. "I'll set your alarm for later."

"But you need help—"

"Ty, I've run a restaurant for years. Believe it or not, I can handle a morning open."

Tyler blinks at him and smiles. "'Kay. Come get me if you need me, though."

"Sure."

While Asher showers, he tries not to imagine that he's washing lingering remnants of Tyler's touch down the drain. Part of him trusts that they'll have this again, while another worries because he has no idea what he's doing, or what they're doing. He's fascinated by Tyler's changeability. He enjoys him so much, but he wants to unearth the truest side of him. Tyler has trained himself to be what people want from him; maybe that's his youth or inexperience. Tyler carries a lot of anxieties that Asher is pretty sure he doesn't even realize. Tyler has a need to put everything in order; the only time he seems truly at rest is after Asher has taken him apart in bed. Tyler has so many walls. Asher knows that an actual future where they'd be together and not cruising along with whatever it is they're doing now won't work with someone who can't let their walls down.

Asher's not sure he's ready to let all of *his* walls down. He's only just let himself realize how many he has. Behind them are many big emotional weights he'll have to process. They're heavy and heartbreaking, and Asher worries that Tyler is too young to help him handle those as well.

Asher closes his eyes and rinses the shampoo from his hair and pushes those thoughts out of his head. When he pads quietly back into the room, Tyler is asleep again despite the glow from the small lamp on the night table. He's curled on his side with his fists tucked under his chin. Deep affection sweeps through Asher, through his suddenly tight breathing and too hard beating heart. He closes his eyes and turns away because it's so much. It's so close to what he once felt for John, to what felt like to fall in love.

But Asher's tasted love, and he's tasted loss and now, he tastes fear, thick in his throat.

Chapter Twenty

WHEN TYLER FINALLY COMES DOWN to work, in the nick of time before someone comes in, his limbs are still coltish.

"You could have slept longer," Asher says.

"Mmm-mmm," Tyler mumbles. His eyes are closed as he inhales the scent of his coffee. "People have enough gossip about us for a while."

"What?" Asher drops his pen. Tyler's eyes pop open.

"Fuck, I didn't mean to tell you that."

"Um, what?" Asher asks again. He closes his eyes and pinches the bridge of his nose.

"Don't be mad." Tyler's eyes are open now. He slides down the counter and nudges Asher's knee with his. "It's restaurant gossip. You know how it is."

"This is not a good thing, Tyler!"

Tyler squares his shoulders. "So, what, are you ashamed of this?"

"Oh my god, *no*," Asher says. He runs his fingers through his hair. Instinctively Tyler reaches to smooth it for him. "I... I don't want to undermine my authority or reputation with them."

"Asher, they love you. They love working here. They know you're a human being."

"You don't understand, Ty. Last time I lost my staff's respect and almost lost—"

"Asher, it's not the same. I promise. Come on, you know these people."

Asher turns away.

"Asher, is this about something else?" Tyler asks. Now is not the time to reveal his insecurities, much less doubts, about what's happening. It's too early—with them and also in the morning.

"No. I don't know. Nothing to do with you," Asher says. "This is… an adjustment. All of it."

Tyler is quiet while he tries to make sense of the faint anxiety buzzing through him; last night, caught up in Asher's touch and confidence, Tyler had left it behind. He puts his coffee down. "Can I kiss you?" he asks.

Asher smiles, takes his hand and tugs him down. "Of course."

Tyler swallows his qualms and lets himself relax into Asher's body. He's steady, so steady, and warm. He exudes a kindness and care Tyler knows has been unlocked for him only. Asher's true self is so different from how he presents himself. Tyler revels in knowing this.

They kiss, careful of each other, but sweet and slow, for long minutes. Asher pulls away every few kisses; he looks into Tyler's eyes as if trying to read something there. He kisses behind Tyler's ear; it's affection without intent to escalate. The office is small, but what they have is big, bigger than he can figure out. This room though, more than any other place, is a space just for them. A little haven. It's ridiculous. It's ugly and cramped, and, when Tyler's too busy to nag and sort the various messes of papers, it's awful.

But when Asher's hands dig into his waist and he breathes in little gasps against Tyler's mouth, that's the only thing that matters.

* * *

THEY DON'T ADDRESS THE STAFF knowing again, although they both take pains to be more discreet. They don't talk about what they're doing or what it means, even though Tyler spends more nights at Asher's than his own apartment. Even when he's not working, he's often at Asher's.

It's Wednesday a few weeks later when Asher clomps up the stairs after a long shift. Tyler can tell by his tread he's exhausted. "You don't have any books," is the first thing he says to Asher when he joins him.

"Excellent observational skills."

Tyler is sprawled on the couch, leaving no room for Asher. Asher hovers; Tyler sits up, then spreads his legs a bit and tugs him down until he's between them, spooned back to stomach. Tyler wraps his arms around Asher and encourages him to lean back. When Asher does, the acquiescence of some small bit of control, leaning on Tyler when he usually is the one doing the holding, is a small victory.

Tyler clears his throat. "Why don't you have books?"

"When would I read?"

"I don't know. Before going to bed? On your brand new days off when you can leave the building but never seem to?"

Asher chuckles. He tips back against Tyler's shoulder and shifts until he's able to see the TV while reclining. "That's what HGTV is for."

"Really?" Tyler resists the urge to kiss the side of Asher's head.

"Yeah?" Asher says. "Is that not usual? Plenty of people fall asleep watching TV."

"I guess. I don't know. I've never had a TV in my room before."

Asher is quiet for a long moment. "I'm sorry if—"

"Oh my god, don't apologize." Tyler squeezes him. "It's okay."

Asher sits. "Is it though?"

"Listen," Tyler says, then sighs. "I know you don't mean anything by it. Or maybe you don't get it. But you grew up rich. And you assume that me not having particular material things have to do with money, right?"

"I wouldn't say it that way."

Tyler sighs and swallows his irritation.

"That was the wrong thing to say, wasn't it?" Asher seems serious and attentive.

"Well, it kind of was beside the point." Tyler struggles to find the words for what he's feeling. Asher takes his hand, and Tyler wonders if he realizes he's done it.

"I'm sorry," he finally says. "Sometimes…"

"Sometimes?" Asher says, and wiggles his hand a little.

"I'm not an angry person," Tyler starts. "It never seemed productive."

"Okay?"

"But sometimes it's hard. There's this feeling inside that I get when I see how lopsided the world is. And how differently people see it."

"I see it differently because of my upbringing?"

"Yes and no," Tyler says. "There is a whole world of people who don't have to explain themselves. Where a normal exists that they never have to question. Where the absence of normal or of things they take for granted has a particular meaning. All these people who never think about the color of their skin. They walk around as if it doesn't matter because it doesn't have to."

"There was a lot in there," Asher says. "I want to be sure I'm following."

"Our worlds are different. And money is a part of it. You grew up with enough that you take things for granted. But for a lot of people this 'normal' equals the automatic assumption that *not* having means deficit. Maybe I don't want to have a TV, Asher. Maybe a cigar is just a cigar."

"I'm sorry," Asher says. His fingers are tight around Tyler's, and he sounds a little helpless and lost.

"I'm not mad at you. It's how the world is. I can't tell you how many people I meet who assume that growing up in Detroit and being black means I'm poor, or uneducated, or all the other things people think. I guess it's not fair to judge your normal by mine if I don't want you to judge my normal by yours."

"No, but you're not judging, are you?" Asher prompts. "You're explaining."

"Yeah. I just… I think sometimes people take their privileges for granted and as the truth."

Tyler lets his own words sink in. He's never tried to say these things. Malik was always the one fighting with his words. But that doesn't mean Tyler wasn't paying attention, or that he didn't grow up experiencing these things. His path was different from Malik's, but it was hard too.

"There's more than one truth, Asher," he says finally.

"I know that," Asher says. It seems only a little defensive.

"You know it, but do you *know* it?" Tyler laughs at himself. "Never mind, I'm not making sense."

"No, you are. I think." Asher ducks his head to meet Tyler's eyes. "Tyler, I don't want you to think I am saying this because I'm not hearing you. I am. I grew up in a largely Jewish community, but that doesn't mean I haven't experienced anti-Semitism. I am not equating this to what you are saying. I'd never thought about it the way you've put it. But I do know that there are multiple truths. I just need to work harder at seeing them all." His smile is a little unsure and a lot kind, and Tyler can't help the way he surges toward him, into a kiss. "Thank you. For talking to me about this. And for being patient."

"What are you doing Friday?" Tyler asks a week later.

"Working?"

"Asher, remember we talked about this. Assistant managers? Claudia?"

"Wait, did I schedule her?"

"Yes," Tyler says with forced patience. Asher squirms.

"Okay, well, then, I'm not doing anything. Because I never do." Asher's laugh is self-deprecating.

"Well, I can help with that. I thought maybe you'd want to go on a little field trip with me."

"Is this one of your 'part of your world' things?" Asher asks, and Tyler smiles.

"Yes. Without the mermaid Disney parts."

"Damn, I really wanted that."

"Oh my god, are you making jokes? Hold on, I have to call the Freep," Tyler jokes, referring to one of Detroit's remaining print newspapers, the *Free Press*.

"No newspapers." Asher is laughing now. "Keep it under wraps for a bit. I have a reputation to uphold."

"Well, your super-boring rep aside," Tyler says, enjoying the way Asher's cheeks are flushed with laughter, "I haven't had much time of my own, but maybe you'll come with me to Affirmations? They have tons of stuff for volunteers to do." He doesn't add that he thinks it'll do Asher good to have activities that don't involve the restaurant.

"Yeah." Asher's face shows genuine interest. "As long as you think it'd be okay?"

"Why wouldn't it be?" Tyler asks. "Haven't you ever been there? You lived in Royal Oak, right?"

"I don't know why I haven't gone. I didn't know about it as a teenager, and we only lived in Royal Oak after we opened the restaurant. I guess I've always been too busy."

"Well, it's amazing. Sometimes I think they saved my life. They have an incredible workforce development program to help kids get ready for jobs. Well, they have lots of stuff. Trust me, you will be welcome. You're coming with me Friday."

Asher rolls over, bumping over the uneven tile kisses his cheek.

"Can't wait."

Chapter Twenty-One

"So you brought me to a thing," Asher says. "Does that mean I get to take you to a thing?"

"Of course," Tyler says. He's looking out the window of Asher's car as they drive down I-75 on their way back to Idlewild. It's a gray February day, the kind of day when it hasn't snowed, when everything is dingy, and the ice that lines the gutters is mottled black-gray and embedded with litter. It's the kind of day when winter seems never-ending.

But it's warm in his car, and Asher has had a whole day with Tyler. He spent the day seeing him surrounded by people who know him in a completely different context. Tyler's known some of them since he'd first started going to Affirmations. They have hundreds of stories from when he was a teenager. Here he's shared secrets that predate Asher. Idlewild-Tyler doesn't exist in the place he just shared with Asher.

Almost everything about Tyler was different today: the way he held his body, the speed of his walk, his voice, the way that he talked and the tone of laughter lacing his sentences. And although every bit of it was novel, Asher doesn't sense that this is the truest Tyler either.

"Well, are you going to ask me whatever you want to ask me?" Tyler asks. He turns toward Asher in the seat and curls one leg on the seat underneath the other.

"Oh yeah," Asher says. "I was going to ask if you wanted to go to that Red Wings game with me."

"Which Red Wings game?"

"Don't you remember a while ago when you found that Hanukkah card from my brother?"

"Oh my god, I had completely forgotten about that!" Tyler says. "He gave you the tickets, didn't he?"

"Yep."

"And you're asking me to go? To a sports thing?" Tyler asks, disbelief clear in his voice. "Why would you ask me...?"

Because you're my best friend, Asher thinks. *Because you light everything up.* It almost comes out of his mouth but he scrambles at the last minute to hold it in. "Because you said you've never been."

"It's not that I don't want to go with you... but, I mean..." Tyler starts. "It's *hockey.*" His tone makes it clear that he doubts anybody would want to go to a hockey game.

"Okay, so first of all, it's more fun in person. I'm not a huge hockey fan. I mean, you've never seen me watch a game, have you?"

"No."

"Right. Sports aren't necessarily my thing—well, not all sports—"

"Wait, so there are sports that are your thing?" Tyler asks.

"Well, I don't know. I mean, I really love baseball. So, yeah, I guess."

"Baseball? *Really?*"

"Yeah," Asher says, grinning. "There are people who actually like baseball." He rolls to a stop at a red light. Tyler fiddles with the window switch. The windows are locked, so it doesn't go anywhere, but he keeps clicking and clicking and clicking it.

"That's cool, man," Tyler says. "Not the baseball. The stopping at the light. I mean the baseball is fine, but—"

"Tyler," Asher interrupts his rambling. "What?"

"Oh just... I hate when people act as if they don't have to follow the law just because they're in the city. Like, red lights exist for a reason! This is not a lawless place."

Asher laughs lightly. In many parts of the city, people don't stop at lights if they don't have to. No one is around; he doubts he would get a ticket if he did run it. But he agrees: laws exist for a reason, and not following them, or thinking you don't have to, perpetuates the way people think about Detroit.

"I know we've talked about the fact that I grew up in the suburbs," Asher says, "But I have been in the city for a while. I wouldn't be here if I didn't have a vested interest."

"Been in?" Tyler says. There's a slight edge to his words, but Asher can't tell what Tyler is insinuating. Or if he's even insinuating something. Maybe Asher's reading into the conversation. Ever since their talk the other night, Asher's found himself second guessing a lot of what he says and thinks. It's not a bad thing; Tyler's opening his eyes. But everything seems uncertain, as if he's on unsteady ground.

"You know what I mean," Asher says. They're both still smiling but somehow tension seems to have landed in the car. The air in the car is not precisely strained, just a little off.

Clearly Tyler feels that too, since he won't meet Asher's eyes. His fingers go still on the window button. He takes a deep breath and then turns back to Asher and when he does he wears a smile on his face. It widens, and his eyes get brighter. January stumbled ugly and gray into February and they've had days and days without real sunshine. Asher thinks that perhaps Tyler's eyes are the most vibrant color he seen all winter.

"So these are the kinds of things that you did?" Tyler asks. "When you used to come in the city as a kid?"

"I guess maybe when I was older. When we were little, my parents wouldn't bring us at all. One time, *Phantom of the Opera* came to the Fox, and I begged and begged to go, so my mom had my aunt bring me."

"Wow, your parents really hated the city."

"I told you." He laughs suddenly. "Sometimes I think back to that shit and wonder how on earth they were surprised when I came out."

"Were they? I don't think anyone was surprised when I did. Maybe at how long it took me."

"How old were you?" Asher asks as he makes the turn into the parking garage. It's so dark that it takes his eyes in a moment to adjust, and so he slows the car. Despite that fleeting tension, he's reluctant to park and get out, because he doesn't want this day to be over. Tyler's eyes are steady on his.

"To Mom, youngish I think. Everyone else? I think the end of high school. Somewhere around there. So maybe seventeen or eighteen. You?"

"Fifteen. Didn't feel young but now it does. Maybe because I held on to it for a while. I was so scared."

"Why?" Tyler asks. He puts a hand on Asher's and threads their fingers together.

"I don't know. Well, we were pretty religious. I didn't think there could be a gray area for them; I wasn't sure if there was for me, because back then, faith was very important to me, too. I didn't know if they could accept me. I didn't know if God could."

"And now?"

"They struggled to figure out how to put their faith together with who I was. Reconciling their faith so they could provide a community that would still welcome me took a long time. But they did it." Asher looks up at the ceiling of the car with his hands tight against the wheel and the muscles of his arms taut. "It was hard, and weird. I was a teenager, you know, not really all that rational." Tyler's chuckle is a barely there laugh that carries heavy emotion despite its quiet. "But I grew up. John helped me, too, to see the unconditional love under it all. They chose to change everything about the way they understood the world in order to support me. But watching that struggle while in the middle of my own 'crisis' was really fucking isolating."

"Did you reconcile it all for yourself?" Tyler shifts to get more comfortable and fiddles with an air vent.

"I thought I did. I don't know. Teenage Asher was not that self-aware." He sends Tyler a wry smile. "I mean, I think that's when I started to feel a rift. I don't believe in God anymore, so it doesn't really matter, does it?" A sudden upwelling of emotion crowds his throat. He breathes deep and tries to swallow it down. He's never told anyone that.

"Do you want to talk about this anymore?" Tyler asks. His voice is incredibly gentle.

Asher shakes his head. It's a cliché, that he gave up on God when John died. Secretly, for a very long time, Asher's known it's because he thought John's death meant that God gave up on him. He swallows the need to cry and looks away. When he looks back, Tyler stares at him intently.

"What? Do I have something on my face?"

"No," Tyler says softly. "I love your face."

Tyler takes a deep breath, and Asher does as well. It's not an admission of love, but it's a lot. The air is flavored with anticipation and expectation and uncertainty. It might be the start of the openness between them he craves, even though on its heels comes a terrible anxiety.

"Thanks," Asher says. "You—"

"Thank you for trusting me with that. I want to know more about what your life was like too," Tyler blurts. "If you want to share it with me."

"Yeah." Asher does want to. But right now, Asher has reached his limit. He changes the subject. "So, is that a yes on the game?"

Tyler giggles high and sweet. "Yeah, yeah, I'll go to the game with you. I can't promise not to be bored though."

"You're going to get totally into it," Asher predicts. "It's very hard to get bored at a Red Wings game. The energy will convert you. Especially if it's a good game."

LATER THAT NIGHT, THEY FIND themselves in Asher's bed, not sleeping. Tyler runs his fingers through the crook of Asher's arm delicately over and over, until Asher has to stop him by putting his hand on top flat against Tyler's.

"Tickles," he explains.

"You're ticklish?" Tyler props himself on his elbow to gaze down at Asher. The corner of his mouth curls on the right side.

"No," Asher says, hoping his face doesn't give him away. When Tyler reaches for him with mischief in his eyes, he takes Tyler's hand and rolls so that he's flat on his back with his hand next to his head.

"Don't even think about it," Asher says. Laughter lights his face and brightens his voice. "Or I'll start tickling you."

"Go ahead and try. I'm not ticklish."

"You're kidding."

"No really," Tyler insists. "I'm not ticklish at all."

Asher runs his fingers up Tyler's side, trying to tickle him. Tyler regards him with quiet eyes.

"Wow. I didn't really think there were people who aren't ticklish."

"Have you been tickling a lot of people recently?" Tyler teases.

"Every day," Asher deadpans. "That's how I'm keeping the business alive. I just walk through the dining room tickling patrons. They never have any idea what hit them, but they tip well."

Tyler giggles and his eyes crinkle. Slowly he pulls his hand from under Asher's and then cups his cheek. Asher is still running his fingers over Tyler's skin, but lightly now. Tyler shivers into the touch. He gives Asher one little kiss and pulls back and searches his eyes.

"Will you tell me more?" Tyler asks.

"More what?" Asher blinks.

"About what it was like for you, growing up."

"Well," Asher's not sure what Tyler is looking for, and so he's not really sure he has what Tyler wants him to give. Their conversation earlier and the emotions that came with it still haunt him. Tyler nudges him; Asher is still half draped over him. Tyler settles on his side, so Asher does too, until they're face to face on the pillows.

"You said your aunt brought you to the Fox when you were a kid. How much did you come into the city after that?"

"I don't know." Asher is grateful Tyler's taking the conversation in a lighter direction. "Not too often, until Eli got a driver's license. My parents wouldn't let him bring me to baseball games, but sometimes he would anyway."

"Really?" Tyler smiles. "Did you guys get in trouble for it?"

"Only got caught once," Asher says. He sighs. When it happened, it seemed as if it were the worst thing in the world, but as a memory it makes him laugh. With almost fifteen years between then and now, nostalgia is easier, because what made an impression was that Eli had taken him to a Tigers game. Asher remembers basking in the attention, because although they weren't close due to their ages, Asher hero-worshiped him. It was playoff season, and Asher had wanted to go to a game so badly it was as though every holiday had rolled into one. "It was worth it though," he says to Tyler. "It went to eleven innings—that's how we got caught."

"Eleven is more than usual?" Tyler asks.

"Oh my god, you really do hate sports, don't you?"

"Hate is a strong word." Tyler yawns. Asher kisses the tips of his nose and Tyler blinks sleepily.

"Nine," he whispers. "There's usually only nine innings."

"Were you very late?" Tyler asks.

"Yeah."

"Why didn't you leave?"

"You never leave a Tigers game when they might win! No, I don't know. We kept meaning to but then something would happen. Eli lost his car for a month that night."

"Was he pissed?"

"Oh yeah. But not at me. Still, he told me later that it had been worth it."

"Mmm." Tyler's eyes slip closed. "Did they win?"

"No." Asher settles more comfortably against his pillow. He finds Tyler's hand in the sheets between them and folds their hands together. "Fuckin' Yankees."

Tyler snorts out a laugh and then closes his eyes. Before Asher knows it, he slips into sleep, and then Asher does as well.

Chapter Twenty-Two

"Do you do this often?" Asher parks carefully. The asphalt under the car is badly cracked and pitted.

"No, actually." Tyler unbuckles his belt and looks around. It's hard to tell which warehouse door is the right one because they're not marked. He checks the address on the phone again. "Come on."

"If you've never been here, why use it now?" Asher asks. The wind whips his voice away. *Fucking March.*

"If you're gonna work in Detroit and talk about change, local sourcing is a good idea. I met Aurora at the Eastern Market, that day I went with Joy and you wouldn't come. Aurora is a local source for produce."

"You make it sound like I'm a bum. I had to work!"

Tyler tosses him a sunny smile and doesn't respond.

Asher follows him across the lot to an unmarked door and waits while Tyler rings the bell. He's not sure he gets it, because he is aware of Detroit's urban farms—lots of people are. It's one of the things about this city that inspires him. He doesn't say anything because a lovely young woman with midnight-black skin answers the door and lets them in with warm smiles.

"Hi, Tyler! Asher, I take it?" She shakes their hands. "I'm Aurora. I'm so glad you could come over."

"Thank you for having us," Tyler says. The room they walk into has a cement floor and high ceilings. The lights are a little grimy, and it's freezing cold. It's clearly what it seems to be—a truck bay in an old warehouse converted into a home base for a business.

"Do you want something to drink?" Aurora asks.

"Water would be great," Tyler says, and looks over at Asher, who nods.

He's driven past this place on his way to the Eastern Market, but he's always assumed these were empty warehouses and loading docks.

"Are all of these other containers in use?" he asks when she comes back with bottles of water.

"Most of them. People come and go. The people next to us do trapeze lessons."

"That's so cool. Like for acrobats?" Tyler asks.

"Maybe? Mostly I just know because sometimes they have groups of little kids, and the noise carries."

Asher picks at the label of his water. "Have you guys been in this space long?" he asks.

"No, this is an experiment. We had grant money, and we thought it might help to have a professional space."

"So this is new for you?" Asher asks.

"Only the last few months. The farm got to be big enough and do well enough that we decided to try to work on the neighborhood. We wanted a community center but were having trouble with the funds. Carter worked with some of our volunteers to get us a grant from a community agriculture coalition, and we thought a professional space might help."

"That's very cool," Tyler says. "Carter is your partner?" He's bouncing in his seat.

"Yes. And thank you." She gives him a kind smile. "We've been accused of becoming one of those urban farming collectives that sells out." Her lips turn down in a frown. "I promise, I'm not—we're not—in it for the money. Not for ourselves. Our hours are spotty because some of us work other jobs, and this is all volunteer-run. Carter is having trouble finding a job, so you might see the most of him."

"All right," Asher says.

"I mean, if you decide to go with us," she hurries to add. "I know that our professional website isn't up yet. We have one person who is tech-ish, but he's hard to pin down. But we can talk here, or you can come to the neighborhood and see what we're doing and get a feel for it?"

Asher's been skeptical since Tyler proposed this source. It's not that he doesn't want to source locally; he thinks that's a great idea. But this is a small enough collective that he's pretty sure they'd have to order from other sources as well. That sounds like an administrative nightmare. He takes a moment to think it over. Apparently it's a second too long. Aurora clears her throat.

"Why don't I start with some literature about us, before you commit to a field trip?" she says. She goes to her back room, and Tyler turns to him.

"What is your problem?"

"What—? I don't have a problem!"

"You're doing that taciturn quiet thing," Tyler points out.

"What? I don't even know what that means."

"Taciturn? Dour? Stern? Grumpily not speaking?"

"That's not what I'm doing," Asher says patiently, although the words do give him pause. "I'm thinking. This isn't an idea I ever would have thought of."

"Well, you're coming off as rude," Tyler says and rolls his eyes. "I know you don't mean it, but please, stop. You're making her nervous."

"I am?"

"Among other things," Tyler says under his breath. Asher lets it go.

"So here," Aurora bustles back in. A strong gust of wind rattles the rolling door of the dock, and wind rushes under the crack, and a draft comes in from above them. She wraps her thin cardigan around herself.

"Cold, girl?" Tyler says carefully.

"Always," she says. She smiles at him. "It's always cold in here. I can't wait for summer. I always forget to dress warmly. I'm not usually the one in here."

"Oh?" Asher looks up from the papers he's scanning. He hands them to Tyler, with the price list on top and the company philosophy—he got it from the website, but he's not sure if Tyler read it— "How come?"

She shivers violently when the wind smacks hard against the building again. "Ugh, March," she says, and he smiles sympathetically, then reaches for his coat. He stands and wraps it around her shoulders. The look he gets from her is part wary and part thankful.

"Do you mind?" he asks.

"Very thoughtful," she says. "Thank you."

Tyler clears his throat to get Asher's attention. He's through looking at the papers.

"Yeah, if you have time, we'd love to go out to the co-op sometime." Asher says. He makes an effort to smile and to make it genuine.

"Yay!" she says, adorably girlish, which cracks Asher up.

"We can set up a time to meet you there then?" Asher asks.

"Of course. I'd call Carter, though. He would be your best bet for more flexible times. There won't be much exciting stuff for you to see right now; we've only started building greenhouses. But it's great in the spring. You can visit us any time." She stands and hands him his jacket, which he takes reluctantly. Aurora fishes around on the table before coming up with a business card. It has her information on it, as well as Carter's.

"Thank you, Aurora," Tyler says. He pulls her into a hug when she comes around the desk. Asher envies Tyler's ease with people as much as he admires it.

"We'll be in touch," Tyler promises and puts a gentle hand on the small of Asher's back as they turn toward the door. It takes him until they get to the door and have to separate to realize he's done it.

* * *

THE DAY OF THE HOCKEY game, Tyler has to talk himself into acting excited. Asher obviously is, and Tyler doesn't want to put a damper on his evening. Walking through the tunnel from the parking ramp to the Joe Louis Arena gives Tyler a tiny bit of comfort; he has no idea why. It's dingy and old, but he likes the way sound echoes through it. When they come out into a beautifully big-skied day, he spots the people mover behind them.

"It's been so long since I've been here, I didn't think people still use it," Asher says, gesturing behind him. Tyler shrugs but doesn't answer. He takes it all in. The Joe is a little old and a little shabby, and not pretentious at all. He loves it. Asher's told him they're going to move the Red Wings to a new arena. Tyler's knows very well how much commerce the new baseball and football stadiums have brought to Detroit, but considering the horrific state of the city's schools, the amount of money invested in building a new arena is appalling. In the car, Asher talked about the nostalgia many people feel toward the Joe but also how ridiculous it is that so many people don't seem connect the idea of how much money goes into these projects that could go elsewhere.

"Because unless there's another sickout," Tyler says, referring to the recent teacher strike in Detroit in protest of the conditions of the schools, "people don't see, or don't want to see these things." He feels a little bad for saying it.

They're quiet until they get to the arena. A huge crowd of people waits to get in, smushed by the doors. People surge up a large set of stairs and are spit out of the tunnel behind them. There's a line of port-a-potties to the left, which makes no sense, because there are bathrooms inside. A group of men walk by, shirtless, with red and white paint on their faces and chests. Even Asher stares.

"Do you ever think about how homo-erotic that shit is? Do they paint each other, then bro-high five?" Tyler whispers into Asher's ear. He snorts, bites back a grin and squints into the sunshine.

"You're so weird." Asher looks over, and Tyler knows how much he wants to take Tyler's hand.

Of course he doesn't. It might not be safe in this public space for a display of any sort. But Tyler looks back calmly, makes a fist, and holds Asher's gaze with a small, coy smile.

They flash their tickets and take a moment to empty pockets for the metal detector. Asher sets it off repeatedly until they realize it's his belt.

"That's a big fucking buckle," Tyler observes when Asher puts it back on. "How did I not notice that? It's practically cowboy."

"Shut up, you," Asher says. "It's the only one I have."

"No, it's kind of sexy. Do you ride horses too?"

"I need to shop for new clothes soon," Asher says around a smile and a sigh. "It's been years." He checks their tickets and leads Tyler through the push and pull of bodies going in conflicting directions. No one seems to respect the unspoken rules of directional walking in a crowd.

"You know, online shopping is a thing," Tyler says. He can't tell if Asher hears him. Once they climb to their seats, which are high up but center ice, which Asher tells him is awesome, Tyler sits carefully.

"It's colder in here than I thought it would be," he says and tries not to shiver.

Asher laughs. "It's probably the presence of all the ice," he teases.

"No shit," Tyler says back. Asher's expression is fond, as if he can't believe that he's here with Tyler. Tyler feels so lucky then and so seen. He doesn't let himself stop to wonder why he likes it because historically, being so seen has left him terrified. Asher takes off his coat and gives it to Tyler.

"But you'll be cold," Tyler protests, even as he puts it on.

"You know I run hot."

"If you're sure."

Asher's coat is big on him; the sleeves hang past his hands. It's lovely. The inside is lined with soft fleece.

Soon the lights dim and there is a sudden, roar from the crowd. Tyler jumps. The players for the other team are announced and come out; the crowd boos and hisses. Spotlights come on and the lights begin to throb and spin. A giant fake octopus is lowered from the ceiling to the beat of an Eminem song. The building is sparkling with the electric energy of the crowd.

They're standing, because everyone else is. "Is it always like this?" he whispers into Asher's ear. Asher is clapping and cheering along with everyone else. Tyler thinks this might be the weirdest moment of his life, because it's as if a sudden, alien Asher has landed on this earth. *Who is he?*

"Yeah," he shouts back. He doesn't take his eyes off the ice. The music transitions to another song, a medley of Detroit artists, and the noise in the arena somehow manages to get louder as their players begin to take the ice.

Eventually things calm down and everyone sits as the game begins. "You okay?" Asher asks.

"Oh, yeah," Tyler says. "I've never seen anything like this before. I feel like an anthropologist in a strange environment."

Surprise and delight cross Asher's features. Then they melt into that fondness that spreads warmth through Tyler's body. He tries to calm down, because it's almost too much, but he can't seem to help it. "I'll make you a bet," Asher says. "By the second goal, you'll be cheering along with the rest of us."

Tyler's is deeply skeptical. He must make a face, because Asher laughs. "I doubt it."

Asher whispers into his ear, and it sends delighted shivers through his body. "Want to wager?"

"What did you have in mind?" Tyler tries to keep his tone even.

"If I win, you have to tell me something you've always wanted but have never received. And I promise to do it."

Tyler clears his throat; his voice wobbles. "So if I win, you can do anything you want to me." He looks directly into Asher's eyes. "Anything." This time Asher looks away and bites his lip. His color is high. The arena is filled with catcalls and the sound of the puck being slapped by the players' stick-things. To their left, a large group is getting a cheer started.

Finally, Asher turns back to him and holds his hand out. Tyler takes it and they shake. "It's a deal."

Tyler looks forward blindly. He knows exactly what he'd do, given free choice, what he's never done but always wanted to try. The thought of asking for it, or actually doing it, is both exciting—incredibly exciting—but also terrifying.

Suddenly a roar from the crowd with everyone surging to their feet, breaks him out of his thoughts. They must have scored. He gets to his feet, because everyone else has. But it seems that everyone is cheering because a fight has broken out. Someone's helmet skids across the ice, and players are throwing punches, which must surely be ineffective with the amount of padding they're all wearing. The refs skate in and start pulling people out, as do other teammates.

"Yeah!" Asher yells.

"Why are we cheering for this?" Tyler asks. The commentator announces penalties and half the crowd begins to boo. Tyler can only assume it's because one penalty is called on their guys.

"I don't know." Asher shrugs. "It's hockey."

It's a terrible explanation, because the whole thing seems barbaric.

"You don't know? I thought you liked hockey?"

Asher laughs. "I do, but I was talking to you."

As the game continues, though, Tyler begins to understand. He had no idea hockey was such a physical game, with guys crashing into each other and body checking each other into what Asher calls the boards.

Despite himself, Tyler begins to find himself following the game. The excitement of the crowd is infectious, and by the time the Wings score a second goal, Tyler is out of his seat clapping and stomping.

* * *

"Oh my god, I'm so tired," Tyler complains when they get in the car. A long line of cars blocks them from backing out. "How on earth are we going to get out of here?"

"Eventually someone lets you out. Maybe one in ten people here aren't assholes."

Tyler laughs and closes his eyes. "It's not even that late," he murmurs.

"Maybe you expended too much energy cheering," Asher says. Teasing and lighthearted. Tyler nods. "Hey, can you check if I'm clear?" Tyler turns and judges how much room they have on his side.

"It'll be close but I think you can clear it." He talks Asher through. They escape scraping the bumper of the car on Tyler's side by centimeters.

"Ugh! I hate this," Asher complains.

"Traffic?" Tyler's not even pretending to try to keep his eyes open.

"No, how they shuffle us into exits that make no sense. I always get lost when they turn us this way," Asher complains. Tyler opens his eyes and sees what Asher means. He's been pushed into one line for an exit.

"How do you get lost? You live in the city."

"I haven't come to a game in years. I always got lost going home to my parent's house or back to wherever John and I were living." Asher explains. They're spit out in the only direction they can go, and ahead he can see the Ambassador Bridge, lit up and graceful. Tyler's heard it's in terrible condition, but right now it's beautiful. To their left, Windsor is sprinkled with late-night lights. He's never been to Canada.

"Do you think you can find your way home from here?" Tyler asks. They're herded through an intersection that's closed in one direction where cops are gesturing for them to keep going. Asher makes what seems to be a random choice, and they end up on Fort Street. "Never mind."

"No, I think I can get home from here. I have to get turned around."

"It's so pretty right now," Tyler says. It's very quiet in the car and he resists the urge to turn on the radio. He doubts Asher has the same taste in music. The silence is welcome, though.

"I know. I love when they light things up at night. Like the Renaissance Center..."

"Really? Ugh! I hate those buildings," Tyler says. Asher glances at him.

"Why?"

"They're ugly," Tyler says. "There are so many awesome buildings in Detroit. I love the older buildings. Do you know how many different architectural styles there are? The churches alone—" he gestures to the giant church they're now passing. "The way the train station looked. All of those buildings Downtown… the towers just don't fit in."

"I see what you're saying."

"You like them?"

"I don't know. I think I like what they represent."

Tyler makes a face at him.

"I just… the idea of the city being visible. I like that people can see that we're still here."

Tyler hums noncommittally. He understands what Asher is saying, but is also resentful. "The thing is, we've always been here," Tyler says. "We're invisible to so many people, but we ain't never left. We've been keeping this city alive through all the shit corrupt assholes have done. Outside of this city, it's corruption and crime people see, not everyday folk working to make lives." Tyler surprises himself with his own words. Malik would be proud.

"I'd never thought of it that way," Asher says. His face folds into a frown.

"Look, I'm not saying that it's bad. The city needs things to come back. But… I hate that what we've been doing for years, holding on and putting up with shit and all the smaller stuff we do isn't what gets noticed. Not just community centers and urban farming. Not just art in chaos like the Heidelberg Project. But people holding on, getting through the everyday stuff. We don't need to be saved from ourselves. We need people to work beside us. To listen."

"I hope you know that I know that and that's what I want to do." Asher says, worry clear in his voice. "John and I never intended anything else."

"I know," Tyler says softly. He puts a hand on Asher's arm.

"I'll admit I never thought of it that way, though."

"Well, then, I'm glad we met," Tyler says. He tries to bring levity to his tone.

They drive in silence. Tyler is no longer sleepy. He's thinking of Malik; Malik who seemed to love Tyler's calm to his fiery nature and how he depended on Tyler's even nature to stabilize his own anger. For a long time, Tyler became that stabilizing person and it worked. And it wasn't faking; it was like breathing.

But after a while, it frustrated Malik, who accused him of not caring. He came to Tyler for comfort and later gave him annoyed lectures. It's one of the things about the end of their relationship that completely turned Tyler around, because he couldn't tell who Malik wanted him to be.

He wishes he could tell Malik, *I was listening. I was learning. I wish you hadn't given up on me because I couldn't tell what you needed from me.* Tyler's happier without the constant tension their relationship had become, with Malik always pulling him in, then pushing him away, and his resentment about Idlewild and the work Tyler was doing was hard to take. Tyler had such a hard time striking a balance between Malik-Tyler and Idlewild-Tyler.

"I am, too," Asher says. The silence has stretched so long that Tyler has to connect the words to their conversation.

Asher pulls into the parking garage while Tyler stares out the window. Exhaustion is in his bones. It's not the game, he realizes. He spends so much time with Asher, working early morning opens, and they've just finished inventory. They've been spending too many late nights lost in each other.

"Oh god, I'm sorry," Asher says suddenly when he's parked. "I didn't ask if you wanted to go home."

"Oh—" Tyler says. *Should he?* "Do you want me to?"

"No!" Asher says, then modulates his voice. "I don't want you to feel as if you have to stay."

"I want to. I don't know how much fun I'll be, though."

"You know I just enjoy being with you, right?" Asher says. It's hesitant; a sudden vulnerability comes off of Asher in waves. It rises, too, in himself.

"I guess," he says. He does think so, but they've established a pattern where what Tyler feels, and what he occasionally senses from Asher, is an elephant in the room.

"Tyler—" Asher says sadly. His body is twisted in the small car, facing him; his eyes are wide and earnest.

"Don't worry, honey," Tyler says. He's too tired to try to hide the glittering cadence of his words. Many men Tyler knows and has been with aren't into that. "I know," he reassures him. Asher leans forward, holds Tyler's face gently with both hands and giving him a long and tender kiss that shivers all the way to his toes.

Asher breaks the kiss. Tyler's eyes flutter shut; Asher's thumbs smooth over his cheekbones. They stay suspended in this moment, sharing a look that doesn't hide desire, doesn't hide how deeply they care for each other. It's lovely and unexpected and brutally honest without words—until Asher takes a breath and pulls away. Tyler's skin is cold without him.

That night, they sleep. Asher crawls into bed before Tyler, and, when Tyler comes to bed, Asher automatically puts his arms around him, spooning close. There is no pressure or expectation for anything more than sleep, which is a great relief. Not that he wouldn't like sex right now. But sometimes it's just nice to relax, sink into his own bones and let go of everything else.

Chapter Twenty-Three

ASHER DOESN'T BRING THE BET up for another week. He wants to catch Tyler off guard. Tyler is a beautiful challenge; Asher loves finding tiny cracks in his armor in the moments when Tyler is genuine. Asher tells himself those moments are the result of building comfort they have with each other. But he's never sure, and he'd never bring it up and risk Tyler pulling away. Even when Tyler is totally with him, it's only when he's slid into vulnerability that Tyler really feels present, as if the spaces between them might not exist.

Tyler sneaks upstairs on a day off. He texts Asher to ask if it's cool. Not only is it cool, it's something Asher has been hoping for all day. Sometimes when they're working, tension rises that's job-related. As the business has flourished, so have tense moments and arguments between everyone during rushes when things are on the brink of falling apart and people are in the weeds. Tyler has a tendency to nag whenever Asher leaves the office a mess; for the most part Asher can take it in stride but sometimes even he loses his cool. That's normal though. That's restaurant life. Amazingly, as soon as work is over, they are both able to put it behind them.

Asher goes upstairs, still buzzing from a busy-as-fuck shift. Their profit the last few weeks has been incredible. It'll take hours for him to unwind, or it would if he were leaving the shift alone. He knows the staff—most of them—feels the same. He overheard some of them talking about going to a club to burn off the energy that wound them up all day. He remembers those days clearly.

Thank god Tyler is here, because he's the perfect outlet for Asher to focus this energy on.

He finds Tyler curled in his bed with a book in hand. Lately books have been appearing in the loft when Tyler leaves them behind. Asher wonders if it's a hint or forgetfulness.

He crawls onto the bed and hovers over Tyler on all fours. Tyler sets the book aside and gives Asher a lazy smile. He puts his arms around Asher and pulls him closer. Asher takes him in the kiss, uses his mouth as persuasion and seduction. He can sense electricity snapping between them.

"Hi," Tyler says, breathy and light, when Asher pulls away to start in on his neck. "Good shift, I take it?"

"You have no idea," Asher says. His body is plastered against Tyler's; Tyler pulls him closer and closer. He wraps one leg over Asher's and uses his calf to pull him close. Asher is already painfully hard. He sucks on Tyler's neck, then mouths his way down to Tyler's collarbone. Tyler is wearing a feminine lightweight top with a very loose neck. He pulls Tyler to a sitting position; the shirt slips off one shoulder. The drape of it, the juxtaposition of Tyler's slim but obviously masculine body paired with that top, make Asher crazy.

"Fuck, Tyler," Asher groans. He gets onto his knees and pulls Tyler up too. His hands are under his shirt, against his beautifully young taut stomach. "You are so sexy."

"Yeah?" Tyler shudders under his touch. Asher makes no move to take his shirt off. "It's not too—"

Asher stops his words with a kiss. It's less measured, less controlled.

"So this is something you like?" Tyler asks eventually. Both of them are breathing harder. Asher senses what's behind the words; he can't address them full on, but the last thing he wants is Tyler latching on to something just for him. Asher's not sure, but he worries that Tyler does that.

"I like *you*," Asher says. He shrugs out of his own shirt which Tyler has unbuttoned, then lifts his arms to Tyler can work off his undershirt. "God, everything about you turns me on." He reaches down and pulls Tyler closer with his palms cupping Tyler's ass.

"Oh," Tyler says faintly. He takes his own shirt off, which Asher regrets, but he lets it go when Tyler unbuttons his pants.

Once they're naked, he pulls Tyler over him. "Remember?" He whispers against Tyler's mouth.

"What?" Tyler pulls way.

"Our bet? You totally lost."

"Oh my god." Tyler says. "I did totally forget."

"You have to pay up now," Asher says. He touches everywhere; Tyler's body is so suited for his hands.

"What was the bet again?" Tyler asks, a tiny note of wariness in his tone.

"You have to tell me something you've always wanted to do but never have."

Tyler pauses. "How do you know there are things I've never done?"

"Are there?" Asher counters. Tyler smiles.

"Okay, yeah there are."

Asher rolls them over, but keeps most of their bodies carefully apart. It's so easy to get carried away when he's with Tyler, who makes it so easy to loose himself, who gets Asher out of his head, helpless.

"Tell me your secrets," he says, singsong in his voice.

"I don't know if you do—I mean… I've never asked someone for—"

"Tyler," Asher says, and looks at him with as much naked honesty he can. "I do everything. *Everything.*"

"Really?"

"Is this so surprising?"

"I don't know? I've never been with someone who didn't want—or assume—"

"Really?" Asher has to admit he's flabbergasted.

"Of course. Look at me," Tyler says, flabbergasted himself.

Asher shakes his head. This conversation is going in a weird, serious direction. "Well, I am down for anything. So you tell me."

Tyler hesitates. "Unless… please don't feel pressured."

"No, really, I love bottoming. I want to do something that you ask for, that's all for you. And I want you to want it and to be comfortable."

"No, I want to," Tyler says shyly. "I just don't know what I'm doing. I don't want to disappoint."

"Oh god, honey, that's *not* gonna happen. I'll talk you through it, if you want." He says it low, going for seductive.

"Yeah?" Tyler says. His voice is so high it betrays his excitement.

"Grab the lube," Asher says quietly. Tyler does; his hands shake. Asher has to trust that that's not bad. He's a little shaky himself.

He talks Tyler through everything, praising him and making sure to touch him, though after a bit it's hard to concentrate. It's been a very long time since he's done this with someone, and he's almost forgotten how amazing it feels. He closes his eyes and grinds down onto Tyler's fingers.

"God, please—" Asher says brokenly. "Fuck me now, oh, *fuck*—"

He opens his eyes when Tyler pulls his fingers out slowly. They glisten with lube in the low light. Asher tears the foil wrapper of the condom for him. Tyler kneels close to him and moans when Asher rolls it on.

"I can't believe—" Tyler whispers.

"How do you want me?" Asher asks.

"I don't know," Tyler says, there is so much uncertainty in the words and in Tyler's face that Asher's heart cramps. Here is a boy unused to asking for himself, scared of what he wants.

"Tell me what you fantasize about." Asher runs his hands up Tyler's body. "When you're alone."

Tyler closes his eyes and breathes out slowly. "Can it be like this?" he asks. "Face to face?"

"Oh fuck, yes." Asher pulls Tyler over him, perhaps a little roughly. He's desperate and hungry with the promise of what's to come. He pulls a pillow to himself with a flailing arm and with Tyler's help pushes it under his ass and hips. Tyler coats himself with more lube—way too much, but that's good.

"Talk to me, please," Tyler says quietly. The need in his voice changes the tone. Asher is awed by the gift they're giving one another; the moment is intensely intimate, and he feels so laid bare. He can tell Tyler does, too.

"Slow," he whispers, then whimpers when Tyler presses against and then slowly into him. Asher closes his eyes and exhales and bears down and tries to relax. The pressure and fullness are a lot to take but also exactly what his body craves. "You're okay, keep going," he encourages. He opens his eyes; Tyler's are wide; the green is almost swallowed by his pupils.

"Are you okay?" Tyler asks.

"Yes. I'm fine. Don't—" Asher moans when Tyler pulls out, then pushes back in; he moves inside Asher in incremental thrusts. "Don't worry about me, honey. Do what you want; do what feels good."

"Oh my god." Tyler stops and presses his forehead against Asher's shoulder. "This—"

"I know." Asher rolls his hips. "Please, *please*—"

Tyler takes a deep breath and bites down Asher's shoulder. It hurts a little but is right, perfect, and, when Tyler begins to really fuck him, it's uninhibited. It's fast and sloppy. Tyler's arms are under him, holding him close with fingers gripping his shoulder blades. They're tight against each other, sweating and rocking and, for once, Asher doesn't think at all. He lets go and gives himself over to Tyler and lets him take him wherever he wants, however he wants.

AFTERWARD, ASHER CAN'T BRING HIMSELF to move. He winces when Tyler pulls out and takes off the condom. Tyler wipes him up with his discarded undershirt. With clumsy fingers Asher pulls Tyler back in, tangles them together and closes his eyes. One of them is shaking through the aftermath. It might be him.

It has been a very, very long time since someone has pulled him so thoroughly apart. He gets Tyler's arms around him and hopes he will hold him tighter. Usually Tyler who needs holding after they fuck; usually he's doing the taking apart.

"Asher, are—"

Asher shakes his head and tucks his face into Tyler's neck. They're both sweating, and it's too hot. Asher squeezes his eyes together because that blissful wash of white, that feeling of being pulled out of his head and put into someone's hands, is fading, and, in its wake, the memory of the last time he felt this and of the only other person in his life who has taken him there.

And now he knows who is shaking. Tyler runs one hand in the gentlest arc, slow and rhythmic like the push and pull of sea fans in currents of blue water. John and Asher went to the Mayan Riviera for their honeymoon and there they went scuba diving. John trailed off after fish at a sedate pace, happy to zigzag his way through the water. But the calm—the silence other than the living song of pops and crackles of the reef—mesmerized Asher. He watched the sea fans and the anemones as they let the currents move them; he felt himself moved by those same currents.

Asher has never again felt peace the way that he did in that moment. And now—now it's too much—it's a memory Tyler's snatched from a box of memories Asher refuses to acknowledge, much less touch.

"I need to shower. I'm gross," he says suddenly. He plasters on what he hopes is a convincing smile and hopes Tyler won't want to shower together. His shower is too small for that, and right now, Asher needs to fucking pull himself together.

"Okay," Tyler says. His smile is less than genuine. Asher can't read it, but he sounds different. Uncertain maybe? He forces himself to get up rather than try to draw whatever it is out of Tyler and fix it. Two vulnerable men who have been play-acting at confidence will only lead to places Asher isn't willing to go.

This wasn't meant to be serious. In the shower, Asher closes his eyes and puts his forehead against the plastic shower liner. He has known from the start that he must be careful with Tyler: with his youth, but also with his tricky vulnerability. Tyler hides it well, but betrays it in ways Asher only sees because he pays close attention. He's wanted to get underneath Tyler's carefully pieced-together persona, but it never occurred to him that perhaps he's been playing the same game.

Asher wasn't expecting his own vulnerability. He wasn't expecting this. He puts a hand over his chest and forces himself to breathe, because his chest is tight. The edges of panic press outward from inside his currently thin skin.

He's over John. He's had years to grieve. Why, then, in the last months, has he felt it so much more? Lifting Idlewild, meeting these new people who have helped make it possible, meeting Tyler—he feels the joy of it, he does. But so often lately, the crush of missing John strikes at the strangest moments and he is aching for the only person who really knew Asher *before*.

Until now, Asher's never felt this aching heartbreak when he's with Tyler. Panic, a fluttering, frenzied thing, begins to beat so hard inside Asher's chest he has to sit, right in the shower. Water beats against his head and runs into his eyes and down his face. He has no idea whether or not he's crying.

Asher hasn't seen it, but he recognizes now, that Tyler is the antidote; he's the balm. He remembers John for Asher in their time together, but with kindness and care. So it doesn't hurt him, and, if it does, it's easy for Asher to fit right back into this new, different skin, to become this man who is willing to take Tyler places he's never been before.

Asher takes deep, calming breaths and stands. He wipes his face and reminds himself that outside of this bathroom is a young and vulnerable man Asher's taken apart as thoroughly as he's been deconstructed. He has to take care because tonight he can't give Tyler his heart or any more of himself than he has already. He's reasonably sure he'd fall apart if he did.

Tyler's not the only one who can pretend. He just does it differently. And, if he stays in the shower, the hot water will run out, and he wants to leave Tyler the option of showering.

He wraps himself in a towel. The mirror is steamed over, and Asher doesn't bother to wipe it off. Something will show on his face, but he can only try to power through, to steer Tyler toward the shower and take those extra moments to compose himself.

Tyler is still in bed, curled on his side the way he does. His eyes are open though, staring across the apartment sightlessly. He's very still.

"Mmm, hey," Asher says. He keeps his voice low and tries for affection and warmth. He kisses Tyler's exposed shoulder. Tyler rolls over a little. His eyes shine, but Asher can't tell if it's from happiness or sadness. He pushes past that and runs his hand down Tyler's arm. Tyler scoots back a little, and Asher sits next to him, then kisses him very softly. "Want to shower? I left you hot water."

Tyler scans Asher's face, reading his expression. Finally, he smiles. "That would be nice. I can get out of your hair after, if you want."

"No," Asher makes himself say. The fact that he realized that Tyler is what makes his grief better scared him, but not as much as being left alone with it. For one blinding, crazy moment, Asher wonders if the only way he'll be able to keep it together will be to always be with Tyler.

Tyler pulls away and sits. Asher lets him go. While Tyler's in the shower, singing loudly, Asher finishes drying. He moisturizes and pulls on underwear. He changes the sheets because Tyler appreciates that. He contemplates picking up, but his bed is much too inviting and he's very weary. Instead he gets Tyler a glass of water and sets it on the nightstand, then crawls into bed. He picks up the book Tyler's been reading and loses a few minutes to it. By the time Tyler's out of the shower, he's blinking sleepy eyes open and his body is so relaxed he could melt right into the mattress. Tyler gets ready for bed, and Asher dog-ears his own spot in the book, chapters behind Tyler's.

"Do you mind?" he asks, tilting the book so Tyler can see.

"Of course not. That makes me happy," Tyler says. "I'll have to leave it here."

"You don't have to, I don't want to take it away—"

"No, I want to." Tyler climbs into bed and pulls the book away, putting it on the makeshift nightstand on Asher's side. "Double win: you reading and sleeping better *and* an excuse to keep coming back."

Asher settles on his side and opens his arms so Tyler can spoon into them. "You need excuses?" he says into the dark.

"Do I?" Asher senses uncertainty in the question. Maybe the vulnerability in the question is aided by the dark. Maybe it's bravery, being able to expose himself when not looking at Asher. Maybe it's Tyler unwilling to let go of what they'd shared.

Pretending that they both hadn't been shaken would be too much of a lie. Not when Asher has the responsibility of making sure he doesn't hurt Tyler.

"Of course not." Many other things could be said. But this will have to do for now. He kisses the back of Tyler's neck, snuggles close and closes his eyes. Tyler's fingers find Asher's, which are wrapped around his waist, and hold on tight.

Chapter Twenty-Four

TYLER WAKES BEFORE DAWN. ASHER is on the other side of the bed, his back to him. His body is heavy in sleep; his back expands and contracts with the long, slow breaths of exhaustion. The memory of last night rushes over him in waves: too much and too heavy.

Tyler slips out of bed. He dresses in last night's clothes. He goes downstairs as silently as he can and makes coffee. It's Sunday, brunch day, so he has some time before they have to open.

He carries his coffee back upstairs and then settles at the window facing Woodward. From here, he can see the sun break over the buildings. The sky begins to pink slowly, spilling into sorbet orange, chasing darkness into gray-blue. The sky is strewn with thin clouds that halo brilliantly in the coming sun and brighten the edges of the buildings.

Tyler rests his head against the brick wall and breathes in the scent of his coffee. He feels… so much. There's only so much he can to do to keep those feelings at bay.

He turns and watches Asher sleep. His face is completely at rest. His hair is a riot. Tyler is so fucked, fucked because he is so utterly, deeply in love.

He's in love and smart enough to realize that this probably won't end well. Last night was the most vulnerable Asher has ever been. Tyler's never experienced anything like it; nor the fucking and being able to move someone into that place: the not-thinking, giving-over-to-it, helpless-in-someone-else's-hands place. Tyler's mastered the art of putting himself together after sex and disguising the moment. He wonders how long it has been since Asher trusted another human in this way. He has a pretty good idea. He had no idea how put-together Asher is until, with Tyler's kisses and touch, he let him in.

Tyler is not willing or ready to give this up, which means he has to walk carefully, gain Asher's trust, show him that Tyler won't hurt him, that Tyler can be a safe place for him to open up to all of the things he's been holding in. The coffee is bitter on his tongue, and his muscles ache from the night before. He wants Asher's trust, but Tyler's not sure he can trust Asher not to hurt him or leave him, not to let him down.

Once the sun is fully up and traffic along Woodward begins to wake, Tyler slips back downstairs. He makes Asher coffee. He roots around and finds croissants and heats them, then gets some raspberry jelly and leftover whipped butter. He slices some melon and arranges it on a plate.

Asher is stirring when Tyler takes it upstairs with everything precariously balanced. Despite the fact that he's worked at Idlewild for months, he's still working on carrying many things the way the other servers do.

"Morning," he sings softly. Asher grunts and pulls the covers higher, then buries his face in Tyler's pillow, which he's clutched in his arms.

"I brought you some breakfast and coffee," Tyler says, voice still low.

"Time 'izit?" Asher says from within the pillow.

"Nine."

Asher sits. "Thank god for brunch Sundays," he says, rubbing his eyes. "Best decision we ever made."

The *we* roots into Tyler's stomach, which is warm and happy. When Asher refers to their work as a shared venture, it is validating and lovely. Tyler has no desire to take credit for Idlewild, but he's so proud of the work they've done, and that he's been a good part of what they're making. He loves when Asher acknowledges that he understands that as well. It's not selfishness when Asher doesn't, it's the imprint of his lonely struggle before he decided to restart.

Tyler puts the tray down on the floor, then presses the coffee into Asher's fumbling hands. His eyes are still heavy with sleep. Tyler resists the urge to kiss him back into the sheets.

"I made it how you like it," he says instead. He's rewarded by a sweet smile. "And breakfast."

Asher sits straighter, sits cross-legged under the sheets, and Tyler sets the plates between them. Asher's eyes light up; this is one of his favorite breakfasts. It's simple, but Tyler's noticed by now that Asher has simple tastes—funny, that, since he runs a restaurant with a rotating menu of complex and beautiful small plates.

"Ty, you are the best." Asher's voice is still a little graveled with sleep. He leans forward carefully so as not to disturb the plates and kisses Tyler on the cheek.

"Here," Tyler says, feeding him a piece of melon to cover his reaction to the words and gesture. Asher holds his wrist and nibbles it carefully from his fingers. He nips on the end of one, and shivers roll down Tyler's spine. They don't have time for more than breakfast, but the promise is lovely.

They eat without speaking, feeding each other with small smiles and touches. Afraid they'll betray too much, Tyler's eyes flit away whenever they meet Asher's. They don't acknowledge the night before in words, but Asher doesn't seem to be fighting closeness. Perhaps he's too sleepy.

Once they've eaten, Asher clears the plates away. They still have some time before he has to go down. He coaxes Tyler onto the couch where they watch the morning news in a tangle of limbs. Every now and then he kisses Tyler's cheek or neck or hand. He's so openly affectionate, Tyler can't help but begin to build hope.

"I was thinking, I wanted to take you somewhere," Asher says after a while.

"Where?"

"A surprise?"

"Mmm." Tyler puts his head on Asher's shoulder, sleepy and content. "Sounds good."

They nail down plans for their next day off—before dinner shift—and eventually drag themselves off the couch.

"I can lend you clothes," Asher offers. They lingered too long for him to offer Tyler a ride home.

"Um." Tyler blushes. "I might have brought a spare set? This happens so often, you know and I, I thought—"

"Don't worry so much," Asher says with a smile. "That's good thinking." Tyler sighs with relief.

Dressing together breaks the lovely spell morning spun around them. The sun spilling in through the windows is too bright. The more put together Asher is, the more armored he seems. Tyler is ready sooner; his hair doesn't require the attention Asher's does.

"I'll go down." He wraps his arms around Asher's back. He's short enough that he can't see over Asher's shoulder and into the mirror. But that's okay. He's not sure he wants to see the look on Asher's face. His body is tight, guarded. Tyler kisses between his shoulder blades and ignores it. "Take your time."

"Thanks," Asher says. He turns and kisses Tyler's mouth, fast and hard, before turning back to the mirror.

By the time Tyler has the cash drawers ready to go and is pulling the back-of-line pans together to help the cooks prep, Asher comes down. Tyler can smell him before he sees him. Asher's cologne is distinct: cedar and vanilla and something else Tyler can't place. By the end of most shifts Tyler can only smell it when their bodies are together. He likes that even better.

"How's it going?" Asher says. He steps behind the salad station and crouches to check the coolers.

"Fine." Tyler ignores the tiny pit of doubt in his stomach because Asher's tone is strange. It's the most pulled-back he's ever seemed, at least since they've grown closer.

Tyler has to remind himself that Asher is far more fragile than either of them realized and that perhaps Asher hasn't owned that yet. He must tread carefully and with compassion.

The back doorbell rings, and Tyler sets down his clipboard. "I've got it," he says, and leaves Asher alone, in the sanctuary of his kitchen.

* * *

"So this is our destination?" Tyler says, stopping as they wait to cross Kirby along John R. They're going to the Detroit Institute of Arts. It's a lovely building, a mix of Beaux-Arts and Renaissance Revival architecture. It's sprawling, and the landscaping is lush with burgeoning spring.

"Yep," Asher says brightly. Tyler smiles at him. "Is this okay?" He crosses the street in the middle, ignoring the crosswalk half a block down and the construction everywhere.

"Of course." This is meant to be a place in the city Asher is showing him, and he almost hates to burst his bubble. "I've been here lots of times, I love it."

Asher turns his face to try to hide his surprise. Tyler rolls his eyes and reminds himself of his promise to educate Asher gently. "I'm black, honey, not uneducated or cultured."

"Oh god." Asher stops and meets his eyes, "I didn't mean—I mean, I'm sorry. I shouldn't—"

"Relax," Tyler says, and risks giving his hand a squeeze. "I'm about sixty percent joking."

Asher closes his eyes. "You're much kinder to me about this shit than you should be."

"Eh." Tyler waves this off. He doesn't want to tell Asher that he's waking him to things he's been raised not to see. He's doing it through action. "Let's go in. We can show each other our favorite parts."

"Yeah?" Asher smiles. It's unsure and makes him look years younger. These little moments are always a revelation to Tyler. Tyler's always known Asher doesn't have his shit together and yet projects an inherent composure. Experience has taught him that one has to get very, very close to catch a glimpse behind the veneer. It's almost painful, how hungry for these moments of intimacy Tyler is. He can't delight in them right now though, because he doesn't think they were meant to be shared yet.

He waits a moment, offering Asher a sunny smile while Asher pulls himself together.

"Lead the way then," Tyler says, and follows half a step behind Asher.

Chapter Twenty-Five

IT TURNS OUT THAT THEY both love the Rivera Court the most.

"Want to go there last then?" Asher offers. Tyler nods: he's not looking at Asher. Instead he takes it all in, slow and deliberate. "Why don't you pick an exhibit, and I'll pick one?"

"Or we could wander," Tyler says.

"Wait." Asher stops. "Is this me trying to make a plan, and you wanting to just do whatever?"

Surprised, Tyler laughs. "I think I like this. Role reversal."

Asher laughs too, to cover the pang of anxiety he's been burying ever since last night. He resists the urge to take Tyler's hand and leads them down the promenade. Tyler lingers in the Native American art section. He has a much longer attention span for exploring the rooms; Asher doesn't mind. He sits back and watches Tyler. The movement of his face as the art moves him, interests him, surprises him. He's completely and utterly unselfconscious. *I'd follow you anywhere, to see you look like this.*

Instead of saying this, or something more foolish and risky, Asher takes Tyler's hand and tugs him toward the prints and photographs room. The museum is almost empty. Rather than drop his hand, Tyler laces their fingers together.

Eventually they wander into the Rivera Court. There's no guided tour at the moment.

"I've done it anyway—have you?" Asher asks.

"Yeah, I came with Malik when they had the Frieda Khalo and Rivera show," Tyler tells him.

"I did too."

Tyler smiles brightly. It's a lovely sunny day, so the room is bright and the high ceilings appear loftier. They sit facing the north mural and take long moments to look. The frescoes are bright and busy; everywhere the eye falls is another image, another symbol, more to think about. Asher prefers to sit and look rather than take the guided tour. He'd rather think about what he's looking at, and he loves seeing something new every time.

"You ever notice his self-portrait in there?" Asher asks Tyler.

"No! Where?"

"On the right, between the conveyor belts," Asher says and points. Tyler gets up to examine it more closely. Asher is happy to watch him move in the sunlight.

"It's crazy to me, sometimes. How many people come to see them and how cool they are, but don't try to understand them?" Tyler finally says when he sits back down.

"I don't know."

"Everything he thought—that people thought the future held— what the auto industry and Ford, science and life—and where it's all at now," Tyler muses. "Do people think about it all?"

"Sure. I mean… I don't know. I guess it depends. I mean, look at the scientists." Asher points up. On the top right is a fresco of scientists formulating poison gas, and on the left are iconographic images of doctors and scientists vaccinating a baby. "I think it's a pretty balanced depiction of the harm and the good scientific advancement can make. I've always seen these as a commentary on possibility and potential consequence. The way that science and technology were becoming, and became, the new religion."

"You sound like Malik," Tyler says, then stiffens. "I shouldn't say that shit, should I?"

Asher takes a moment to assess his reaction. "No, I think it's fine." The truth is, it is.

Tyler had finally told him about that dinner with his family when Malik had shown up. He seemed worried that maybe Asher wouldn't understand why he was asking to structure his hours more and dedicate time for his family. Of course Asher had understood. Tyler's ties to his family fill Asher with faint longing. Tyler hesitated to tell Asher that Malik had been there and the resolutions they'd come to. And yes, initially they made Asher insecure, but a more logical part of him understood and admired Tyler's gift for forgiveness and caring. Asher doesn't think he has that anymore, if he ever had.

They don't speak after that. At some point Tyler's stomach growls, loudly, and so they decide to eat. Rather than eat at the museum, Asher convinces Tyler to go to a Midtown restaurant.

"To check out the competition," he says, and Tyler beams. They end up at The Jolly Pumpkin, where Asher plies Tyler with too many beers. He's never seen Tyler drunk. It's only four; they're in that twilight hour before dinner picks up and lunch is too late to really be lunch at all. Asher didn't like his first beer so he gave it to Tyler. They're sitting at the bar, backs to the room. Asher approves of the open but slightly industrial air of the place. The ceilings are high and exposed, and there are long cafeteria-style tables of scarred wood in the middle floor.

"Did you know that President Obama came here once?" Asher asks to distract him when he orders.

"Yes. Wait. Did you just order another beer?"

"Come on, we need to know what great beers there are."

"Asher, we're not a beer place," Tyler points out. His protest must have been token, because he starts in on the beer when it's delivered.

"Well, you never know what the future holds," Asher says, surprising himself with the honest-to-god optimism of the statement. Not that he thinks they'll become a brewery, but because down in his bones he trusts that Idlewild has a future. Tyler delicately wipes foam from his lip and smiles.

"It's a good feeling, isn't it?" He knows exactly what Asher is feeling. Asher tilts his head and lets himself see, without his own walls up, the boy in front of him. He's so lovely; he wore a lovely green lightweight scarf and a heather gray cardigan to the museum. It's warm in the restaurant, and he's taken them off to reveal a boatneck cream-colored top. Asher wants to bite his collarbones; he wants to tuck his face into Tyler's long neck and against his delicate bones. He wants to see the smile on Tyler's face and his green eyes steady on his.

"It's a great feeling."

WHEN THEY GET BACK TO Idlewild, Tyler is still tipsy and a little too handsy. He'd been like that in the car, palm hot against Asher's thigh, squeezing and stroking. He'd also promised Asher a blowjob when they got back to the restaurant if he could sneak Tyler upstairs and then described what he wanted to do in detail. Amused, turned on and very happy with the way their day went, Asher assures Tyler he can do any and all of that.

Of course, the sneaking in part doesn't go as planned, because Jared is taking a break in the back. Tyler is giggling and clumsy; Asher has to put physical distance between them to keep Tyler from touching him. They exchange awkward conversation with Jared until he can usher Tyler into the office, which is marginally more subtle than taking him upstairs. Asher knows his relationship with Tyler is an open secret with the staff; still, he realizes that if he takes Tyler upstairs he won't have the willpower to come back down. This doesn't stop Tyler from pushing him roughly into one of the chairs, which rolls and bangs against the wall.

"Easy there," Asher says, his laughter cut off as Tyler drops to his knees lightning fast. "Ty—"

"Shush, you," Tyler says. He's focused on Asher's pants, and despite knowing this is a terrible idea, it's hard to resist. "Bet I can get you off in five minutes or less." Asher's not sure about that, but he is already mostly hard. Tyler strips off his scarf and sweater; the neck of his shirt slips to the right exposing some of his shoulder. Tyler smirks at him, confirming that he knows by now that this gets Asher going. Asher arches back, acquiescing; perhaps it's the thrill of knowing people are outside the door, or Tyler being aggressive and forward, but in the end, Asher's pretty sure he hasn't come that fast in years.

"YOU EVER HEARD OF JOHN'S Carpet House?" Tyler asks. He drowses with his head on Asher's stomach, tangled in Asher's sheets. The mindless drone of the television blurs behind them; lying this way, Tyler reports that he can hear every breath Asher takes and that his stomach is louder than the TV.

"No," Asher says. Tyler lifts his head and smiles; Asher was half asleep. He sighs and fidgets, moving to accommodate Tyler when he scoots up and leans on an elbow.

"How do you feel about jazz?"

Asher smiles. "You're so random. And awake." He yawns through Tyler's laugh.

"Well?" Tyler asks. He runs his fingers in small, light circles over Asher's belly and chest. Asher twitches again and covers his hand. Unlike Tyler, Asher is very, very ticklish.

"I like it, I think. I don't listen to a lot of it," Asher says. "I'm guessing this Carpet House is a jazz place you want to take me to?"

"Yeah." Tyler frees his hand and uses it to tug some of Asher's curls off of his forehead. Asher closes his eyes; he loves having his hair played with. "But not now because it's a summer thing."

Asher commands himself not to show any signs of distress. Things have been going beautifully between them, but it's definitely light and fun and playful right now, and Asher's been working hard to keep it that way while he figures out whatever is going on in his mind. Any hints of the kind of intimacies they'd begun sharing leave Asher steeped in melancholy and worry. He *wants* these things with Tyler—the promise of something they can do together in the summer—but he's also terrified. It's so easy, being with Tyler, and Asher knows that his own vacillating desires have become irrational. And that it's unfair, how he wants to push Tyler to let down his walls and trust him, when he won't do it himself.

Asher rolls onto his side and props himself on his elbow, pushing down any semblance of distress and smiling with genuine warmth. The pad of Tyler's fingertip skates along Asher's neck and shoulder and he shivers; he hopes Tyler can't hear the strong beat of his anxious heart. Asher isn't dumb; Tyler doesn't want to scare him off. They are careful in this dance, this delicate and fraught balancing.

"Well?" Asher prompts. He holds Tyler's elbow and raises an eyebrow. "Tell me about it."

"Sorry, I was thinking." Tyler shakes his head. "Down on the corner of St. Aubin and Frederick, there are these jazz and blues concerts. One of those outdoor places where you go, set up a chair, listen to some good music and eat great food. People grill and sell food. Musical legends have played there, and also their kids. There's a peanut guy who sells peanuts. I'm making this sound weird, aren't I?"

"No, this sounds cool. Have you gone often?"

"Actually it's been a few years."

Asher frowns. That's definitely by a bad area, down by Chene. "And it's outdoor?"

"Yeah, like a whole block. They keep it all going on donations. I think it's been going for twenty years or something."

"That sounds really cool. I can't believe I've never heard of this," Asher says.

Tyler smiles. "It's not even one of the secret ones."

"Secret ones?"

"Things people do in the city. You know the guys who make benches out of reclaimed wood for the bus stops—I think it's called *Sit On It* or something? Those are cool. Artistic, and some of them have shelves for books under them. I think I've seen some at the Eastern Market. And that's just one thing. There's so much happening in the city people don't see. Like, people know about the urban farms and the Heidelberg Project but there's so, so much more."

Asher's hand runs up and then down Tyler's arm, landing on his hand. Tyler takes it.

"I can't wait for you to show me all of these things," Asher says, swallowing down fear.

"Yeah?" Tyler smiles shyly then he crowds closer to Asher and kisses him, gently putting him on his back.

"I swear you have a fourteen-second recovery rate," Asher mumbles against his mouth.

"I bet I can get you there too," Tyler teases, and then does his very best to make good on it.

Chapter Twenty-Six

WHEN TYLER WAKES IN THE morning, he finds himself alone in the bed, again. Either he was sleeping very deeply or Asher snuck out early. Tyler checks his phone, which has been charging on the floor next to the bed: it's still pretty early. He groans but makes himself get up, rubbing the sleep from his eyes.

Half awake, he searches the crates Asher uses for clothes in order to find some of his own and then showers. He turns the water up hot, as hot as he can, and slowly wakes himself. He's half slathered in body wash when it hits him that he's using his own. He keeps his clothes here and his books. He's been telling himself—as he's sure Asher is—that they're keeping things light, but Tyler's practically moved in and is constantly unsure of where he stands. When he goes downstairs to greet Asher, will he find him moody and distant or sweet and affectionate?

"Morning," Tyler sings when he lets himself into the office. Asher's got his back to him on his side of the desk. He doesn't turn around.

"Morning." He doesn't sound upset, but distracted. Tyler opts not to try to give him a kiss.

"What needs doing, boss?"

"Check the lines?" Asher does turn then. Circles bag under his eyes, but his smile is real. "I got the drawers. Delivery's in a little bit so I'll hang out here."

"Okay," Tyler says. Asher is still sitting, which Tyler takes to mean he doesn't want Tyler to approach him.

In the quiet kitchen, Tyler looks around blindly. This up and down, this unsureness, is almost worse than when he was with Malik. He'd ask himself it is worth it, if he weren't aware of how deeply and helplessly in love with Asher he is. It's nothing like it was with Malik, and Tyler refuses to give up.

"I'LL SEE YOU LATER, SWEETIE," Tyler says to Claudia. It's been a slow shift, a waste of everyone's time. Asher's been in the office for most of it, which is unusual, but it's not as though they needed him. Tyler won't ask to stay. Instead he kisses Dia's cheek and waves goodbye to Santos.

"Call me if you need me," she says. He turns, and rolls his eyes, because when has he ever called her? They're not close outside of work, not that he would be averse to it. They just aren't. But he stops when he sees her face.

"Everything okay?" he asks her.

"Is everything okay with you?" she counters.

He laughs to cover his surprise. "Of course, why wouldn't it be?"

She looks him over; she starts to say something and then changes her mind. She wears her hair in a high ponytail again, and her long curls bounce and catch the light. "Of course you are," she says; her tone strikes him as insincere or ironic. He smiles tightly.

Of course, the truth is that he's not okay. He's not precisely not-not-okay either. He's not anything. Or maybe he's too much. *Who the fuck knows?*

What he is, is confused.

He's so deep in thought he makes it halfway to the bus stop before he realizes that he's left his apron, and his money, in the breakroom. The back door is open. His key is in his apron, which is apparently not on the counter where he thought it was. He's about to open his locker when he hears Claudia speak.

"Tyler seems off." He hears her say.

"Tyler is fine," Asher responds. Tyler ducks behind the wall, hoping he hasn't been seen. He hates to be that cliché, but if Asher's gonna talk to someone about him, maybe he can figure out what the fuck is going on between them in this weird stalemate.

"Don't mess with him." There's almost a note of warning in her tone. It warms Tyler a little. He doesn't need to be protected, and certainly doesn't need anyone warning Asher off, but it's not unwelcome to be cared for.

"Dia, why would I be messing with him?" Asher sounds weary.

"Because that boy is head over heels for you. There are practically hearts floating over his head when he's with you. Lately, when you're not together he's definitely sad. Or upset? Something."

Asher is quiet; Tyler tries to still his breathing so he can hear if he responds.

"I promise I have no intention of hurting him, if that's what you're worried about. Things are a little confusing right now; he's young, and he's just come out of a relationship. We're... he's a really special kid, and we're just a stop on his way. Once he figures himself out, he'll be long gone."

"That's the excuse you're going with?" Claudia asks. Tyler can picture her face perfectly, her knife-sharp sarcasm and tilted head, her too-direct eyes. He has no idea what Asher does in response; it's either non-verbal or he doesn't respond at all. "There are so many things wrong with what you just said—"

"*Claudia*," Asher says. The warning is clear. "I can't right now. I promise to be careful with him."

"I didn't mean just him," she says. "I gotta go finish getting things ready. I'll see you later."

Tyler slips out of the back door before Asher comes back and catches him eavesdropping. He stands outside, leans against the brick of the wall next to the door, and tries to rearrange his thoughts. In the span of a few seconds Tyler's learned too much—he's not felt the years between them as keenly as he does now. Asher called him a kid. A fucking *kid*. And, icing on the cake, he thinks Tyler's just going to leave Idlewild?

The worst, though, is that Asher—that Claudia—talked about how Tyler needs to figure himself out. *I have*. He loves Idlewild. He wants to see a future here. Has he jeopardized that with this affair? It seems stupid that he's never let himself experience the weight of his choices before. Tyler doesn't need to figure himself out. He knows who he is: the boy who travels the in-between spaces, who bridges things. He's a conduit and a chameleon. *There's nothing wrong with that, right?*

A sharp wail pierces the air; close by a siren goes off, and behind it, the blare of a fire truck. The noise moves away and so does Tyler, lest he get caught loitering. Above all things, he cannot lose Asher or Idlewild, which means he needs a plan.

* * *

"So I was thinking..." Tyler says without turning his chair around. He tries to keep his tone light and casual, non-invested.

"Hm?" Judging by the lack of screeching, Asher hasn't turned around in his chair either.

"I heard that *Lights on Tamae* is out on Netflix."

The chair makes its horrific noise. "Remind me which one that one is?"

Tyler closes his eyes, takes a deep breath and makes his body appear relaxed. He turns too. "You know, the one we saw an ad for when you were pretending not to watch the Hallmark channel the other day. You said something about wanting to see it."

"I was not!" Laughter laces Asher's protest. "It's out? Do you want to watch it?"

"If you do," Tyler offers; politely refraining from more teasing. It strikes him that in order to get Asher on "dates" he has to invite himself over. It's never seemed weird. He's always been welcome. Hell, he might still be. But everything is so fraught.

He cannot let Asher slip through his fingers. The thought fills him with panic.

"That sounds good," Asher says. His smile is natural. It's as if he has no idea what's going on. *How can he breathe through all of the unspoken subtext in this room?* Tyler waits for Asher to extend an invitation.

"Hey," Asher nudges Tyler's knee, "Where'd you go?"

"Huh?" Tyler blinks at him.

"You're a million miles away," Asher says. "Is everything okay? I was going to ask if you want to hang out tonight, but if you're tired—"

"No!" Tyler forces himself to laugh. "I mean, no. I'm fine. I'd love to stay."

"Want a snack?" Asher asks when they get upstairs.

"Oh, I can get something," Tyler says. He starts go downstairs.

"No, no," Asher pulls him back with a hand around his waist. "I wanted to know if *you* want one. I'm fine."

"Oh, well then. I'm okay too."

Asher pauses but then smiles and reels him in for a kiss. It's sweet. Asher is being so *normal*. Maybe nothing's changed. Maybe Tyler's imagined the whole thing—their relationship getting more serious. He didn't imagine Asher's words though, and that's definitely what he needs to work on.

Asher pulls back and smiles into Tyler's eyes. He *can't* be imagining this, not when Asher looks at him like this; not when just his hands around Tyler's waist make him bright and liquid; not when Asher's body and breath and smile are so *his*. He lets Asher lead the way to the couch. As part of Tyler's plan, he's thought of all the things Asher seems to like the most about him.

First: Tyler in more androgynous clothes. He has no idea why, and it took him a while to pick up on it, but he certainly can't object because that's an aesthetic he'd pick for himself anyway.

Second: malleable. Not in a bad way, because he loves it, and he takes pleasure in giving himself over to Asher most of the time. He's unsure of himself now, and he needs to be all the things Asher wants. He can definitely pretend. Asher is much more comfortable with that dynamic; Tyler's no fool. Asher needs that, needs to feel in control in order to control his fears. Tyler can give him that.

Third: vocal. Asher loves when Tyler talks; he gets off on coaxing Tyler's wishes out of him. Tyler doesn't want to be anyone's burden, and he wants to bring Asher as much pleasure as he gives Tyler.

Fourth: Tyler knows that Asher tops. For some reason, this is something they've never done. They've done plenty of other things, and it's not a secret that Tyler loves bottoming. Asher has somehow figured out that it's all other things that Tyler's not used to receiving; he's lavished those upon him. But this is definitely something he can give Asher he hasn't before, and he has a pretty good idea it'll make Asher happy.

Tyler's wearing a caramel-colored knit turtleneck with a long pocket that goes down one thigh. The color does great things for his eyes, and the elaborate drape and shape of the neck make his jawbones particularly striking. His jeans are insanely tight and ripped up, cut to mimic women's jeans. The outfit is definitely working, because even though the movie is on, every now and then Asher kisses his neck or runs a finger along a line of exposed thigh where his pants are ripped. Asher turns and kisses behind Tyler's ear; his hot, wide hand grips Tyler's thigh, high and hard. Tyler shivers; it's crazy how well Asher knows his body. He's so good at unspooling all of Tyler's defenses that he's wound so tight around himself.

Tyler clears his throat. He has to keep himself together, because he can't stick to the plan if Asher drives him into incoherence.

He turns his head and kisses Asher's forehead. Asher closes his eyes and breathes him in.

"So are we not watching the movie?" Tyler whispers.

"Depends on you," he says. Tyler likes that Asher gives him choices. Right now, though, Asher wants him. Carefully he climbs into Asher's lap and straddles him despite how tight his pants are. Tyler kisses him, dirty and hungry.

By the time they work their way to the bed, they're undressing in a clumsy hurry, and by the time Asher has him naked, it's very hard for Tyler to think through his plan.

"Fuck me," he finally blurts out.

"Really?" Asher pulls away.

"You don't want to?" Tyler asks, a little surprised.

"Of course I do," Asher says. "So long as that's what you want."

"Oh my god, fuck me already," Tyler says. He laughs and rolls over. He knows that if he can see Asher, he'll fall apart. He always does.

Asher takes his sweet time, though. He works and works until Tyler begs, and when he's finally there, rocking into him, he's so slow and gentle Tyler can hardly stand it. He's been in love and he's made love. But this is a whole new level. Asher always surprises him—so reserved everywhere but in bed, where he's so deeply sensual and focused and giving it's crazy.

When it's over, Tyler can hardly speak. Asher runs his hands over Tyler's skin with reverence. Tyler wants to close his eyes and let himself be touched, glowing under Asher's fingers with his heart lit.

He orders himself to roll over. He takes Asher's face in his hands and strokes his cheeks. "Was that okay for you? What can I do?"

"You don't have to do anything," Asher says. His eyebrows shoot up, surprised.

"Are you sure? I feel as if I'm not keeping up my end of the bargain."

"Bargain?" Asher sits abruptly. "You're making this sound as if it's a business transaction," he points out. Tyler sits too.

"No, I mean—I just want to be sure you're… that I'm giving you—"

"Tyler, you just have to be with me."

Tyler sighs; Asher makes it so hard to let Tyler be what Asher wants. His words in the conversation with Claudia ring in Tyler's head. He doesn't trust Tyler's youth. He doesn't trust his maturity or his commitment to Idlewild—commitment in general must be something

Asher doesn't trust from him. Asher thinks Tyler doesn't know what he wants or who he is.

He wants Asher, and he wants to be what Asher needs.

It's impossible to reconcile Asher's hesitance with a man who kisses him so tenderly, who made love to him with so much focus and care that Tyler had to hide his face in the pillows to wipe away tears.

"Asher," Tyler says. "I can't—anymore." His words lose steam. "I'm so confused."

"What can't..." Asher's voice trails off. "Do you not want to be here anymore?"

"No, I do." Tyler fights off tears and that miserable, failing feeling in his chest. "I can't tell what you want from me."

"This?" Asher says. He sounds as lost as Tyler. A sudden flare of anger spears through Tyler. He bites back words that will push Asher away.

Instead, he gets up and searches out his briefs. He is way too naked. Asher stands and finds himself clean clothes as well. Tyler stands with tank top in his hands, unsure what happens next. He has no idea where his pants or sweater are.

"Come sit," Asher says. His voice is soft and gentle. And closed. With his clothes on and in that moment of quiet, Asher has pulled himself back in. Any uncertainty or vulnerability is gone. "We should talk."

It's not meant to be patronizing and Tyler knows Asher doesn't realize it is, much less mean it to be. But it's as if Asher's trying to coax him into a calmer state. As if Tyler's out of control or too emotional.

Maybe he is. But he's not showing it and he can't stand the thought that Asher thinks he needs to teach Tyler from some grown-up high horse. Tyler's not a kid. And besides, Asher's a mess too. He might project calm but inside is a tangled, lost man. Tyler's seen the potential Asher has for a happier life, for a rebirth. And he can see himself as a part of that, if only Asher would let him.

Chapter Twenty-Seven

ASHER TUGS TYLER DOWN TOWARD the couch. He tries to keep his face and expression neutral; the contrast between what they shared in bed and this angry, closed-off boy is startling.

"Tyler, why are you acting this way?" Asher asks. He reaches for Tyler's hand, but Tyler pulls back and won't look at him.

"Please don't treat me like I'm a child," Tyler says. It is calm, measured, and, although he doesn't mean it, dangerous. The thread of anger under the words is clear. Anger on Tyler is new, unsettling but also good to see.

"I'm not," Asher frowns. "Are you planning to act like one?"

"Are you kidding? Fuck this." Tyler pulls his shirt on.

"No, no." Asher stands and tries to take Tyler's hand again. Tyler snatches it away. "I just want to talk. You are upset right now, right? I know it can be hard to talk about this stuff, but you can talk to me."

"Sure," Tyler says. His sarcasm is ugly and raw. "You gonna teach me to talk about my feelings now?"

"What—"

"What do you know about it? When do you talk about it?" He puts a finger on Asher's chest. It's gentle, even if his words aren't. "When you won't even let yourself see what's in there?"

"What are you talking about?" Asher steps away.

"What was John's favorite color?" Tyler asks.

"I'm sorry, what?" The change in conversation throws him.

"Where did you get married? When?" Tyler continues, though Asher hasn't answered.

"Up north, in Mackinaw, when the leaves were changing," Asher answers. "Green." Tyler's asking him to prove something. He has no idea what it is. Even though his chest is tight, he pushes through.

"What were his favorite foods?" Tyler's eyes are bright, almost as if he's going to cry. "Did you guys want to have kids?"

Aching, raw and hard, rolls razor-sharp through him. He clears his throat around tears he refuses to let go.

"We—we did," he says. He turns his back to Tyler. Despite himself, tears come, blinding him until he blinks. "Why are you doing this?"

"How did he die?" Tyler asks. His voice is unbearably soft. Asher covers his face; he's holding his body so rigid it hurts, but it doesn't stop the shaking.

"What the fuck?" Asher says when he can trust himself to speak.

"You want to talk to me about my feelings? Let's talk about yours. About John. The man you won't talk about unless I make you? The man you pretend to be over, that you won't let yourself grieve?"

"What the hell do you think—you think you know anything about it?" Asher's face washes red. He tries to take a deep breath.

"You think I'm too young to understand these things?" Tyler yells. Things are spinning out of control so fast. "You think I'm gonna leave, that I'm some kind of mess that needs puttin' together? What a joke! *You're* a mess. *You* can't move on because you haven't let him go. Because you can't let yourself feel it. *You're* the one who's left everyone in your life who knew him."

"You don't know what you're talking about," Asher says. He's still turned away, with his hands braced on the top of the couch. He wipes his tears away with his shoulder. "I haven't walked away from anything. I'm still here, aren't I?" He faces Tyler and gestures to the building around them. It's a weak argument and a bad defense, but he can't stand to listen to any truth in Tyler's words.

"I remember," Tyler says, taking a breath and trying to modulate his voice. It's nearly impossible, because he's crying now too. "A long time ago, before this all happened. You told me you wanted to be with someone again, one day. That you were ready."

"So? Maybe I am."

"Really? Look," Tyler says. "*Look.*" Asher turns. Tyler's pointing to the stack of boxes labeled with John's name piled in the corner. "You've never unpacked them. Will you? Let yourself see those things, and touch the things that were his and let them go?"

"Shut up," Asher says. "Stop, *stop*, please."

"I don't want to hurt you." Tyler takes a breath. "And I won't lie. Maybe I've been hoping that might be me. That maybe… that things have changed. Because I thought I felt that."

"Tyler," Asher says, helplessly. Tyler brushes his own tears away.

"But you won't let me in. As soon as I think you might, you turn me away. You close off. You make it about me to deflect. Because you don't have room for what you really want."

"No," Asher says. "That's not it at all."

"Oh." Tyler blinks and his shoulders sag, "I… I shouldn't have assumed. I just thought—"

"No, that's not what I—"

"I'm so dumb, I knew this… I knew I shouldn't fall in love with you. You're such a mess, and I knew it."

"I'm a mess?" Asher says. He takes a breath, and Tyler can see him battling to get himself under control. "You don't even know who you want to be! You can't even be yourself. Everything is a performance with you. You're everything you think people want you to be. You're the most charismatic goddamn man I've ever met and you use it all up on other people."

There's dead quiet then. Tyler struggles to breathe. "Is that how you see me? No wonder you can't trust me to be grown-up enough to handle a relationship," he says. His voice is a mess of tears and anger and fear.

"That's not what I mean." Asher runs his fingers through his hair and makes a noise of pure frustration.

"I heard you talking to Claudia," Tyler says. A long silence while they both shudder and compose their bodies follows.

"Maybe you shouldn't have been listening. Maybe you should have talked to me about it, instead of all of this."

"Whatever," Tyler says. Asher can tell he said the wrong thing, only he's not sure what it was.

Tyler locates his pants, pulls them on and shakes off Asher's hand. He doesn't bother to put his shoes on, just grabs them and thunders down the stairs. Asher follows him, barefoot as well.

"Tyler, please, please don't leave," Asher says. Tyler's never heard that tone. They're both crying.

"You need to think your shit through," Tyler says.

"Listen, please—"

"No, really. This isn't going to work if you can't let him go. You can't make room for both of us."

"Tyler," Asher says helplessly. "I want this to work." He says it, baldly, plainly. It's not an admission of love, because he can't, not in these circumstances. But it has to be enough; he needs it to be.

"Maybe I've got my own shit to work on," Tyler admits. "But I don't think you've given me as much credit as I deserve. I'm not a kid. I might be younger than you, but I'm not a child. You can't see me as one if you want this."

He spares Asher one last look, Asher, who doesn't say anything else to keep him there, who doesn't make promises or admissions or acquiesce because he realizes that Tyler might be right. Tyler pulls on his shoes and walks out the door.

THE KITCHEN IS CAVERNOUS WITH silence after the bang of the door shutting. Asher wraps his arms around himself. He's cold; the air blowing in through the door was cold. Tyler didn't have a sweater on.

He must have left it upstairs. Asher wants to grab it and run after him. He's sure he won't be welcome, though.

Asher wipes his face clean and works his way upstairs. It's too quiet. Asher turns on another movie for the noise. It's the title suggested after the movie they hadn't watched ended. His bed is a rumpled mess. The sheets should be changed. But that doesn't matter. None of it does.

What if that's the last he ever has of Tyler?

Despite the fact that he orders himself to be calm, Asher can't hold in the pain that wracks him at the thought. He sits heavily on the couch, covers his face, and cries.

Once he starts, he can't stop. He cries harder and he can't stop himself from replaying the words Tyler threw at him and he can't breathe properly. Asher grips the edge of his couch and orders himself to breathe evenly. When he has himself under control—on the fine edge of it, because the smallest thing will push him over—he stumbles into his tiny bathroom and washes his face. He turns the shower as hot as he can stand it. He showers until the water runs cold; he stares at the white wall in front of him, numb and hulled out.

He strips the sheets mechanically and forces himself not to think of Tyler. And when he lies down, he turns his back to the stack of boxes Tyler forced him to acknowledge because seeing them right now might make him acknowledge them in a completely different way.

WHEN HE WAKES, THE BOXES are the first thing he sees. He's wrapped himself around Tyler's pillow. It still smells of him. And it's way too much, having Tyler redolent here, where Asher sees him, so sweet and giving, and that pile of boxes holding of everything he's packed away and never opened again.

For the first time, Asher really lets himself think of John—not of missing him, but of what John might say to him now.

He'd probably agree with Tyler.

Asher rolls out of bed and dresses. He goes downstairs and makes coffee. He preps for the day and, when the door rings, he lets Claudia in without words. She takes one look at him and her eyes soften so much it's almost unbearable. She pulls Asher into a hug that's as surprising as it is needed.

When she pulls away she looks into his eyes for a moment, reading him. He can't hide the evidence of so many tears. Finally, she nods.

"Give me the keys," she says gently.

"You're on bar," he says.

"We'll be okay. I've got this."

He closes his eyes. "I don't—"

"I know you want to work through this and pretend nothing is happening." Asher winces; how transparent is he? "But I think you can't, because if you work we'll have two guys all kinds of fucked up on the floor."

Of course, she's right. Tyler works today. Asher's wondered if Tyler will come in and what the fuck he'll do, or what he can say. But Claudia is right. He's not ready and he can't trust himself to hold it together. "If he doesn't come, call me. I don't want you two short." She nods.

Upstairs, he's hemmed in. He's been living—hiding—in this space, completely sequestered. The brick is crumbling and the exposed ceiling is unfinished, raw and uninviting. The window frames are all splintered wood, and the tiny kitchenette has ancient appliances. He can't even think about the bathroom. This isn't a home. This was supposed to be temporary, a Band-Aid solution, a project he left undone. But it's become an island he's stranded himself on. *What the fuck is wrong with me?* He almost never leaves this building unless Tyler makes him go. Asher doesn't want to admit this to himself, but he was the one to cut off ties with his family. It's been comfortable to tell himself that they did it—that he wasn't close to his brother, that his parents were distant. As kids he and Eli weren't close, but when Asher thinks back to the time after John's death, Eli was there: helping him with Idlewild, distracting Asher by watching baseball and drinking a beer with him, reaching out. And when he'd gone home to Montana... Asher had let himself drift away.

John's family though… they were such a reminder of John, of the life that they'd shared and how Asher felt like one of their children. Putting himself back together had taken a Herculean effort, months and months of perfecting distracting himself and putting his pain away. He couldn't do that when John's mother called to invite him to Thanksgiving dinner, or when they would come to the restaurant to check on him nor when they'd email and, when he stopped responding and answering the phone, sent cards.

Asher had been so heartbroken it never occurred to him that by shutting them all out, he might have doubled their grief as well.

When he sits at his tiny table, he makes himself think honestly. And when he does, it's clear. He has made no plans to find a new place to live. He's happy that Idlewild seems to be on the upswing, but that itching, too-tight feeling he's been fighting is that he's so *sick* of being here.

I have the self-awareness of a fly.

Asher lingers over his coffee. His niece Julie has sent him a card for holidays and birthdays for years. He knows Eli buys them and she only signs them. The first few years, the cards came with indecipherable scribbles; only recently have hints of letter formation and her name been present. This was Eli's way of reaching out to him, because he's been unreachable and he hasn't seen it through the story he's been telling himself.

He hardly knows his own niece, and that realization is a punch in the gut.

Asher stares into an empty mug, in the claustrophobic silence of his apartment, at his fears and failures. He has a lot of fixing to do. He's not sure where to start. If he wanted to reach out and mend fences with John's parents, would they let him?

In the corner of this small hole he's called home is a stack of boxes with his husband's name on them: things he couldn't bear to part with. He sat motionless at their kitchen table as Eli and his parents brought him things and asked him gently what he wanted to keep. They boxed them for him. Two boxes came from Steve and Amber, John's parents, things from John's childhood and adolescence that were left in their house, things they said Asher might want to keep. He has no idea what's in any of the boxes.

Unpacking these gifts of memory will hurt unbearably.

How on earth could he have thought he'd moved on? Tyler was so right.

And Christ, Tyler. Tyler with sweet spring grass-colored eyes and soft skin who is small boned and graceful and clumsy by turns, a beautiful and eye catching, enthralling, thrilling man. Tyler makes him laugh. He has taken the time in the last year to open Asher's eyes to so many things he's taken for granted. He has changed the way Asher looks at this world. He has taken Asher's love for this city and amplified it with kind guidance. Asher thinks back over the last year and marvels at the realization that only in the last few months has he really laughed and let himself take part in joy.

Asher is so in love, and so terrified. And Tyler is right, too, because there's not room in his heart; it seems impossible to imagine himself letting Tyler in fully, to imagine himself open to loving someone the way he once loved John.

Losing one best friend was too much, and not letting it break him cost a lot, and Asher realizes most of cost was pulling himself in and erasing the things that involved *feeling*.

Right now though, Asher *is* alone. He never planned on being alone forever; he aches for what he had once but he's created an impossible, impassible situation for himself. A new relationship would never be the same, but Asher doesn't want loneliness.

Over the years, it's been easier to tell himself that he wants to fall in love without actually meaning to give himself that gift and risk. Right now there's a restaurant full of people who believe in him and in Idlewild, people who have kept a dream and a wish he and John had. In that kitchen, or maybe in the office or entertaining customers, is a man he loves so much it hurts. And Asher can choose. He can walk away and try to live a safe and perhaps empty life. He's lived this long like that. He hasn't been truly happy, but he's survived, and that's meant a lot.

Don't I want more than survival?

Asher's surprised to find that the answer is yes. Unequivocally *yes*.

Although his first instinct is to run downstairs and find Tyler, he can't make a relationship work if he can't promise to honestly to work on healing his own grief, to open himself to the risk of more heartbreak. *What if I'm not strong enough to do what I must do to move on?*

Asher strips out of his work clothes; he's suddenly so exhausted, it's as if he hasn't slept in years and then ran a marathon. Naked, he evaluates his body. He's not bothered by his body, but he remembers what it used to look like. He used to love to run. He and John would take turns waking the other early in the morning and egging each other on. The best were the lovely mornings when they'd get distracted, when they'd end up fumbling with sleepy hands but willing bodies, crashing into and against each other in the winter dark.

He wonders if he's capable of running any more. He's not old, but sometimes he really feels his age. Right now is one of those times.

Down to his boxers, Asher climbs into bed. His eyes heavy, he blinks his way awake long enough to think of what the next steps have to be. What he wants most right now is Tyler.

Chapter Twenty-Eight

TYLER WORKS THROUGH HIS SHIFT in quiet misery as best he can. He almost breaks down and leaves when Claudia greets him with sympathy in her gaze. That sympathy and Asher's absence speak volumes.

It's a struggle, pretending when he's out on the floor. Tyler smiles and is friendly, but he makes mistakes ringing up food. He mixes orders and drops two plates. No one says anything; they just hop in and help. Finally, Claudia takes pity on him—or the customers—and takes him off the floor. She puts him in the kitchen with orders to make some freaking salads and listen to music.

Jared takes Tyler's spot on the floor. He doesn't complain at all, just takes Tyler's apron with a smile.

Tyler is surrounded by people who seem to care more for him than he deserves. Asher is right: Tyler is many things, but rarely himself. And while Tyler stands by everything he said to Asher, Tyler can see how Asher was right. Tyler doesn't trust anyone with his real self. Hell, he doesn't trust himself. He was a boy with big dreams and a burning need to make his family's life better, to make them proud. He played every role he could to get through school, through relationships, through the miserable, choking sense of failure when he realized he couldn't be a doctor. He wants Idlewild so badly; he believes this is his place. Tyler's was afraid for months to tell his family this; he was afraid to show Malik how happy this job makes him.

Tyler has always bridged other's expectations of him. He's the in-between boy. He's erased himself so much that, when he tries to find his borders, he's not sure where they are. He thinks of his mother, his sisters and everyone at Idlewild and realizes that no matter how lost he is, people wait, who, despite his fears, will still be there when he's finished crossing the bridges to his real self. It's a humbling thought. *How could I have thought my self-worth should be defined by other people's desires?*

It's a lot to digest, but Tyler can't let himself wallow, because above him somewhere is a man he loves desperately. Tyler isn't sure he'll ever get to give that love to Asher, but the best love he has is the one coming from that deep, real kernel of self. Tyler might doubt himself, but he has much faith in his love for Asher.

Tyler works the rest of his shift with his ear buds in. It's easier to do his job when he doesn't have to pretend to be okay. People leave him alone, and he can focus on reading his tickets and getting food out. When the lunch rush eases, he cleans his station methodically, perhaps too methodically. But it's good to put his focus so completely on something he doesn't have to worry about.

* * *

HE DOESN'T SEE ASHER. HE doesn't hear from him. Tyler has scheduled days off in the middle of the week. He spends those days thinking through all of the things he and Asher said to each other.

He wishes he'd been kinder.

He could have been more patient.

He let his fears cloud the support and honesty he could have offered Asher.

Asher isn't wrong about him. Being many things doesn't have to be a bad quality. Tyler doesn't ever want to tamp himself down, or limit himself, but he has been doing just that. He doesn't need to force himself to be something because he's scared of being alone. He has no idea how he'll do it, but he thinks that he can be all of the things that are true without using them to hide.

Malik wasn't right for him; he understands that now. How had Malik seen Tyler in the end? How desperate had he made himself? The thought makes his skin crawl. Tyler doesn't want to be that man; it was never a part of his plan.

* * *

"MAMA?" TYLER CALLS OUT. HE leaves his key in the door in case she isn't home.

"Tyler?" He follows the sound of her voice into the kitchen, where she's rolling out dough and watching a daytime show on the tiny TV he bought for her last year. "What's up, baby?" She wipes her hands on her apron and hugs him carefully; there's still flour on her hands. He doesn't care. He holds onto her for a bit longer than he usually would.

"Hi," he says.

She gives him a shrewd look and points to a chair. "Sit. I'll make you some hot chocolate."

"Mama." He laughs. "I'm not a kid." When he was little, her answer to scraped knees and broken hearts had always been hot chocolate. He has never known why, nor asked.

"You need it. I can tell." Her tone brooks no response, and so he sits and waits. She makes it the good way, in a pan with a little spice and a lot of flavor. She settles across from him with a mug of her own, even though he knows she won't drink it. She never does.

"All right baby, talk to me. What's going on?"

Tyler fiddles with the handle of his mug. It's chipped and very old, with an almost completely faded picture of Mickey Mouse and the Disney logo on it. They've had it since he was a kid.

"You in trouble?" she asks. He shakes his head. "Didn't think so. Not you." Her voice is very kind. She trusts him so much, to be a good man, to make the best choices.

"I'm sorry." Tyler swallows the ache that rises in an ugly, hot tide in his throat.

"For what?"

"I promised you all I'd be a doctor. I was gonna make something of myself. And I failed." Tyler risks a sip of the chocolate, but it's still way too hot.

"Tyler Deshawn, do not let me hear you say these things about yourself."

"Mama," he starts.

"What's this nonsense about?" She takes his hand and squeezes it.

"I wanted to make you proud; all of you. Take care of everyone."

"Tyler, you *have*."

"But not like I promised," he protests. "I couldn't hack it. The classes were too hard. I knew I'd never make it in med school. I blamed not going on the money, but that wasn't really it. It didn't feel right." He puts a hand over his heart.

"And what you're doing now?" she asks. "Does it feel right?"

Tyler hesitates. *Working at a restaurant isn't the same thing as being a doctor, right?* "It does. But it's not the same."

"Tyler. What you do brings people happiness. They go to that place for fun. They go to have a good time. You think this world doesn't need people who do that work? Who run grocery stores or serve drinks? Who help bring back a restaurant that meant the world to someone?"

Tyler bites his lip. He'd not thought of it that way.

"Ain't nothing wrong about serving people, Tyler. This is a good thing. It's a great thing. And you—you were made for this work, baby."

"What do you mean?"

"I don't know where you learned to be so organized—not from me, and your worthless father didn't have an ounce of it in his lazy body. But you make order. You make things stable; you right things. You smile, and people can't help but smile back. That's a gift."

"What if it's all an act?" he says, risking his biggest fear.

"Son, don't think I can't see what you do and who you are. I see how you change. But I've known you your whole life. I *raised* you. And baby, you are something special. Not everyone is born with that light." She taps his chest. "Don't you go thinking there's anything wrong with that. Don't pretend it ain't there. You know better."

Tyler looks away, then takes a long drink. The chocolate tastes of comfort and home and safety.

"What's this really about?" she asks. *Damn, she's always been so perceptive.* Tyler takes a deep breath and meets her eyes.

"I fell in love."

"You haven't before?" she asks, no judgement in her voice.

"Yes. But not like this. Nothing's ever felt like this, Mama," he admits. Her hand is still on his, and she squeezes it again.

"Good." He's surprised to see tears shine in her eyes. "Don't get me wrong. I got a lot of love in my heart for Malik, too, but I knew he wasn't right for you."

Tyler huffs out a laugh. "You couldn't tell me this?"

"Maybe one day—boy, do I hope—you'll have a child of your own, and you'll know you have to step back and let him learn on his own."

Tyler lets this sink in. The opening music of a daytime drama comes on.

"You afraid of losing him?" Mama finally asks. Tyler nods. "Son," she says as she waits for his eyes to look into hers, "no matter what happened in school, you ain't never failed. He love you?"

"Yes, but it's so messed up and—"

"Then you'll make it work." She's sure and unflinching. Her faith in him is ballast and courage. He nods. He's not sure taking a risk on Asher will work out, but he's more sure that he can't give up on trying.

Chapter Twenty-Nine

You're not working tomorrow.

Asher sends the text before he can think too hard about it, then puts his phone down. Unsure when, or if, Tyler will respond, Asher doesn't want to tempt himself. Staring at the screen will only make him want to keep texting until Tyler responds.

No...? Asher squints at the response and then re-reads his own text. Fuck.

Sry, forgot the ? at the end of that text

Okay?

Damn, Tyler is making this hard on him. Maybe texting was a bad idea, but Asher can't trust how he would sound if he called Tyler. As it is, his hands are shaking and his heart is pounding. When Asher woke up two days ago, he made himself coffee, grabbed a quick breakfast he wasn't going to eat and sat down with a pen and paper. If he detoured into the office to take one of Tyler's favorite pens, well, no one had to know.

Could you maybe come in and help me with something?

Unable to help it, he does stare at his phone after this one. Tyler doesn't make him wait.

Asher, I don't know if that's a good idea

Asher types a response so fast he has to fix typos three times.

Not for work. Can you help *me*?

Okay

Tyler's response doesn't really give clue: Does he really want to? Is this a pity thing? How mad is he? Of course, minus things like emojis, text is never a good medium for conversation with heart or heat, so Asher can't expect that.

He is tempted to dress himself up the next night. A good thirty-five minutes pass as he stands in front of his crate of clothes naked, debating with himself. Eventually he talks himself around to something more casual. A T-shirt that's unbelievably soft and his oldest jeans. They're a little tight, since he's a little heavier, but don't look bad. Everyone, it seems, wears their jeans tight nowadays.

"Asher?" Tyler's voice floats up the stairs. *Fuck.* His hair is still wet and he's forgotten to grab food.

"Come up," he calls. He rubs the towel over his hair and ties to calm his racing heart. Tyler is beautiful and guarded in all of his lovely bones.

"Hi," Asher says.

"Hi back." They stare at each other; Asher feels stupid.

"Okay, this is—"

"What did—"

They both laugh, Tyler more lightly than Asher. Asher gestures at the couch.

"So, I need to talk to you about a few things before I ask you for this favor."

Tyler sits on the edge of the couch, face tilted up toward Asher, who is still standing. "Okay."

Asher paces back and forth, thinking through what he wants to say. This is harder than he thought it would be. But when he passes the couch a third time, he notices that stack of boxes; either they're mocking him or pushing him, but what must be done must be done. He sits next to Tyler and takes his hand, which Tyler gives with the slightest hesitation.

"The thing is…" Asher clears his throat and tries to breathe. "That I'm in love you, and you were right."

Tyler's eyes get wide then, as wide as Asher has ever seen, and his hand spasms. "You—wait. What? About what?"

"Gosh, like, everything," Asher says. "Wow! I sound like I'm thirteen again."

Tyler laughs. Asher wants him on his lap, he wants Tyler's fingers in his hair and his mouth on his and the words given back. Tyler lets himself be pulled forward and swings a leg over and sits on his lap. Asher frames his face with his sharp cheekbones against his palms and his lovely and slightly pointed ears under his fingers and with one thumb brushing his lips. Tyler sways, easy and pliant, into the kiss.

AFTER THE KISSING—LOTS OF IT—TYLER settles, heavy and relaxed, into Asher's lap. His face is tucked into his neck, and even though Asher's head is angled back at a strange angle, he'd be happy to sit here and let his legs fall asleep under Tyler's weight.

"You said you needed help?" Tyler pulls back and prompts him.

"Yeah," Asher says. Tyler hasn't said the words back; Asher's uncertainty and fear are overwhelming, but he forces himself to focus. His head is still against the back of the couch; for once he's looking up at Tyler. "Since you're so organized and anal—"

"Hey!"

"I thought," Asher starts, laughing and squeezing Tyler's waist, which makes this easier to say. "Maybe you could help me clean out some boxes."

Tyler is very still, and his eyes, soft and direct. "Asher," he says, "Are you sure?"

Asher takes a breath and reminds himself that he can *do* brave—he can also do hard and he can do strong. Survival is all of those things.

"John loved to eat baked brie," he says.

"Huh?" Tyler's eyebrows draw together.

"He loved to experiment with things to put on it and he hated when people baked it into puff pastries." Tyler crawls off his lap, and cold seeps into Asher's bones immediately. Tyler snuggles close though, tucking his feet under Asher's leg so his knees curl against Asher's chest. Asher drapes his arm around them and turns his head toward Tyler. His eyes burn, but tears don't fall—not because he won't let them, but because they aren't there yet. When he speaks again and his voice cracks, he knows they're coming.

"John wanted kids. He had names picked out. He knew he wanted three, and he had alternates and sub-alternates, and I hated most of them."

"Did you want kids?" Tyler asks. Despite the quiet in the apartment, his voice is so soft it's barely a whisper.

"Yes." Asher closes his eyes, and Tyler's cold fingertips collect the tear that rolls down his check. "More than anything. Still do." He chuckles and opens his eyes. "Maybe not three. Who knows, though?"

"Yeah," Tyler says. He strokes the back of Asher's hand.

"And he—" Asher clears his throat and tries again. His voice wobbles so much it's almost impossible to get the words out. "He went to the store one night, late, after I'd nagged him because he kept forgetting to pick up contact solution when it was his turn."

"And?" Tyler prompts after a long pause while Asher struggles to breathe. He's not sure why this is so hard to say: because of Tyler maybe, because he's not just sharing the facts, but sharing John with someone new.

"And he was hit by a drunk driver."

"Oh, honey." Tyler's own tears spill over, and Asher catches them the way that Tyler had caught his. "Did you—I don't mean that you should—"

"I don't blame myself," Asher says, understanding what Tyler wants to ask. "For a while I think I did. But..." he pauses to gather the right words. "I know now that maybe I've buried a lot, and that I've stagnated, that I could have been growing these last few years and haven't. But I promise, I did have some peace after a couple of years."

"Good. That's good," Tyler whispers.

"I wasn't the one driving the car that hit him. That's no one's fault but that man's. John and I squabbled all the time. I think all couples do. We do." He offers Tyler a wan smile.

"Well, I don't know about squabbling," Tyler teases.

"And fighting, yes. Sometimes."

Tyler is quiet for a long time. "Are you saying… do you want to be a couple?" He sounds so painfully raw and unsure; Asher understands. He cannot stand the thought of not exposing this. Of not giving Tyler every bit of honesty, no matter how scary it might be.

"Aren't we already? Haven't we been?"

Tyler tilts his head and smiles; his smile is brilliant and pierces right through all of Asher's uncertainty.

"When I say I love you, that's part of what I mean. What I want."

"Oh?" Tyler's face is a study of joy and hope and fear.

"Yes." Asher kisses Tyler softly and, with their foreheads together, whispers, "Tyler Heyward, I do love you so."

"Oh!" Delighted shock in his voice now, Tyler closes his eyes and tucks his face into Asher's neck, as if he wants to hide it. Asher lets him. He's not sure why Tyler wants to hide; if this time the words have hit Tyler differently, or if they suddenly make sense.

"Tyler," he says, then stops. He has to say this right, if he can. "When I say I love you, I want you to know that I love *you*." Tyler is quiet; the only indication that he's heard Asher is the tiniest shudder. "Ty, sweetheart, would you look at me for this?"

Tyler shakes his head. "Please," Asher says. He runs his fingers along the bumps of Tyler's spine and wishes he could kiss each one. He wants to whisper every word into Tyler's skin and hopes he'll let Asher in. "I want you to see me when I say this."

Tyler moves back. His lips are pressed together, hard, and his eyes are too bright. Asher cups his neck and takes one of Tyler's hands, which has Asher's shirt clenched in it. "I need you to know that I see you, when I say it. This." One tear spills over and drips down Tyler's cheek. Asher catches it with his thumb.

"You are so many things; you can be so many people, and there are so many versions of you. I love that." Tyler's eyes dart away. His body shifts. "But you don't have to be any of them here. You can be any of them; I just want them to be honest. I'm sorry I said those things the way I did. I think…"

"You think?" Tyler prompts, voice gone hoarse with the effort of holding back tears.

"Sometimes it's like you are whatever version of yourself you think other people need. I don't know if you're faking it or doing it to please others." Tyler lifts a shoulder and a rueful, fleeting smile moves over his face.

"You don't have to please me by being who you think I want you to be. Not here. Here you can be whatever feels best. I love each part of you, but I just want it to be *true*. When you're with me." Tyler's brows are drawn, and his eyes are distant, deep in thought. "Does that make sense? It's hard to explain."

"I guess. I don't know—Asher I'm just… I don't know if I can. Maybe this is just me?"

"Do you love that about yourself? Does it feel real?" Asher asks.

"Maybe sometimes? When I'm not thinking about it. When I'm not faking it because I'm scared."

"I don't want you to be scared with me," Asher says. "And it's okay if it takes a while for you to trust me. But… do you want to?"

Tyler nods. "I do." Asher's smile is wide. Every emotion Tyler brings out in him—more than just love—makes it hard to breathe.

"Then that's all I need, right now. And I'll keep telling you, and showing you, that I love you and that I won't leave you as long as you want to be with me."

"Oh god," Tyler says. It's broken and wet with tears and whispered into Asher's neck again. "I love you, too." Asher almost doesn't hear it, tucked in between tears and so soft.

"Could you," Asher says. He takes a breath and realizes he's shaking. "Could you maybe kiss me now? Again. I mean—"

Tyler laughs, and it's a wet, happy sound, thick with happy tears, and when he kisses Asher, he tastes a little of those tears and a lot of homecoming.

AN HOUR LATER, THEY'VE HARDLY moved from the couch, other than when Tyler went to get tissues and tea.

"I'm not eighty," Asher says.

"No, but you are sniffling," Tyler says. "And we don't have hot chocolate."

"Hot chocolate?" Spicy cinnamon steam floats up from the mug; despite his protests, Asher wraps his hands around it. The warmth seeps into his hands and the sigh he releases after he sips is deep and exhausted.

"My mama always makes hot chocolate when we're upset or hurt or need comfort." Tyler says and shrugs.

"I don't feel any of those though," Asher protests.

Tyler just smiles. "Comfort works for many things, Ash."

Asher closes his eyes. He feels more hollow than he can remembers. Tyler's never called him that. No one has. It's incredible that after so many lonely years, he can have something new.

"Tired?" Tyler asks. With gentle fingers, he plays with a couple of Asher's curls. Asher slides down a little until he's leaning against Tyler bonelessly.

"Yeah."

"Do you want to get into bed?" Tyler asks. Asher demurs and makes an attempt to sit up. He's forgotten about the tea and almost sloshes it all over them. Tyler catches it in time.

"No. We should talk. About, you know. The stuff."

"The stuff?" Tyler asks.

"Don't tease," Asher says. He bumps shoulders with Tyler and gestures toward the boxes. Tyler takes a long time to think. "This is about more than just the boxes, right?"

"Yeah," Asher says. He's being clumsy with this and perhaps unfair. He's at the edge of his reserve; his vulnerability is exhausted. Right now, he wants to be caught by a partner who can carry some of his load.

"You need to move, I think," Tyler says. He speaks very slowly, either because he's trying to spell it out, or because he's unsure. Asher looks up at him. Tyler's gaze is direct and serious.

"I think you should, too." Asher says. He takes the deepest breath he can and then takes the plunge. "With me?"

"Really?" Tyler asks. He covers his mouth to hide his wide smile. Asher tugs his hand down and then catches Tyler's laugh with his lips. It's a kiss full of promises and joy.

"Absolutely."

"Oh god! I get to make so many lists!" Tyler says when they break apart, causing Asher to laugh helplessly.

"I see. You don't want to live with me for *me*, you just want to organize things," he jokes.

"Been my plan all along, old man," Tyler says, snapping his fingers and poking his belly; Asher laughs harder. He tries to squirm away, and they tussle on the couch until Asher has them flipped and has Tyler pinned beneath him. It's not graceful, and he almost falls off a couple of times, but he perseveres.

"This seems like the right time to take things to your bed, don't you think?" Tyler says, breathless and sassy and lit up. Asher's got his hands over his head and keeps his lips just out of reach.

"Our bed," Asher corrects.

"I take no responsibility for that mattress," Tyler says. "We'll get a new one."

"We can get a new everything," Asher says, and it's a promise for so much more. Tyler leans up to kiss him, and that too feels new.

Epilogue

"SWEETHEART, WHAT ARE YOU DOING?" Tyler stiffens then melts back into Asher, who's come home from work early. He didn't hear him come in, but his arms coming around him from behind are welcome.

"Decoration for fall," Tyler says.

"Do you decorate for every holiday?" Asher asks. Tyler turns to face him.

"Is that okay?" Everything is still so new; sometimes Tyler doesn't know how he'll land on his feet if he does this all wrong. But Asher is always sure even when Tyler isn't, and he's patient and kind and, it seems, so full of love to give Tyler. Tyler, too, has an endless bounty of love to give.

"I love it. It'll probably help me remember what month it is," Asher says. It's true—Asher is terrible at keeping track of days and time. Even though he no longer lives above Idlewild, it's hard to pry him away at times. Tyler understands; Asher was scared for a long time that it would slip from his fingers, that every last thing he had of John would be taken from him. Tyler does his best to help Asher trust that no one would let that happen.

"Um, so I kind of did a thing," Tyler says. He looks down at the wreath of painted fall leaves and acorns he's holding.

"Uh-oh," Asher says.

"I thought… we could do Thanksgiving. At the restaurant? I might have already asked Mama and my sisters?" Asher is quiet; when Tyler looks up at him, he can't read the expression on his face. "I'm sorry. That was a terrible idea, wasn't it?"

"No," Asher says. He runs his hands through his hair. It's curled at the temples, which means he was working behind the line where the heat and steam broke down the product Asher uses to try to tame it. "I've just not… I haven't done Thanksgiving in a couple of years."

"Not even with your family?" Tyler asks. *How is that possible?*

"They invited me," Asher explains.

"But you found a reason not to go, didn't you?"

Asher nods. He turns away and sits heavily on the couch. Tyler knows now when he can and can't push. Asher's had to learn—to see—on his own that he pushed people away. Tyler tries to be a listening ear, tries not to show surprise, because without family, he doesn't know where he would be.

"Do you…" Tyler sits on the couch. He tucks one of Asher's curls behind his ear. "Maybe we could invite them. To Thanksgiving?" He's met Asher's parents again. They came down to Idlewild for Asher's birthday, which Tyler had no idea about because Asher hadn't said anything, and asked to take him out somewhere. Asher had introduced Tyler as his boyfriend almost defiantly, as if he expected his parent's rejection or judgment. And when his mother smiled, bright and happy, Tyler could do nothing but watch Asher's bewilderment.

That night, in bed, Tyler had whispered love into his ear. "They love you, too," he'd said, over and over. Asher had been quiet, but when he'd made love to him, it was with intensity and focus and passion that made them both fall apart and into each other.

"You think they'd come?" Asher asks. His face wears hope that makes him look young. Tyler's heart breaks a little.

"I think they'd love it."

"Maybe… maybe I could invite Eli. I don't think he'd come, but…"

"He would appreciate the invitation." Tyler finishes for him. A few days after his parents came to dinner, Asher got another card in the mail, signed only by Julie. It contained more tickets, but this time to a Tiger's game. That night, he'd called Eli for the first time in a very long time to thank him.

Tyler reaches under and tries to maneuver Asher's phone out of his back pocket and elicits laughter.

"Right now?" Asher asks, eyes wide.

"No." Tyler clears his throat. He hopes that this is one of those times when it's right, to push Asher just a little. "I think you should call John's parents now, too."

Asher's hand spasms around his phone. Tyler puts his own hand around Asher's. "You don't have to," he says. He tucks himself closer to Asher. "But you miss them; I can tell when you talk about them. They loved you very much, didn't they?"

Asher looks at him. "You have so much in your heart, Tyler," he says. Tyler's not sure what he means but knows that this moment isn't about him.

"You do, too," he says. He kisses Asher and puts his forehead against Asher's. He looks into his lovely brown eyes and says it again, with more force and intensity. "You do." Asher closes his eyes and nods, and when he pulls away, it's to look at his phone.

"Okay," he says. He threads his fingers through Tyler's and uses the other to find the number on his phone, and, when he makes the call, Tyler aches with the trust Asher has in him and his own happiness. He's the bridge, he's the in-between boy, but now, he knows it's a beautiful gift.

END

Acknowledgments

When this book was nothing but a seed, I shared it with a colleague—with one simple question she changed the shape of the story and my approach. So, many thanks to Allegra Smith for unknowingly making this book what it is. With so much gratitude I want to thank Erin McRae for being so excited when I first pitched this story; your encouragement made it very hard to give up. Of course, so many thanks to Pene Henson, who kept me going through every roadblock. Thank you to Lynn Charles and Moriah Gemel for answering my panicked emails and reading the very roughest forms of this book.

This book benefited immensely from the help of the following women who volunteered as sensitivity readers for Idlewild: Rachel Rigodon, Kelle B., and Naomi Tajedler, and as well, Alysia Constantine, who not only read and gave me such wonderful advice, but who kept me laughing when I was going through a very hard time. Nicki Harper deserves all of the thanks for putting up with my rampant comma abuse for the third time in a row.

Even though most of you won't read this, thanks go to everyone in my graduate program who support me in countless ways that make this side adventure possible.

Without my wonderful publisher, Interlude Press, none of this would be possible. I cannot thank them enough for believing in me, putting up with my shenanigans, and encouraging me at all times. Annie, Candy, and Choi, all of the work and dedication you give this company inspires me. Thank you so much.

READING RESOURCES:

Detroit: An American Autopsy by Charlie LeDuff

Detroit City is the Place to Be: The Afterlife of an American Metropolis by Mark Binelli

How to Live in Detroit Without Being a Jackass by Aaron Foley

The Origins of the Urban Crisis: Race and Inequality in Postwar Detroit by Thomas Sugrue

About the Author

JUDE SIERRA FIRST BEGAN WRITING poetry as a child in her home country of Brazil. Still a student of the form, she began writing long-form fiction by tackling her first National Novel Writing Month project in 2007, and in 2011 began writing in online communities, where her stories have thousands of readers. Her previous novels include *Hush* (2015) and *What It Takes* (2016), which received a Starred Review from *Publishers Weekly*.

interlude press
you may also like…

What It Takes by Jude Sierra

Milo met Andrew moments after moving to Cape Cod—launching a lifelong friendship of deep bonds, secret forts and plans for the future. When Milo goes home for his father's funeral, he and Andrew finally act on their attraction—but doubtful of his worth, Milo severs ties. They meet again years later, and their long-held feelings will not be denied. Will they have what it takes to find lasting love?

ISBN (print) 978-1-941530-59-7 | (eBook) 978-1-941530-60-3

Hush by Jude Sierra

Wren is one of "the gifted"—a college sophomore with the power to compel others' feelings and desires. He uses his power as a game of sexual consent until Cameron, a naïve freshman, enters his life. As Cameron begins to understand his sexuality and gain confidence under Wren's tutelage, Wren grows to recognize new and unexpected things about himself. Will Cameron's growing confidence finally break down Wren's emotional walls, or will Wren walk away from his best chance for love?

ISBN (print) 978-1-941530-27-6 | (eBook) 978-1-941530-31-3

Sweet by Alysia Constantine

Alone and lonely since the death of his partner, a West Village pastry chef gradually reclaims his life through an unconventional courtship with an unfulfilled accountant that involves magical food, online flirtation, and a dog named Andy. Sweet is also the story of how we tell love stories. The narrator is on to you, Reader, and wants to give you a love story that doesn't always fit the bill.

ISBN (print) 978-1-941530-61-0 | (eBook) 978-1-941530-62-7

One **story**
can change **everything.**

@interlude**press**
Twitter | Facebook | Instagram | Tumblr | Pinterest

For a reader's guide to **Idlewild** and book club prompts,
please visit interludepress.com.

10/2/18

CPSIA information can be obtained
at www.ICGtesting.com
Printed in the USA
LVHW03s2346070918
589550LV00001B/58/P

9/28/18